Statures of No Limitations

by

Judith Fournie Helms

Cover Art by *Teddi Black*

The Wild Rose Press, Inc.
PO Box 708
Adams Basin, NY 14410-0708
Visit us at www.thewildrosepress.com

Publishing History
First Edition, 2025
Trade Paperback ISBN 978-1-5092-6223-6
Digital ISBN 978-1-5092-6224-3

Published in the United States of America

Dedication

For girls and women of all shapes and sizes, all of whom are beautiful

Siempre adelante

Acknowledgements

Bodyism is too important a subject for me to have risked diving in without a solid support team. I gratefully acknowledge those who provided invaluable guidance, assistance, and encouragement during all stages of the process of writing the story of Heather, Danni, and Marni (and their support team!).

Sincere thanks to Betsy Ashton, James A. Clark, Sue Coryell, Dr. Lynne Foreman, Lauren Hafner, Holly Hale, Lily Helms, Grace Kotre, David Kotre, Diane Langhorst, Max Langhorst, Anne Moore (1947-2023), Todd Schenk, Bill Sparer, Mary Ann Sparer, Mary Beth Trybulec, Denise Tuttle, Rev. Cheryl Wade, Eileen Watson, Mark Young, and editors T. Jeffers and A.B. Westrick. Thank you, too, to the Lake Writers of the Virginia Writers Club, fellow authors and dear friends, who kept me on track through the drafts.

Finally, this book would not have been possible without the encouragement and steady guidance of Ally Robertson, Crimson Editor of The Wild Rose Press. I am most grateful to her and to all of the supportive people at my wonderful publisher.

As always, my deepest appreciation is for my trusted first reader, my husband, Larry.

Chapter 1

Since we only knew one another by voice, we planned to each hold a yellow legal pad so we could easily identify the other two. We'd wisely chosen not to try to describe ourselves, which would've been only slightly more embarrassing than how we actually connected. Having taken an early train from Waukegan into the city, I arrived at the bar first and grabbed a regular-height table with three chairs. I slid my stuffed leather briefcase underneath and ordered a beer from a waiter who was delivering drinks to the couple at the next table. As I scanned the room for yellow legal pads, I made brief eye contact with a man at the bar who looked me over, smiled, then raised his eyebrows. My chest tightened and I quickly averted my gaze. I grabbed the plasticized bar menu and pretended to read it, while my heart raced. I glanced in the direction opposite the bar and caught a glimpse of a woman changing places with her male companion so she'd be facing me, and he wouldn't. The same old ritual.

At the bar, the thirty-something guy in a well-fitted dark business suit was settling his bill, and I sensed he'd be trying to chat me up in a few seconds. I was perspiring, but refused to remove the jacket of my skirt suit since I was wearing a lightweight shell underneath and dreaded the thought of any more scrutiny. My attention shifted to a woman who emerged through the revolving door, and who must have taken up every inch of that triangle. She appeared to be wearing a gray tent over black slacks, and had a yellow legal pad tucked under her right arm. She glanced about the room. I saw her before she noticed the pad on my table, so I rose and waved, relieved she'd headed off the guy.

"Danielle?" she asked.

"I'm Heather. You must be Marnie."

As we shook hands, she said, "Guilty. I probably should've told you I'd be the really fat one, but why ruin a surprise?"

That threw me off balance for a moment and I laughed, too hard. I tried to gather myself as I pointed to our table. We took our seats, and I couldn't help thinking that her girth probably required more space than her chair provided. "It's so nice to finally meet you, Marnie. Would you like a beer while we wait for Danielle?" I was looking at her, but worrying that my overly enthusiastic smile might betray my ill-ease. I literally wiped the stupid grin off my face with the back of my hand and glanced at the door, hoping Danielle would arrive soon.

"Actually, I think I need a glass of wine." She motioned for the server.

Trying to feign lack of awareness of her exceptional heft, I launched over-earnestly into the subject of the latest development in the case we were defending as co-counsel. It had been brought by a litigious middle-aged woman who'd already made her mark with other not-quite-clever-enough fraudulent claims in numerous jurisdictions. Marnie, who was with a Chicago firm, represented a major cola manufacturer. Danielle, also in Chicago, had the distributor. My client was the retailer, a mom-and-pop shop in Waukegan, the city where my firm's office was located two blocks from the county courthouse where the woman's case was pending.

We'd all just received the results of the x-rays of the mouse which the plaintiff claimed had surprised and traumatized her by showing up in her bottled cola. The unfortunate little thing had had most of its tiny bones broken as it was shoved through the narrow mouth of the bottle. Shoved sometime after its untimely death, I hoped. "It seems we've cracked the mouse case wide open."

"Yeah. I know Ms. Spitz is a crook," Marnie said as she lifted the same menu I'd fake-studied. "But someone who could stomach squeezing a rodent into a cola bottle ought to be entitled to something for the gross-out factor."

"I suppose you're right." I sighed, trying to imitate normal conversation when every fiber of me wanted to understand how she'd let herself get so heavy. I added, "She had to overcome any smidge of squeamishness to execute that."

"She executed it? Ghastly. I hope she blindfolded it first."

I laughed, and it helped me relax. "At least the one before ours was less nauseating."

"Wait. Which one was that?" asked Marnie, leaning back in her chair. She looked as relaxed as I felt uneasy.

"She fell and broke her leg, then had her friends carry her to the bottom of the stairs at the restaurant where she was working, so she could make a Workers' Comp claim."

She nodded. "Of course. But I thought burning down her own over-insured house was the most daring."

"Definitely—at least among the frauds we know

of." I took a swallow of my beer. "But I have to wonder how Ms. Spitz could've done so little homework that she didn't realize the presence of the accelerant would be investigated. I can't believe she skated at the criminal trial."

"True. But at least she skated without any insurance money." She smiled. The server brought the glass of wine, and Marnie hurried to take a long sip. "She should be in jail."

My eyes shifted to focus on movement I was sensing, just to Marnie's left side, where a face not a foot above the table was smiling up at me. It was a woman's head at the height where a child's would be. "Heather and Marnie?" she said. I was staring, at the same time trying not to.

"Danielle?" I asked, embarrassment rendering me stupid. Of course she was. Both Marnie and I stood and walked around the table to lean down and shake her small hand.

When we all sat, I saw that her face just cleared the table. My problem-solver instinct kicked in before I could think through protocol. "I have a pile of deposition transcripts in my briefcase." I reached for it and pulled out a stack almost eight inches high. "Would you be more comfortable sitting on these?"

She gave me a flicker of a smile and said, "Great. They don't stock kids' booster seats in bars. I mean, why would they?"

I shrugged, then rounded the table to set the transcripts in place.

She hopped down from the chair and said, "Actually, I usually bring a cushion with me, but I was hurrying to get out of my office and left it behind." Then she stepped on the lower rung of the wooden chair to hoist herself back up.

I returned to my seat and, determined to keep the conversation flowing, slipped into lawyer mode. "So, Marnie and I were just discussing Ms. Spitz's impressive history of insurance fraud."

"I know." Danielle had her hands folded, resting against the edge of the table. "She has a flare for it, poor thing."

"Why 'poor thing?' " Marnie asked.

"I imagine the circumstances that led her to pull those pranks must've been pretty tough."

"Possibly," Marnie said. "Or maybe she could easily hold down a job but prefers the satisfaction of ripping someone off."

I was struck by the contrasting knee-jerk positions on human nature. Marnie said, "Damn. The partners should've asked her at her deposition what childhood deprivations drove her to the larceny."

"Maybe a special interrogatory?" Danielle asked.

"Why not?" I asked, feeling my self-control in overdrive as I tried to keep up with the exchange while acting as though I didn't notice anything unusual about either of them. For some reason, this caused me to blink uncontrollably. "What will you have to drink, Danielle?"

"Gin and tonic." She paused, then asked in a soft voice, "Do you have something in your eye, Heather?"

I lied. "Allergies."

Marnie summoned the server, pointed at our empty glasses, and ordered for Danielle, whom I hoped wouldn't think she was being treated like a child. Of course, this made no sense as no one orders a gin and tonic for a little kid. A few minutes later, once our drinks and pretzels arrived, Danielle said, "You don't have to do this, you know."

"Drink alcohol?" Marnie asked.

Danielle laughed. "Oh no. We have to do that. I'm referring to the elephant in the room."

Marnie tossed back her jet-black, shoulder-length hair, and said, "I may be as wide as I am tall, but there's no call to refer to me as an elephant."

I spat out my beer, which thankfully didn't spray either of them. As I wiped the table with a napkin, I looked at Danielle, and moronically asked, "What?"

"I'm a dwarf."

"No, you're not. You're a person with dwarfism."

They just stared at me. My lame attempt to defend her from herself had fallen flat, and my chest immediately tightened. Unfortunately, I went on, "Isn't it like how we now say, 'an enslaved person,' rather than 'a slave?'"

"No," said Marnie.

"I'm with Marnie, Heather. Traffickers captured or 'purchased'..."—she used air quotes—"African people, then forced them into the role of slave. But I really am a dwarf. I'm three feet, eight inches tall. The word doesn't offend me." The drinks were served, and she took a couple of sips of hers.

I thought about it for a moment. "But 'dwarf' doesn't define you. 'Person' defines you. It's like I'm just a person of above average height, and you're a person of below-average height."

"And I'm a person of above-average weight," said Marnie.

Danielle looked at me. "I appreciate what you're trying to do. But it's not like I don't know I'm a dwarf.

It's taken me most of my thirty-two years to fully accept it."

"But it's the rest of the world that hasn't. Right?" asked Marnie.

"True."

"I totally get it. Look at me."

She surveyed Marnie, from her head to the tabletop, and side to side. "I see your point."

When they both turned back to me, I squirmed in my chair like a restless child. All I could think to say was, "I'm not like the rest of the world."

"I can tell," said Marnie.

"So can I," said Danielle. "That's not why I'm looking at you."

"Then what?"

"I'm just wondering about some things—about your life."

"Me too," said Marnie. "I mean, I have a plethora of assumptions and prejudices—which are probably right."

I took a deep breath. "Guys, you do realize we've just met." I looked at my watch. "We've been talking for under a half hour. And you two want us to bare our souls to each other?"

"I do," said Danielle.

"I'm in," said Marnie. "But I can't do it on an empty stomach. Obviously, I can't do much of anything on an empty stomach."

I wasn't sure how to respond to her self-deprecation, and let it drop. The two of them moved on to compare the merits of the several restaurants on their lists, so we could be sure to choose one that would suit all of us. By the time we agreed, we'd each had a couple of drinks, and I was finally starting to relax a little. We hailed a cab and Marnie gave the driver the address as she slid into the middle of the back seat. I was to her right, with my briefcase on my lap. My slim suit skirt was hiked up from quickly jumping into the cab on the street side so Danielle could take her time hoisting herself up from the sidewalk. I couldn't help noticing that her legs had to stick straight out since her knees didn't reach the edge of the seat. Unintentionally, we both slid in toward Marnie since her portion of the back seat was compressed more than usual. I stared at my briefcase sitting on my knees. It felt like it was filled with bricks.

Once the three of us were out of the cab, I witnessed for the first time something I've seen on a hundred occasions since that moment. Some men looked at me, as they always did. A few people glanced at Marnie in an entirely different way. Many people on the sidewalk, and those walking into the restaurant, stopped what they were doing—their conversations, tapping away at iPhones, hurrying to catch cabs—to stare at Danielle. She didn't acknowledge them, so I kept my silence. But by the time we were seated, I was seething.

I sputtered, "Outside. There were incredibly rude people openly staring at you."

"Pretty much everyone we passed," said Marnie.

"Really?" asked Danielle, whose face was just a few inches above the red checkered tablecloth.

Marnie shook her head and smiled. "You're messing with us."

"A little bit. I do have some vague sense it happened. But I've learned to block it out."

"That works?" I asked, all the while wondering if I would've been one of those people if I hadn't been in her party.

"Somewhat. See, I've been dealing with this since I could walk. For decades it hurt my feelings. It brought me down. Not that I have that far to go." She giggled. "But if I'd let it go on like that, I wouldn't be here today."

"Are you serious?" I asked.

"As serious as a suicide attempt."

"Good God," said Marnie. "We need more alcohol." She waved to a waiter across the room who was clearly not our server. He took pity on us when Marnie basically begged him to bring us a bottle of chardonnay and three glasses. He returned with it on the run. I hoped the others hadn't noticed that the handsome Italian man was making eyes at me the whole time.

I decided I might as well take advantage of his attention. "It was very kind of you to get our drinks so quickly. I don't suppose you could possibly do one more little thing for us?" He and I were basically gazing into each other's eyes.

"Of course, ma'am. Anything."

"We need a pillow to raise the seat for my friend."

The waiter kept eye contact with me for a moment, and then nodded. "I'll just be a moment."

As he hurried away, they both rolled their eyes at me.

"What? Did you want me to dig out my pile of transcripts again?"

"No," said Danielle. "A pillow would be nice." She paused. "Do you always get your way so easily?"

I sighed and looked at Danielle and then Marnie. "There's more to that than what you guys are imagining."

"How do you know what we're imagining?" asked Marnie.

9

"It's what I'd be imagining if I witnessed what just happened."

The waiter returned with a pile of towels, the perfect amount of lift for Danielle, and I thanked him. I raised my glass to the others, and we clinked to my toast "to new friends." I took the long swallow of wine I knew I needed to be able to say what I hoped would help both of them feel more positive about their looks. "Since you two are obviously interested in our differences, I'd like to say something about that." Neither of them responded. "I want to tell you what I see when I look at you. Then you tell me about me. Okay?"

"This should be depressing," said Marnie.

"I'm all ears," said Danielle. She added, "Actually, I'm all head, but go on."

The two of them were the most self-deprecating women I'd ever met, and I thought I had a decent idea of how to correct their negativism about themselves. "So, Danielle—"

She interrupted. "Since we're going to be intimate friends, please call me Danni, with an 'i'."

How she foresaw that the first time we met, I'll never know. I surveyed her features and hair as I spoke. "Okay. Danni, when I look at you, I see an attractive, self-possessed woman with lovely, wide-set blue eyes, fair skin, and a big, absolutely radiant smile. I see that her clothes are well-tailored, and her auburn hair is precision-cut in a flattering bob. She is short in stature, but confident in her movements and eye contact."

"Well done!" said Marnie. "Spot-on. So, what do you see when you look at me?" She put her elbow on the table, chin on her hand, and leaned toward me.

I studied her for a moment before I launched into it.

"A woman with a stunningly beautiful face, clear eyes which seem to contain a hundred shards of different hues of green, a fair complexion with a constellation of delicate freckles sprinkled over the bridge of her nose. I see luxurious raven straight hair, which gleams as it catches the light, and seems to swing to complement every change of expression. Her carriage is proud, and she is completely unapologetic for her figure."

"Aw, shucks," said Marnie.

"Wow," said Danni. "You should be a writer."

"Yeah. Well, I do fool around with short stories. Anyway, it's your turn. And you guys have to be perfectly honest."

"I'm no poet, but I'll give it a try." Marnie took a moment to look me over. "A slim woman, probably five feet eight or so. Perfectly proportioned figure, but a bit busty—in a good way. I believe the word *statuesque* fits: statue-like, tall, and well-proportioned. But the dictionary definition doesn't really make sense because statues actually come in all shapes. I have an adorably grotesque ceramic troll *Igor* on my bookshelf. My folks' neighbors keep an impish gnome in their garden. Also, those fabulous round women sculptures, which I apparently inspired, are displayed around the world. But I digress. The woman looks like a California surfer girl with her long, golden-blonde ponytail, olive complexion, and—"

Danni cut her off. "Oh, let me do her face."

Marnie nodded.

"So, her face is perfect."

I looked at Danni. "I think you can do better. And remember, be honest." I tried to keep my face impassive as she studied it, but I had to work not to laugh at how intently she was staring at me.

"Fine. Good cheekbones, but not too high, elegantly chiseled nose, full lips, neat, very white teeth, nicely arched blonde eyebrows, and hazel eyes…" She leaned in closer. "With gold flecks."

"Of course there are gold flecks," said Marnie.

I pursed my lips and shook my head. "No. Try this. You guys see me on the street. You've no idea who I am. You're alone, thinking to yourself, so you're completely free to be judgmental."

"Airhead," said Marnie.

"Fashion doll," said Danni.

"Bingo!" I said.

"Are you saying that looking like a party girl is a disadvantage to you?" said Danni.

"Of course, it is. I'm a nerd. I read history and science for fun. I'm passionate about my work, my reading, and my writing—and little else. But I'm dismissed as a bubblehead. I have to earn respect, every time, every day." I took a deep breath. "And I have a feeling some people refuse to attribute my success to hard work—if you know what I mean."

"I never thought about it like that, but I guess you're right." Danni sat up a little straighter and added, "That stinks."

"But, frankly," Marnie said, as she swirled the wine remaining in her glass, "judging by how our waiter reacted to you, it's more of a superpower than a disability."

"I'll admit that I use it sometimes, but I try to do it for good, rather than evil. Listen, I'm really not saying that prejudice against my looks is the same as that against dwarves and—"

"You can say it, Heather. I'm called a fat person."

"Shit. I'm not sure I can say that. The thing is, I've always choked at using the three-letter F-word to describe a woman. How about 'plus-size'?"

Marnie lifted her glass to her lips and polished off her wine. "Fat or not, my tummy is demanding that we eat soon."

"Mine too," added Danni.

"There is one other thing about my appearance that's frustrating."

"Let me guess," Marnie said. "If it's not the airhead thing, it must be the threat thing."

"How would you know that?" I asked, and immediately regretted it. I felt my face flush, and hoped they wouldn't notice.

Marnie stared at me, then deadpanned, "That hurt."

"What are you two talking about?" asked Danni.

I waved my hand toward Marnie to answer—trying to redeem myself with her.

"A lot of women don't like to hang out with stunning girlfriends because the contrast is to their disadvantage. But the bigger issue is that many women don't want the beauty anywhere near their boyfriends or husbands."

"Then they're not very secure in their relationships," Danni said.

Marnie shrugged. "Hardly anyone is."

"Yeah. That's what I was referring to," I said. "Would I sound like a whiner if I said it can be lonely?"

"Are you kidding?" Marnie asked. "Of course, you'd sound like a whiner."

Embarrassed, I bit my lower lip, and said nothing.

Danni jumped in. "I don't think that's fair, Marnie.

All three of us have issues because of the way we look. Heather's issues aren't whines just because they're so far from ours."

"Try, in a different solar system."

Mortified, I looked away as I said, "Marnie's right. Sorry."

"Don't be," Danni said. "It's just the other side of my coin with girl pals. Either way, they avoid us. I think it's fascinating. So, what exactly have you two seen?"

Again, I waved to Marnie. She laughed. "Of course, Heather's first reaction was right. I haven't been a victim of that particular type of shunning. But my horrid mother has. She's beautiful, outside and outside. I've overheard her lament her lack of women friends. And apparently, when she and my father are invited to dinner parties, like work-related shindigs, she is always seated as far as possible from any remotely attractive man. It's very real to her. Until I left for college, I heard about it all the time."

Danni said, "It's amazing to me how little people appreciate each other's challenges."

Marnie said, "Wait. You just said how little people *appreciate—*"

Danni laughed. I just shook my head.

After we ordered, we moved on to more traditional first meeting topics; movies, politics, and books. By the time our meals were served, we'd each had a glass of wine at the restaurant, and I was relieved of the perspiring and the blinking that had plagued me earlier. We had a pleasant meal, with no additional discussion about our looks. But by dessert, a comment from earlier in the evening pestered at me until I blurted out, "Why weren't either of you at Ms. Spitz's deposition?"

"Is that an accusation?" Marnie asked.

"Sorry. I didn't mean for it to come out like I'm a state's attorney and you guys are on the stand. But the thing is, the three of us talked through everything on the case by phone, and we signed onto each other's filings. It would've made sense for you two to take plaintiff's deposition with me."

"I know," said Danni. "The thing is, I just work inside the four walls of my office. So, I prepare all the paperwork—appearances and answers, written discovery, and motions. And then I review everything that comes in, like dep transcripts and briefs from the other parties, for the partner I work for. I prepare the status reports and case evaluation letters to the client, but the partner signs them. I confer with co-counsel and the clients, but only by telephone."

"That's crazy," I said. Danni just shrugged, so I continued, "Then what was their reason for hiring you?"

"It wasn't easy for me to get a job in what I wanted to do—litigation. So, after almost a year of rejections, my mom called her sister who's married to one of the senior partners in the firm. He didn't have much of an excuse to not hire me since I've had top grades all through school, Law Review, Order of the Coif, and all that nonsense. Now it's almost six years that I've been practicing with the firm."

I shook my head as I said, "That's not right, Danni."

Marnie spoke up. "I'd like to agree with you, Heather. But I'm not allowed out of my cave either."

"You're saying, because you're plus-size?" I asked.

"Because I'm 'more of a back-office lawyer,' according to the partner I work with. But I finished law school at the top of my class, won the statewide moot court, and now bill more than most of the associates, so I'm in a solid position. I do the same things Danni does. Plus, I research and write most of the appellate briefs for our firm, and for a lot of others that want us on their appeals. I do everything but the oral arguments."

I placed both my hands on the table and leaned in. "Is your name of record on all of those briefs?"

"The partner signs his name. Then, if the thing doesn't settle, he does the oral argument."

At that point, my mouth was literally hanging open. I managed to sputter, "You've both been practicing about six years?"

"Exactly six," said Marnie.

"Almost," said Danni.

"As have I. But I do all the depositions and the court appearances on my cases, I handle my own jury trials, and write and sign my appellate briefs. I argue my own appeals."

"Good for you!" said Marnie.

I squinted at her, as though that would help me understand the woman.

Danni said to Marnie, "I don't think Heather meant it that way."

"I'm not bragging, Marnie. What I do is what all six-year associates in defense firms do, at least in Lake County."

Marnie was dismissive of my concerns. She said, "Well, that's the way it is." Then she looked at her watch, so I also glanced at mine. Somehow, we'd been allowed to linger over our meals for almost three hours.

I said, "We'd better leave a big tip."

"I think the waiter would rather have your number," said Marnie.

I laughed. "I've got the gratuity right here." But I was distracted by the injustice at their law firms. I felt like I'd just witnessed Marnie and Danni get slapped, and my immediate urge was to slap someone back. Once we'd paid our bills and were ready to leave, I said, "It's been an interesting evening—to say the least. Let's get together again soon."

"Absolutely," said Danni.

"Sounds good to me," said Marnie.

On the sidewalk, I bent down to give Danni a quick hug, and leaned in to awkwardly put my hands on Marnie's shoulders for hers. Neither woman resisted, but they didn't really hug back—probably due to logistics. We grabbed a cab to share, and they dropped me at the train station on their way to their respective apartments. I had a half-hour wait and then a half-hour-ride up to my place in Evanston to think through all I'd seen and heard, and get a grip on my anger about the way their firms were treating them. As I sat alone in a double seat on the train, I couldn't stop tapping my finger against the armrest. Once home, I took my little dog out for a quick walk, then paced around my apartment, thinking about Marnie and Danni until I finally grew calm enough to go to bed. While wearing circles in my rug, I'd realized that there was something else, too. Once I'd gotten over my initial surprise at their looks, both women had struck me as especially genuine. They'd made me laugh. I wanted to see them again because, embarrassment notwithstanding, I'd had a lot of fun hanging out with them.

Chapter 2

Ms. Spitz's lawyer dismissed his complaint once he received the results of the mouse x-rays, so Marnie, Danni, and I were no longer automatically in touch. I assumed the others were as absorbed with the press of work as I was. A month had passed since our dinner, and neither of them had reached out to me. I'd been mulling over how unfairly their firms were treating them and what could be done about it. I came up with what I thought was a pretty intriguing solution. I already knew they were both excellent lawyers from their work on the Spitz case. It wasn't easy to dig up the evidence on the plaintiff's prior frauds since she'd used numerous aliases and phony social security numbers in a number of jurisdictions. They'd both been tenacious and creative, giving the woman just enough rope to perjure herself—numerous times. I had to admit my plan was also heavily influenced by the other thing—that Marnie and Danni just might offer my best chance for making true friends, women for whom my looks would be irrelevant. I suspected that, over time, I would be able to see right past theirs, as well.

At a second get-together, I wouldn't have to deal with the surprise of meeting two women my mind's eye had seen so differently from how they actually looked. I figured the chances we could all relax and be ourselves should improve each time we'd see each other. So, I sent an email to suggest a get-together and ask if they'd be willing to come up to my neighborhood for a dinner. Evanston was roughly half-way between Chicago and Waukegan, in distance and in status.

****

Hi, Marnie and Danni, It's been too long. Would you like to get together for dinner? Are you willing to take the train to Evanston so you can see me in my natural habitat? I'd love to visit with you and hope we can find a date that works for everyone. I'm available the following Saturday evenings—

****

Danni accepted right away and explained that she hadn't initiated another get-together because she generally avoided rejection by not asking for anything. Then Marnie wrote to explain she'd been swamped with a knotty appellate brief but expected the light at the end of the tunnel would appear in about a week. We set a date, and they agreed to come north to a restaurant of my choosing.

I selected an upscale Mandarin restaurant, mainly because of its proximity to my apartment building. I hoped that would encourage Marnie and Danni to agree to stop by after dinner, before heading back to the train station. While reserving a table, I explained the need for a pile of towels on Danni's chair, which the owner of the restaurant kindly assured me would be in place. I cleaned my apartment and made sure I had several bottles of wine in the kitchen. The idea I wanted to discuss with them shouldn't be broached in a public setting, since it had the real potential to get all three of us fired.

At the restaurant, I had stashed my umbrella and raincoat, and I was already seated when I saw them walk in through the revolving door. I swallowed hard. Apparently, my prior exposure had failed to inoculate me against being jolted by their forms. I'd always thought a jacket had the magical ability to hide a multitude of sins, but Marnie looked even larger than I remembered in her off-white, iridescent raincoat, and Danni appeared more child-like in her belted olive trench coat and tall rubber boots. Nevertheless, their smiles lit up the room, and I regretted having let so many weeks slip by without seeing them. Marnie threw her things, and then Danni's, on the coat rack near the door and they made their way to our table.

I jumped up to give each of them a quick hug as we said our hellos. Danni noticed that a chair had been readied for her, threw her canvas bag containing her cushion under the table, and sat across from me. Marnie chose the seat to my right.

"Sorry I chose a stormy night to drag you up here. Did you guys have any trouble finding this place?"

"Not per se." Marnie raised an eyebrow.

"Oh, no. What happened?"

Danni smiled. "It was nothing really. We'd just gotten off the train. Since it was raining pretty steadily, we both raised our umbrellas." She was acting it out. "The moment mine was up, a gust of wind thrust me to the very edge of the platform."

"Oh, my god!"

Marnie said, "A guy who was standing there waiting for a southbound train reached down and grabbed Danni around her waist, then twirled her back. It looked like a dance move."

"Thank goodness he was there," I said. "Are you okay, Danni?"

"Absolutely. He actually got down on one knee, in a puddle, to make sure he hadn't hurt me. That's when I saw how cute he was." She glanced at Marnie who nodded in confirmation.

"And a very kind person," I said.

"Very. It's funny, but in all the years I've been outside on rainy days holding an umbrella, I was never lifted like that before."

"She definitely achieved lift-off," said Marnie.

I sighed. "I'm so glad you're okay. And I have to tell you guys that I really miss having a case together."

"I do, too," said Danni. "You two are much more fun than any other lawyers I deal with."

"Ditto," said Marnie.

Once our wine was served, Danni picked up her glass and made a toast, "To new friends." She remembered the one I'd made a month before. We clinked.

After taking a sip, I apologized for not having made sure we'd see each other sooner.

"I agree with the sentiment, Heather," said Marnie. "But you're not our cruise director. Danni and I are equally guilty." She set her wine glass down and leaned back in her chair.

"True," I said. "And you two may make it up to me by agreeing to stop by for a glass of wine at my apartment. It's literally two blocks from here."

"Suits me," said Marnie.

"I'd love to see you in your natural habitat—as you put it in your email." Danni picked up her menu. "Now, what's good here?"

Afterwards, walking the couple of blocks with them was awkward in ways I hadn't expected. With Marnie on one side of me and Danni on the other, it was much easier logistically to chat with Marnie since Danni's head reached just above the level of my waist. The other major issue was that I tended to be a quick walker, so I had to consciously reduce my pace to one that was comfortable for them. And, positioned between them, I was the recipient of many stares, raised eyebrows, and pitying smiles, which must've made up their everyday realities. I am embarrassed to say that I was embarrassed. I put on a fake smile and worked to summon all the maturity I possessed to try to experience it more as eye-opening, which it was, and which almost everything about my friendship with Marnie and Danni had been.

We reached my building, and as I dug in my purse for the key, I said, "At least we didn't need our umbrellas."

"Less risk that Danni would float off," said Marnie.

"Actually, I wouldn't mind blowing away again if that handsome guy would catch me."

I smiled down at the top of her head. I normally dashed up the stairs to my second-floor studio apartment, but I guessed it would better suit Marnie and Danni to take the elevator. I led us there, and then on to my unit. I'd left a couple of lamps burning for our return and for my pal, Chica-the-Brave, but switched on a couple more. I also needed to turn off NPR, which I always kept on as company for her when I left.

As Marnie and Danni stepped into my apartment, my white, five-pound guard dog ran up to them, barking as though she knew they were bent on robbing and murdering me. After a minute or so of my reassuring her with the nonsensical statement, "All gone," she went back to her bed to resume her nap. Once she was quiet, I said, "My ferocious protector is Chica-the-Brave."

"And you named her that because—" said Marnie.

"Ever since I got her as a tiny puppy fluff-ball, she's been aggressive with other dogs—and sometimes people—when she first meets them. The bigger they are, the more she goes after them. But she bites neither man nor beast. It's more like a mad, fearless dash at the newcomer, with lots of yapping—like how she just reacted to you guys. When I walk her, she pulls on the leash, trying to run at anything loud, especially motorcycles and trucks."

As she glanced around for a place to put her umbrella, Marnie said, "I was going to say something about short man complex—but she's a female. Also, I don't want Danni to think I have anything against short men."

I took the three damp umbrellas and threw them into my kitchen sink. "I planned to call her Chica, because I was studying Spanish online at the time. But her personality demanded the additional words."

"I'll bet she's a sweetheart with you," said Danni.

"She's a doll. At night she sleeps with her little head resting on my leg."

My apartment was one large room, with the kitchen and bathroom off to the side. Dressed with linens and pillows to simulate a daybed, my twin bed was pushed against the opposite wall. Two small, floral chintz-covered couches faced each other, with an oval, glass-topped coffee table between them. Since I had only a tiny closet, I'd bought an old armoire and a garage sale oak chest, which I'd placed near the bed. My two large windows faced a Catholic church and grammar school across the street.

"Sweet apartment," said Marnie.

Danni said, "It's so cozy."

"Thanks. It's home."

After taking their raincoats and tossing them on my bed, I put on some jazz. I said, "Red or white?" and both opted for the chardonnay. I asked them to make themselves at home, and Marnie complied by taking off her shoes and lounging on one of the couches, while Danni made herself comfortable on the other. When I returned with a tray holding the wine and glasses, I sat beside Danni. Once we'd each taken a sip of the chardonnay, I took a deep breath, licked my lips, and said, "So, has anything changed at your firms?"

"In what way?" asked Marnie.

"I'm referring to being let out of your caves. Have you gotten to do any court appearances?"

"No change there," said Marnie. "And not likely to be."

"Nor for me," said Danni.

"For how long do you guys plan to put up with that?"

"Just until I retire," said Danni.

"I haven't really thought about it," said Marnie. "It's not how I imagined my career, but it's interesting work and I'm paid well."

"Me too," said Danni. "I love what I do. And I'm thrilled with my paycheck."

I started to perspire before asking my next question, but I managed it. "Do you guys mind saying what you're talking about in the paycheck department?"

"In the low six figures," said Marnie.

"Mine, too," said Danni.

Marnie looked at me and said, "Why? What's

yours?"

"High five figures. Lake County defense firms don't get paid the same hourly that Chicago firms do, so we associates get a bit less."

Marnie said, "Then maybe it's we who should be asking you how long you plan to put up with that."

"It's not the same thing."

"How so?" asked Marnie. Chica-the-Brave came around the corner of the couch, popped up to sit beside her, and promptly rolled over for a belly-rub. Marnie rolled her eyes before obliging her.

Having survived asking the impertinent question about their salaries, I was able to relax into the rest of my spiel. "I think you both know 'how so,' but I'm happy to lay it out. You both went to law school, and you performed exceptionally well, right?"

"True," said Marnie.

"That's right," said Danni.

"Marnie, the last time we were together, you mentioned you won the state-wide moot court competition in law school. And, Danni, you said you really wanted to practice as a litigator."

"So?" asked Marnie.

"So, neither of you is being allowed to do what you're more than capable of, and hoped to be doing. While you haven't spent time in court, I assume you've both read tons of transcripts of court hearings and trials. Was there ever a single performance by a defense attorney that you don't believe you could've done as well—if not better?"

"Okay. I admit it. I would've done better," said Marnie.

Danni hesitated for a moment, then said, "I'll just

25

say that I could've thought up the same or better arguments. But I have no idea if my presentation would be as strong. I just don't have a public speaking background."

I pulled my right leg up under me as I turned to face her. "But you could, Danni. None of us is born making an opening statement."

"That's something I'd like to see, though," said Marnie.

I shook my head. "Seriously, Marnie, don't you yearn to do the thing you were trained to do?"

"I'm already doing most of what I was trained to do—and with excellent results, thank you."

"Face the fact, Marnie. Your name isn't even on your appellate briefs."

She put up both hands, which Chica-the-Brave took as a signal to move on to Danni. She trotted under the coffee table and jumped up to sit between Danni and me. Marnie said, "I concede. I'm basically an excellent ghost writer. But it is a legit, well-paying job."

"Listen, guys, I'm not trying to convince you to covet something you really don't want. I just can't imagine talented, six-year lawyers in litigation practices *not* wanting to get into court. During the six months we worked together, I just assumed you were getting court time, like any other lawyer."

"Honestly," said Danni, "I don't know what to say. I'll have to give it some thought. But why don't you tell us what you think would be so great about having our bodies inside the courtroom."

I took a moment to think, and another sip of wine to be sure my tongue was lubricated. I looked from one of them to the other as I answered. "There's nothing like it.

There's a solemnity to court, a feeling of reverence I used to get in church. I know this sounds corny, but I always feel honored to be allowed to speak for my client, irrespective of the quality of the judge who happens to be listening to me. It's the integrity of *my* work that I can control, which is why it's so important to me to communicate reason and truth…to be a voice that the judges know won't bullshit them. It's being a part of a process that's still sacred and bigger than any one person. And that's just when I'm arguing motions."

I pulled my other leg up under me. "Now think about defending your client in front of a jury. Mastering the facts, exposing the deceit, convincing twelve people, who are taking the time to do their own civic duty, that you're the one who is telling them the truth. Addressing the jurors—owning their attention—empowers you like you'll never experience anywhere else. There's no thrill like having a verdict come in, and even if you've won, talking with the jurors to learn how you can do a better job the next time. Honestly, it's highly emotional. But all the while, you know that everything you did, and everything your opponent did, is fair game as the parties study their appeal options."

They both looked interested, so I took the last sip of my wine and went on. "And then there's the appellate court, where you conclusively win or lose, and potentially change the law. The briefs aren't always the whole story—I know it's possible to change the mind of an appellate judge in oral argument. I've seen it happen. I've made it happen. So, whether you're handling a motion at the trial court, a jury trial, or an appeal in the First or Second District, the Seventh Circuit, or the State Supreme Court, oral argument is the culmination of all of your work."

"So, it's the climax," said Marnie. "I like climaxes."

"It's the apex," said Danni.

I laughed, then leaned forward and emptied the bottle, giving each of us a quarter of a glass. "But it really is, guys. The zenith. The summit. The pinnacle. It's all that. And you're missing it."

"Shit," said Marnie. "There's no point in my going on."

"Okay. Okay. I know I get carried away about this stuff. I just think you two deserve to experience it."

"How do you propose we change our bosses' positions about it?" asked Danni.

"Ask for it. Depending on how strongly you feel about it, possibly demand it. You could present an ultimatum."

"Ouch," said Marnie. "I was with you up to 'ask.' I have to pay my rent. And I prefer to be able to eat and drink—obviously."

"Heather, I love your passion for the courtroom work. But I'm with Marnie. No one is supporting me but me. And I only got the job because of my uncle. Remember?"

"I remember."

Marnie said, "Actually, I think it's sweet that you don't want us to miss out on what you obviously love doing." She finished her wine and held out her empty glass to show me.

I got up to fetch another bottle, then returned with it and stood at the end of the coffee table. I was nervous to be closing in on making my big pitch, and in spite of all the wine, my mouth was suddenly dry. "What if you did have another job to go to if you were to give the ultimatum and then got shot down?"

"First of all," said Danni, "if I give an ultimatum, I'll definitely be shot down. I have a pity position as it is. Yes, I do great work, but it wouldn't be hard for the firm to find a person of average height who could also do a great job."

"And second," said Marnie, "there is no other job. Neither of us has been able to make the kind of contacts and reputations we'd need in order to be confident we'd get job offers—much less ones that pay as well."

I took a deep breath, then sat back down next to Danni. Chica-the-Brave, still between us, had settled in so that her little face rested between her paws, her brown eyes fixed on Marnie. I leaned forward to pour a little into each glass, then set the bottle down.

Danni said, "You have an idea, don't you?"

I hesitated, knowing they'd both think what I was about to say would prove I was a deranged nut.

Danni said softly, "What is it, Heather? What's your idea?"

The kindness in her voice gave me the courage to say it. "We start our own firm."

Marnie's first reaction was a snort, followed by uncontrolled laughter. She actually slipped off the couch and continued guffawing on the floor, wedged between the couch and the coffee table. Danni was biting her lower lip, probably to keep from also cracking up in my face.

I sat stone-faced, looked at each of them, and said, "So, that's a 'yes'?"

Once Marnie pulled herself up off the floor and was able to regain her composure, the three of us talked briefly about my suggestion. Meaning, we all agreed we'd had too much to drink to have a constructive conversation about it that night. But Marnie and Danni promised to start giving the idea some thought.

We chatted about other subjects, and by the time I handed them their things, gave out hugs, and led them to the elevator, it was clear we were all feeling quite mellow. Standing at the front door of my building, I watched the two of them head down the block toward the train station, and I wondered how long it would take me to evolve from seeing their unconventional figures to just seeing my friends.

Back in my apartment, as I washed and dried the wine glasses, I weighed the disruption we would all face against the positives of opening our own shop. We could definitely make sure that Marnie and Danni would get time in the courtroom and in depositions. And, from what I'd heard, partnering to start a new firm was an intimate and intense venture. We would take on a huge debt together, and spend countless hours with each other planning every detail of the launch. We'd also share a secret, our plan to leave our current jobs and take as many of our employers' clients with us as possible. If that were discovered, it could definitely get us booted out of our old jobs before we were ready to go, jeopardizing our careers.

Still, it looked like exactly what I longed for—a chance to develop serious friendships. I tried to convince myself that the sisterhood aspect was a bonus, and the righting of a wrong was my main objective.

Chapter 3

If there were to be any hope of convincing them to partner with me, I'd need to have a business plan that was realistic and promising. At that point, I wasn't sure those two elements could co-exist. I knew a few lawyers who'd opened their own shops, but it would be impossible to approach them for advice without risking that my plan to leave my own firm, and take as many clients with me as possible, would be discovered. Therefore, I had to base my proposal on my research on what issues needed to be addressed.

I spent the evenings and a couple of weekends making a list of what we'd need, rough cost projections, and a simple timeline. I based everything on a Lake County location, for reasons that had nothing to do with logistics or costs, and everything to do with establishing ourselves in a community of lawyers small enough to allow everyone to eventually get to know Marnie and Danni as the amazing people they were. The anonymity of a big city law practice was a positive for many things, but it pretty much eliminated the frequent interactions that brought genuine acceptance. In a smaller county, one would regularly run across the same lawyers, which was why incivility among attorneys was much less a problem. At least, that was my belief as I prepared to lay out my proposal for Marnie and Danni.

We'd met for dinner a couple of times in the interim,

but when I explained I wanted to talk about my plan for our new firm, we all appreciated it wasn't something to be discussed in a bar or restaurant. Danni invited us to her apartment on a Saturday evening in early October. I took the train from Evanston, as I didn't own a car, and wouldn't have driven it into the Chicago Loop if I did. It wasn't a terribly long way from the station to her address, and I was wearing comfy jeans and sneakers, so I hoofed it.

Once Danni buzzed me in the main entrance, I had trouble finding the stairs, so I took the elevator to her apartment on the top floor. I knocked, Danni swung the door open, and as I leaned down to give her a hug, I glimpsed just behind her a large, gorgeous, black and brown German shepherd, alert to what was happening, eyes glued to me.

Danni saw me staring and said, "This is my sweetie-pie."

I nodded. I was a devoted dog-lover, but I immediately remembered something I'd read about German shepherds when I was trying to select a breed: *This breed will kill for you.* "What's his—or her—name?"

"He's a he. And his name is Grizzly."

"I love it."

"He looks ferocious, but he's an angel with me."

"So, you don't think he would kill for you?"

"I know he would. That's why his training is so important."

I threw my purse and jacket on a bench in the entryway and squatted down to say hello to Grizzly. I asked, "May I?" before touching him. Danni nodded, so I ran my hand over the rich, thick fur on his powerful neck. He remained in a perfect sitting position, allowing me to pet him, my fingers deep in his luxurious coat. I glanced at Danni's attractive furniture, all mission and arts and crafts style. The chairs were softened with richly patterned deep orange and gold brocade fabric.

Marnie hadn't arrived yet, so Danni took me out on her balcony to see the cityscape, which enchanted me with the warm glow of lights just popping on in skyscrapers, mid-rises and the city streets below us. There were a couple of metal chairs, so I grabbed one to get down to Danni's level. She remained standing as we chatted. I said, "How do you manage to get Grizzly the exercise he needs?"

"He needs a lot. Normally, I get up early and take him to a large dog park not too far from here. There's room for him to run full-out when he plays with the other pups. And I have a friend I pay to take Grizzly on long walks around noon and then again around five o'clock every week day. I usually get home by seven, have my dinner, and spend forty-five minutes working with Grizzly on training exercises, before his last walk to do his business at bedtime."

"Forty-five minutes a day of training is impressive."

"Do you think so? When he was a puppy—basically, until he was three—I spent at least an hour and a half every night."

"That's amazing. I just trained Chica-the-Brave to use the pads, which took a few minutes several times a day for about two months until she became reliable."

"What else did you train her to do?"

"Sit. Also, she walks well on a leash, but I can't claim to have trained her in that. She just likes to be a few steps ahead of me, walks when I walk, stops when I stop, pretty much from the beginning. Why? What else can Grizzly do?"

"Sit, roll over, crawl, shake, fetch, bow, play dead, come when called, stop on a dime, growl and bare his teeth when requested, and attack when absolutely necessary."

"Phenomenal. So, you just give a command and he does it?"

"I control him mainly by my facial expressions. But he also knows my voice commands for each behavior, since I may need to instruct him when he can't see me—like when I'm in another room, and I need him to come."

I scrunched up my face. "How can you do that with just a look?"

"Watch this, Heather. I'll call him, then have him lie down, just using my face. Grizzly! Come!"

Within a fraction of a second, Grizzly bounded onto the balcony, then stood completely still, staring at Danni. A second later, Grizzly was lying down at her feet, but I hadn't seen her do anything in particular with her face.

"That was sensational! Would you mind asking Grizzly to do something else? I just want to really focus to see if I can tell what you're doing." I kept my eyes glued to her face.

She smiled. "Sure."

I caught Danni wink her left eye and, sure enough, Grizzly rolled over.

"Wow! Is dog training your hobby?"

"I'm not sure that would be the right word for it. It's more like breathing. It's something I must do."

"Why?"

"I live in a city. I'm three feet eight inches tall. I'm a victim waiting for a purse snatching—or worse. I feel safe enough without Grizzly on my way to and from work because it's rush hour. But I need to take him out for a walk after dinner every night, and sometimes I need to go out in the evening for something. If I feel the least bit nervous, I have Grizzly bare his teeth, which works every time."

I studied the muscular animal. "Someone would have to be suicidal to mess with you. But I still don't understand why he has to be so phenomenally well-trained."

"If he weren't, what do you think would happen if someone bothered me?"

"He'd attack?"

"Exactly. German shepherds are profoundly protective, Heather, so he could seriously hurt someone. Like I said before, I know he'd kill for me. Of course, he's always on a leash, but that's just for show. I don't have the physical strength to have any impact whatsoever on what he does. If Grizzly weren't reliably responsive to my commands, I couldn't keep him."

"Makes sense. But why facial expression rather than a whistle or something like that?"

Danni laughed. "Of course, this isn't the usual way. It's just that my face is near to the level of Grizzly's, so I started working on it, basically to see if I could do it. For me, this takes no physical strength at all. Plus, while I might not always have a whistle with me, I always have my face with me."

I laughed. "Good point."

We heard Marnie on the intercom, Danni hurried to buzz her in, and we both met her at the door. She gave us each a quick hug and approached Grizzly. "Oh, what a handsome doggie you are."

Grizzly bowed, and I burst out laughing.

"That was incredible!" said Marnie. "How did he…or she…understand what I said?"

"*He* didn't," said Danni.

I said, "Danni controls Grizzly's every move with her facial expressions."

Marnie looked at Danni, then at Grizzly. "I believe that. Your faces are pretty much at the same level. It's logical. You know something? You and Grizzly could always get work as a circus act: the midget and the monster."

For once, Danni didn't laugh. She said, "You are a funny woman, Marnie. But I should tell you that 'midget' is pejorative."

I said, "I would think the suggestion of a circus act might be, too."

Danni looked up at me and smiled. "Actually, I love Marnie's warped humor. I just wanted her to know about that word—in case she comes across any other dwarves." She glanced at Marnie. "And, I have to warn you that a lot of them are quite strong."

"They wouldn't have to be particularly Herculean to take me down. I'm in terrible shape." She paused. "Okay. Go ahead, Heather. Hit me with a good wisecrack. Perhaps something about me also having a promising career on the midway."

"Marnie, you do very well at insulting yourself. You don't need my paltry attempts."

"Very true," she said, then let loose her endearing, hearty, unrestrained laughter. She slipped out of her jacket and threw it on the bench, next to mine.

I was taking in a rich aroma. "Do I smell bread baking?"

"I made some baguettes to go with our lasagna. A salad. And a little dessert."

"Sounds wonderful," I said. "Thanks, Danni."

"Would you guys like a quick tour?"

"Definitely," said Marnie.

I nodded.

"Great. Don't guess I need to say this is my living room, and that little alcove with the table is my dining room." As we approached the rectangular oak table and six chairs, I noticed a gorgeous inlaid wood pattern around the edge of the piece, and that the whole set glowed in the lamp light.

"It's all so beautiful," I said.

"Thanks. Most of the pieces were gifts."

Marnie asked, "Why did you decide to go with full-sized furniture?"

Danni smiled. "Come over here." She led us around the table to the head, where the only seat with armrests was located. When she pulled out the chair, which was on wheels, we saw the extra, fitted cushion which raised the seat up about six inches. She said, "My friends and family are all average size people, so this works out best. But wait until you see my bedroom."

We stepped through the door behind the dining room into her bedroom, which was decorated in more arts and crafts style furniture, with a stunning orange, yellow, and black paisley coverlet on the bed. Everything was about fifteen inches shorter than normal. Danni smiled. "This is my space. So, I had everything custom made to make me feel comfortable."

"It's lovely," I said, as I looked at all the beautiful pieces.

"It really is," said Marnie. "It makes me feel a little

like that animated princess."

"Marnie!" I said.

"You know, with your black hair, fair complexion, and beautiful face, you are a ringer for her," said Danni.

"Thanks."

"But I'm afraid there aren't six more dwarves here."

"You guys are terrible," I said.

"I am," said Marnie.

I just shook my head, which I realized I did a lot when I was with them.

Danni showed us her bathroom, where everything was suited for average height people, but with a long stool at the sink. "If I ever buy a place of my own, I'll customize my bathroom, and have another, traditional one for guests." Her small, modern kitchen was also full size, with a couple of foot stools at the ready. I noticed two crystal plates sitting on the granite countertop, holding attractively arranged veggie and cheese appetizers. Danni offered wine, and we agreed on a chardonnay that I poured. We each grabbed a goblet from the counter and headed back to the living room.

"You are so interesting, Danni," I said. "I have a ton of questions I'd love to ask you. But I think we should talk business first, before our wine consumption impairs us."

"Good plan," said Marnie, as she settled herself on the cushioned couch. She added, "Danni, can you wrinkle your nose, or whatever, and get Grizzly to sit beside me so I can pet him?"

I'm not sure what Danni did to make it happen, but she may've lifted an eyebrow. Within a second, Grizzly was up on the couch, his head resting on her lap.

Marnie laughed out loud. "You are too cool, Danni."

"Of course. That's everyone's first reaction to me."

Danni and I each took one of the small recliners, which were oak, with padded, brocade-covered seats and backs. I took a deep breath and dove in. "You are both too cool," I said. "Way too cool to be hidden away in your work caves."

"You'll need more flattery than that to convince me to leave my gilded cage, Heather," said Marnie.

"I could come up with more. Remember, I'm a writer. But I think we all know you two won't decide based on anything but a realistic plan that will both get you into the courtroom and guarantee some level of financial security."

"Very true," said Danni.

I took a quick gulp of wine, then set my glass on the coffee table. "I've been doing some research, and the truth is, this won't be easy."

"Shocker," said Marnie.

"I can get into the weeds with details of all the things we'd need to put in place, licensing— probably an LLC— taxes, insurance, staffing, office space, blah, blah, blah."

"That's a lot of important 'blah, blah, blah.' Isn't it?" asked Danni.

"It is important. But there are two major obstacles we have to figure out before it makes sense to worry about any of those other things."

"Let us guess," said Marnie, cocking her head and pointing a finger at her temple. "Clients. We need to know we'll have work to do."

"That's one."

"Financing," said Danni. "Even assuming we have plenty of work, we need to be able to pay ourselves enough to keep up with our rents and bills until our profits catch up."

"You guys are good," I said.

"I figure we must not be too stupid, or you wouldn't want us as your law partners," said Marnie, as she dug her fingers into Grizzly's coat.

"Those are pretty significant hurdles, Heather," said Danni.

"She's right. Let's move on to the appetizers," said Marnie, who was in the process of standing up.

I was a little annoyed at being dismissed. "Do you two always give up so easily?" I realized how ridiculous my comment was just after the last word left my mouth, and I bit down on my lower lip. To their credit, they didn't say anything. "Sorry. Of course, you don't. But wouldn't you at least like to talk through how we might make this work?"

Marnie sat back down. "Heather, yes, I was being flippant. But it was only because I honestly can't imagine how we overcome either of those hurdles. Danni and I have made it clear that our clients won't follow us because they don't realize the degree to which we've been controlling the fates of their files. They think the partner who signed everything also planned the strategies, and carefully guided our work. They barely know us, except as names on line-items on billing statements."

"You would have to supply the work for the three of us," said Danni. "And from what I've heard about other firms that have splintered off, they almost never get as many clients to follow them as they think they will."

"Everything you guys say is true," I said. "I'd just like us to be creative and think of a way to make this work."

"I think it'll take more than creativity," said Marnie. "Maybe Danni could hypnotize them with a wink of her eye."

"I wish I could. I would truly love to practice law with you and Marnie, Heather. I really am sorry I don't have any business to bring with me."

"And that's only one of the two insurmountable hurdles," said Marnie, leaning in to set down her empty wine glass. "What about funding? None of us owns a home we could use as collateral for a loan. I doubt any bank will give us one based on our good looks." She paused. "Well, Heather, you might surprise me on that. But I don't think even you have good looks enough to cover three people."

"Hey!" Since I was completely deflated, I went along with the hilarity of defeat. But I was getting in one more question before I'd surrender the stage to appetizers. I started sweating, just like when I'd asked them their salaries. "So, do you guys have any money?"

"Well, Danni's a little short," said Marnie.

I groaned.

She ignored me and continued, "As for me, I have a little bit, but it's already committed to rent, groceries, and of course, student loans. I don't have much in my 401k yet."

"Ditto," said Danni. "I'm sorry. I'd be thrilled to finance us if I had anything to do it with. What about you, Heather?"

"Same story. And my parents don't have any extra money, either. My two younger brothers come to me for loans." I let out a long sigh. "I guess it is time for appetizers."

"I'll tell you what," said Marnie. "If any of us can think of a way to deal with either of the big hurdles, I'll help work on the other."

"Me, too," said Danni.

"Maybe one of us will win the lottery," I said, as I rose, shoulders slumped, to help Danni fetch the trays of hors d'oeuvres.

"If I win, I'm off to Europe," said Marnie. "But I'll send postcards."

"Thanks, Marnie. Great team spirit," I said.

She laughed and got up to stretch her legs.

An hour later, at dinner, I asked Danni if she had any friends who were dwarves. She said she did, all people she'd met at a regional meeting of Little People of America.

"It's a club?" asked Marnie.

"It's a national organization of people under four feet, eight inches tall, and their friends and relatives. There are also some members who are medical professionals who have little people as patients."

"Do you attend those meetings often?" I asked, while buttering one of her crusty home-made baguettes.

"I should." She paused for a moment. "I'll never forget walking into my first LPA get-together, about five years ago."

"Was it heaven to be with people who looked like you?" I asked.

"Just the opposite. I walked into the ballroom of this hotel where the members were gathered for the cocktail hour and looked around. I found the sight of the dwarves disturbing. And some of them had physical anomalies in addition to small stature and shorter limbs. See, all of my life, I'd existed among people of average height. My first thought was, 'Do I look as strange as they do?' I was confused and embarrassed at my reaction. Fortunately, someone approached me and introduced me around. Once I started chatting with people, I was able to relax. I got to know a couple of women a bit, and we exchanged contact information. Since then, I've heard my reaction isn't all that uncommon."

"That must've been discombobulating," I said.

Marnie set down her utensils and took some water. "I get it, though. I'm trying to imagine what it would feel like for me to walk into a room full of fat people. I don't think my first reaction would be 'how cool—their bodies are just like mine!' I think I'd go straight to denial and tell myself I really don't look anything like those folks."

"That's where my mind went," said Danni. "I think it's just that we have cultural norms, and anything we see that deviates too much is jarring. It's by getting to know people as individuals that we start to see through that stuff."

"I agree," I said. "That's why I want us to practice together in Lake County, where the legal community is so much smaller than Chicago. After you have a few cases with the same opposing counsel, he or she will start to get to know you. I think that's how you become 'Danielle' rather than 'the dwarf lawyer.' That's why I've been so enthusiastic about my plan."

"It's a great plan," said Danni. "We'll keep our eyes peeled. If anything changes that would allow us to pursue it, we'll talk about it again."

"Unlikely. But sure," said Marnie, as she picked up her fork and knife, and dug into her lasagna.

I sighed, I hoped only to myself. I needed to focus on enjoying my time with my friends. Later, I'd get back to fretting over the fact that my idea seemed to be fizzling.

Chapter 4

We fell into a pattern of seeing each other at least every two weeks. Sometimes we took in a movie, or something playing at the Goodman, or Second City, before a late dinner. But our conversation was always the highlight of the evening, so we tended to just find different restaurants to try in Chicago or Evanston. I'm not sure when it was that I decided I was developing an immunity to the stares and comments. But I did like to think I was getting there, and I always looked forward to our next outing.

One evening in mid-November, we found a restaurant styled as an old-time English pub, just west of downtown. The place was all wood, buffed to a glow, with gleaming brass railings and hanging lamps. The waiters wore black bib aprons and either had British accents or did a good job of faking. I appreciated that we were seated in one of the several alcoves along the back wall, behind the bar area, and didn't care whether it was to hide us, or to provide us with some quiet for conversation.

The cozy, cocoon environment made me feel especially mellow. Once we had beer mugs in hand, I made our traditional toast, which I improved by omitting one word. So, we clinked our mugs "to friends." We seemed always to have so much to talk about that I'd never before found the right moment to ask Danni to educate me about dwarfism. I'd read several articles online but had a number of questions I figured she could answer for me.

"Danni, I don't mean to tokenize you in any way, but I wonder if you'd mind telling us a little bit about your kind of dwarfism? My guess is that it's achondroplasia, from what I've read."

Marnie said, "Wait. You haven't also researched obesity, have you?"

"Of course not. It's just that there are over a hundred kinds of dwarfism, and I'm interested in Danni's journey."

"Oh! Where have you been travelling, Danni?"

"Marnie, stop," I said. "Can't we have a conversation without your wisecracks for once?"

"Doubtful. Can't you just work around me?" She raised her eyebrows and gave me a crooked smile.

"What? Are you claiming you are constitutionally incapable of not making a joke? Like the pressure of holding in a punchline would make your head explode?"

"It might. And that, Heather, would be a huge, unsanitary mess. Of course, I don't know because I've never held one in."

"Liar," I said. "I'm sure you didn't constantly spout jokes in church, or at school."

"You might be surprised. I was the only student regularly in detention, who also had top grades."

I sighed. "Anyway, Danni, is there anything you'd like to share about it?"

"I don't always feel like discussing it, but sure." She nodded to me and then to Marnie before launching into it. "The dwarfism community refers to others as average size people—whether you are a smidge over four foot, eight inches tall or six feet or more. We refer to people of our height as dwarves when we're speaking of medical issues. *Midget,* which is really offensive in general discourse, is acceptable when we speak of the medical condition, a very short person with normally proportioned limbs. Outside a medical discussion, most of us prefer to be called persons of short stature or little people."

I couldn't believe I hadn't thought to ask her about her preference before.

"But you're good with 'dwarf.' Right?" asked Marnie.

"Yep."

I let out a breath and smiled at her.

"You're right, Heather, that I have achondroplasia. I'm lucky, as dwarves go, because I don't have special medical issues. I say 'lucky' because some people with dwarfism do have chronic health problems. See, there are hundreds of types, like Heather said. I keep up with one friend I met at an LPA meeting who has something called SED. Her arms and legs are normally proportionate, but she grew up with a tremendous amount of instability in her ankles, knees, and hips, as well as her spine. So, she had her first operation at age two, and over the years, she was frequently taken to the hospital as soon as school let out in the spring, for repair of the irregular bone growth in her legs. She was in either a leg cast or a full body cast for up to twelve weeks, and then she needed three or four weeks of physical therapy when she got home. Thankfully, once she reached puberty, all that ended."

"That's terrible," I said.

"I can't even imagine it," said Marnie. She wrinkled her forehead and pursed her lips. A couple of seconds later, she said, "Nope. I can't do it."

The waiter arrived and we all ordered the fish and chips special. Marnie was ready for a second beer.

Danni said, "Another LPA friend has a form of dwarfism with a completely different genetic mutation. She grew normally until she turned two years old. Her parents had no idea their daughter had a kind of dwarfism until she developed an abnormal gait as a toddler, and they got her assessed. Now she has to watch for any signs of osteoarthritis, because she's at high risk."

I said, "What a shock for her parents—not having had a clue."

Marnie said, "Can't imagine that one either." She took a long swallow of the beer that had just been delivered. "So, was there something in your parents' history that's behind yours?"

Danni leaned forward and smiled at her. "Not at all, Marnie. They're both of average height. It's just a genetic mutation—1 in 25,000 births. I can have children, but depending on a lot of factors, they may or may not have dwarfism."

I said, "Then how do you feel about having children?"

"Honestly, I haven't thought much about it." Her furrowed brow and the squint of her eyes convinced me it was probably true.

"Was your childhood hideous?" asked Marnie.

I said, "What a question!"

Marnie cocked her head, as though it hadn't occurred to her that her phrasing might've been offensive. "Well, Heather, mine was. So, I just assume I'm not the only one."

Danni studied her beer mug for a moment. Then she

looked up and said, "When I look back on my life, I guess I'd say that it would've helped me to have the perspective of an adult when I most needed it—in my teen years. It's always hard to have people judge you based only on your appearance. Even an unusually attractive person like you, Heather, feels frustrated at being judged by assumptions people make based only on your looks. Try to imagine dealing with the jokes, the taunts, the stares and pointing that are dished out to a dwarf on a daily basis. Then try to envision dealing with it at age thirteen. I don't know what the statistics are on suicide attempts by people with dwarfism, but mine was on my thirteenth birthday."

"Oh, no," I said. "I'm so sorry." The pressure was starting around my eyes.

She gave me a little shrug, then said, "My family planned a nice party, but, unlike other years, there wouldn't be a separate party with my friends. My small group of girl pals dumped me when they started getting interested in boys. They never explained why they stopped asking me to things, or why everyone found a reason to decline my invitations. No one went out of her way to be cruel to me. They just didn't want to socialize with me anymore."

"Danni, that's awful," I said.

Marnie said, "The little shitheads."

"I understood. I mean, I understand now. My looks hurt their prospects. And at thirteen, their ability to attract boys was paramount."

"They're still shit-heads," said Marnie.

"Anyway, I made a plan to sit in the driver's seat of the family car, garage door closed, with the engine running. I didn't realize that Dad had put some nails in one of the side windows of the garage, so it always stayed open a few inches. It was because he used nasty smelling solvents for the hobbies he did out there. Anyway, I nodded off, but my folks were looking for me and found me before I dissolved my brain."

"What did they say?"

"Mom said, 'Sweetie, the family arrives in a half hour. Go put on the dress we picked out. And tomorrow morning, I'm taking you to see someone you can talk with to help you get through this.' I don't think they told anyone else, since nobody tiptoed around me at the party. I had fun with my cousins, and aunts and uncles, like I always did."

"Did therapy help?" Marnie asked.

"Very much. But the biggest contribution to my mental health was my decision to focus all my energy on my studies. Then, to my surprise, when I arrived at college, my dorm roommates were friendly and supportive. It's not like they took me to social events with them, but they were always pleasant. We lived together in apartments for the next three years, as well. After graduation, they both returned to their hometowns in Florida to be teachers, but we exchange Christmas cards."

Marnie said, "Can anything be done to stretch legs and arms for dwarves?"

Danni smiled at her. "Yeah. It's called limb lengthening. They say it used to be excruciating, but the centers that do it today claim to have the pain under control. Over time, many patients can see increases in leg length of nine to twelve inches. The arms can be done too, although that's less common. I've heard that each surgery can cost over $100,000."

I said, "Oh, my God. Not many people could afford that. Do you know how it's done?"

"There are different approaches, but the most common is to pin a metal frame onto the bone to be lengthened. Then the bone is cut through. As new bone formation takes place at the fracture site, it isn't allowed to heal as it normally would. Instead, the cut ends are pulled apart, a tiny bit each day. It usually takes several months for the bone to reach the desired length. Once the patients heal and can finally stand, they go through a course of physical therapy."

"That sounds like torture," said Marnie.

"Is that why you decided not to do it?" I asked.

She tilted her head and smiled at me. "How do you know I didn't? Maybe I was two feet, eight inches before I had the procedure."

Marnie choked on her beer and positioned her first two fingers to show a two-inch space. "Thumbelina."

As Marnie wiped the table with her napkin, Danni laughed, then said, "I'm kidding. I did know about it, but, number one, my parents couldn't afford it. And number two, at my height, another ten inches wouldn't have made me an average height person anyway. To me, it wasn't worth the cost—even if we'd had the money— the pain, and the risk of complications, just to come out the other end at four feet, six inches, still with short arms and a larger than average head. I mean, either way, I wasn't going to look like everyone else."

"I see that," said Marnie. "But if they'd stretched your legs a couple of feet, and you still had short arms, you could've looked like a young Tyrannosaurus Rex."

Danni burst out laughing. "If I did, I wouldn't need Grizzly to keep people away."

I said, "You know, you two are both insane."

"I didn't used to be," said Danni.

"I'm just jealous. Why haven't you rubbed off on me?" I asked.

Marnie winked at me. "I'm working on it."

I thought about it. Maybe developing a warped sense of humor wouldn't be a bad idea. But it would take a hell of an effort to catch up with Marnie.

The waiter arrived with the plates of steaming pieces of fish in golden crusts, surrounded by browned and seasoned bits of potatoes. I took a small bite of the fish and focused on the mild meatiness that was almost sweet. I was digesting Danni's presentation of the details of dwarfism when it struck me how smoothly she'd educated us. The whole time she was explaining it, she maintained solid eye contact, taking time to alternate her focus between Marnie and me. She modulated to make points both through her surprisingly commanding vocal projection and by taking it down several notches to, basically, a whisper. She anticipated all the questions I wanted to ask, before I even thought of them. I said, "By the way, Danni, I don't think you have to worry about whether you'd do well in oral argument."

"Really?" she asked.

"You're good," said Marnie. "I can't tell you how much it pains me to say this, but you're almost as good as me."

I said, "You would be effective in court, Danni."

"But guys," she said. "I wasn't arguing. I was just reporting facts."

"Doesn't matter," said Marnie. "You're great at making a presentation. It'll translate to legal arguments."

"Yeah. It will," I said. "Arguments in court are 'just

reporting facts' in a way that helps your client and persuades the judge or jury to do what you want."

"Maybe," said Danni.

Marnie wiped her mouth with an extra cloth napkin, then asked, "But why are we even talking about court? I believe we all said we're in agreement that Danni and I will never get there."

Danni said, "Not exactly. What we agreed to is that if we find a way to overcome either of the big hurdles, we'll revisit the other."

Marnie said, "That's true. But unless someone has something to announce, there's no change on that."

"You're right," said Danni.

I just shrugged, and we moved on to other topics. I knew there was no point dwelling on my frustration, so I was working on focusing on the here and now when I had the chance to hang out with my friends. The importance of staying in the present was something I'd been taught in a mindfulness meditation class—but it wasn't easy.

Chapter 5

I reveled in uncharacteristic happiness, getting to know my new favorite companions. I couldn't say that my feelings were sisterly, since I'd never had a sister, and I didn't imagine my love for my two younger brothers was quite the same thing. But Marnie and Danni brought out in me an unexpected sense of respect, admiration, protectiveness, and the complete absence of competition. Although the three of us certainly had different strengths and weaknesses, we were fundamentally equals. It wasn't that there was nothing to be competitive about, it was more that, as a group, it lay outside our repertoire. It was clear to me that if we ever did start a law firm, we'd always be equal partners, irrespective of periodic unevenness in our successes. While there was no reason to believe we ever would really be able to practice together, I couldn't shake the premonition that we would. Presentiment or not, I couldn't think of a single thing I could do to advance the ball in that direction. Except that I did start playing the lottery.

None of us was dating, although Marnie saw men every weekend for hook-ups. As always, I had more than enough invitations, from men both appropriate and not, but I turned them all down. I encased myself in the bubble of suspicion that the guys wanted to get to know my body more than my soul, and I had no idea how to burst out of it. My friendship with Marnie and Danni didn't help either. Every time a man asked me out, the bubble problem was compounded by the fact that I'd evaluate whether it would be more fun to do whatever he offered, or to hang out with my friends. The answer was obvious, so that was what I did.

One night in early December, we were out for a Mexican dinner at a family-owned restaurant on the near north side. Marnie sat on one side of the booth, and Danni and I were on the other. Mariachi music was being piped in, but it was low and I was catching snippets of conversations from other tables, which made me wonder if others could hear what we were saying. We were all dipping warm corn chips into spicy salsa, and sipping cold beers. I kept my voice low as I explained my dilemma.

"Obvious solution," said Marnie. "You should only date blind men."

"My contacts list is full of them—for my own reasons," Danni said.

"I'm serious," I said.

"What?" Marnie asked. "You're prejudiced against the blind?"

I just shook my head. "Do you guys think I'm being irrational?"

"I'm not in a position to judge anybody else's love life," said Marnie.

"You're not irrational, Heather," Danni said. "I've read that fabulously wealthy or famous people sometimes lament that they can't be sure why someone wants to be with them. And it's not something the rest of society would sympathize with all that much since they're already so privileged."

"Yeah," said Marnie. "You should call a Hollywood power couple for advice."

Danni said, "I can see why it's a problem for you. I was thinking of suggesting you correspond with someone on a dating site, but those sites require you to post a picture."

"Not to mention," Marnie said, "they're actually twelve-year-old Russian trolls."

"Then what?"

"We can't tell you, Heather," said Marnie. "I think it has to be organic. It'll happen when you least expect it."

"Promise?"

"I wish I could. If I had the power to do that, I'd guarantee something for myself."

That made me flush. Even though I really wanted their advice, I was being insensitive to bring it up, when Marnie and Danni faced the problem with far fewer prospects. "Sorry, guys. I shouldn't moan about it."

"Not at all," said Danni. "My expectations are just so low that I tend not to dwell on it."

"Have you dated much, Danni?" asked Marnie.

"Not much." She paused. "To be perfectly honest, not at all."

"Have you thought about whether you'd prefer to date another little person?" I asked, pushing the basket of chips between Marnie and Danni since I knew I'd keep grabbing as long as they sat in front of me.

"I think I'm really open about that. I tend to judge people by interests and character rather than looks. But neither variety has been exactly beating down my door."

"Their loss," said Marnie.

"Thanks."

Marnie also pushed the basket away, so it was basically sitting on Danni's vinyl placemat. When a waiter passed our table, she raised it to him to take away. "What about you, though? Are you trolling, Marnie?" asked Danni.

"I'm a strong believer in making things happen. I won't be waiting around for someone to fall in love with me before I enjoy what my body tells me it needs. I've had real dates—first dates—friends in college set up, but I'm not everyone's cup of tea." She paused. "Let me correct that. I'm not anyone's cup of tea."

"Are you saying that because of your weight?" I askcd.

"I'm sure it doesn't help. But I think it's more my personality."

"You mean the fact that you're shy and retiring?" Danni grinned.

"Exactly," said Marnie, who then laughed heartily. "It's like I told you guys before. I can't help myself. I call things as I see them and seem to have zero capacity to keep my mouth shut."

"You're hysterical, Marnie," said Danni. "Someday you'll run into a guy who enjoys your humor as much as Heather and I do."

Marnie said, "I don't think you should speak for Heather."

"You're right." She turned to me. "Sorry, Heather."

I smiled. "Marnie is the perfect confluence of irreverence and insight." Looking at Marnie, I added, "You only make me uncomfortable because I'm not used to stark honesty. But I'm getting there."

"Thanks, guys," said Marnie.

I nodded, then took a long sip of beer. "But I am

curious about the one-night stands? Where do you dig up all the guys? Do you ever want to see any of them again?"

Marnie leaned back in her seat and placed her folded hands on the edge of the table. "It's simple, really. I like sex. I don't have a steady boyfriend for reasons I've already mentioned, so I just use the hook-up sites. I post my headshot, which could lead to a lot of embarrassment if I didn't also mention my height and weight. So, I do. The thing you two may not realize is that there are plenty of men who go for fat women."

"What are the men like?" I asked.

"If you're asking whether they're also fat, the answer is almost never. I try not to be prejudiced against the rounder guys, for obvious reasons, but I'm more attracted to the ones of average girth."

"You invite them into your apartment?" asked Danni.

"Yeah. I feel safer in an environment I'm familiar with. I'll have a guy over for a Friday evening, then boot him out after the sex. I have no desire to wake up in the morning with a complete stranger in my bed."

"But, Marnie, doesn't using your weekend evenings like that cut into your chances to meet someone you might actually care about?" asked Danni.

"If someone were to set me up on a blind date, I'd go. No one has done that since college. And the fact that plenty of guys like sex with large women does not mean they pick up fat girls at bars. It's more of a stealth operation."

"Well, maybe you'll meet someone at a party," said Danni.

"How many parties brimming with promising men

do you get invited to, Danni?"

"None."

"Ditto." Marnie finished off her beer.

"Do you feel safe with the guys in your apartment?" I asked.

"So far, so good. It's not like they're all prizes. But I get something approximating what I'm looking for out of it."

"What's that?" I said.

"Sex," she said fairly loudly.

I may've imagined it, but I thought the people in the booth behind Marnie sat up straighter at the word.

Marnie added, "I'm sure you've heard of it. It's all the rage in Europe."

Danni laughed. I just shook my head, then said, "Guys, let's try to keep our voices down."

Marnie put her index finger to her lips, then continued at the same volume. "It's not that I'm unaware of how women can pleasure ourselves—what with all the technological advances in that realm." She looked at Danni, but spoke to me. "Now look what you've done, Heather. You made me make Danni blush. And maybe the people behind me."

I felt my face grow hot, but no one in the next booth turned to glare at us.

Danni spoke softly. "If I ever talk about sex with anyone, it'll be you two. But that's a big *if.*"

"The thing is," said Marnie, "I'm a very tactile person. For me, joy is feeling the heat in another's body, running my fingers along the smooth mound of someone's butt, using my tongue to explore the crevasses of—"

I jumped in. "Whoa!" I quickly surveyed the booths

and tables near us. "We get the picture, Marnie. But what if you could get all of that with a steady boyfriend, who genuinely cares about you?"

"If you have someone in particular in mind, sign me up. If not, don't judge me."

"I'm not judging you. But I'll keep my eyes open."

"Thanks, Heather. But I don't know. Remember how Danni said these things have to happen organically?"

"Even organic gardens need watering," I said. "And in the meanwhile, please be careful with your hook-ups. If you ever start to feel unsafe, just text me."

"Or me," said Danni. "I live closer and have an assassin to bring with me."

Marnie said, "Yeah. Grizzly could probably handle it—unless, of course, it's more than one man."

"Gross," I said.

Danni's eyes popped out.

Marnie said, "I was kidding."

The waiter arrived to take our orders.

Chapter 6

Each of us went home for the Christmas holiday that year. I went to southern Illinois, Marnie to Missouri, and Danni to Indiana. I didn't return to Evanston until the evening of January 2nd. I'd rented a car for the seven-hour drive, and by the time I dropped it off, took a cab to my apartment, and unpacked, it was almost eight o'clock, and I was a wash rag. I saw that I'd received a text from Danni asking what time I might be available for a call. The three of us texted often, emailed occasionally, but never talked by phone, so I immediately worried something was wrong. I texted back: "Any time." My phone rang within a minute. I said, "Hi, Danni. Is everything okay?"

"Oh, yeah. Just fine. I was afraid you'd worry. Sorry. I thought I'd text first because I didn't want to call while you were driving or something."

"Not a problem. I'm safely ensconced in my cozy apartment." Once my heart rate slowed back down, I said, "How was your Christmas?" I plopped down on the couch to give Chica-the-Brave a belly rub while I chatted.

"Really great. My mom owns probably fifteen boxes of holiday decorations, and I think she put them all up. I felt nostalgic sleeping in my old bed, but it did bring back a lot of the darker things I haven't thought about for a while. I loved seeing family and old friends, but I feel better now that Grizzly and I are back in our nest. How was your holiday?"

"Good. It's always nice to see my parents, and, of course, my brothers and their wives. But, like you, I'm happier now that I'm back in my own orbit. So, do you want to get together with Marnie for dinner on Saturday?"

"Sure. Absolutely, Heather."

"Great! I'll text her."

"Wait. There's something I need to talk with you about."

That sounded ominous. I wondered what in the world couldn't wait five days and include Marnie. I stopped rubbing, and my puppy used her wet nose to get my hand moving. "Of course. What is it, Danni?"

"Over the past week, I spent a lot of time with my sister, Delaney."

I almost blurted out,

Your sister? How the hell could you not have told us you have a sister? Instead, I said, "I didn't know you *had* a sister." I was no longer doing any belly-rubbing.

"She's my twin, actually."

My God, your twin? is what I almost said. Instead, I said, "Really? Identical?"

"No. If we were identical, she'd be a dwarf, too. And she's not."

About a hundred questions popped into my head. Chica-the-Brave gave up on me and jumped down from the couch. I asked, "Can you tell me about her?"

"I adore Delaney, and always have. See, she's my guardian angel. It's not like she babies me or treats me like her inferior. It's just that, since I was very young, she helped me, commiserated with me, and she protected me."

"What did she do?"

"Here's an example. When we started school, the principal said they generally separate twins so they can grow independently. But Delaney absolutely refused to go to kindergarten unless we could be together. Mom understood what my sister was doing and supported her. Delaney looked out for me, but she never made a big deal out of it. She'd hand me things I couldn't reach, find a stool for me when I needed one, and hoist me up the first step of the school bus, all quickly and surreptitiously. She avoided bringing any extra attention to herself or to me."

"Nice sister."

"Yeah. She is. When we turned ten, we were old enough to go to sleep-away nature camp. We both reveled in it, but it was Delaney who scooped me up onto her back to carry me when a hike was too long or too rigorous for me. She didn't ask one of the counselors. She just sailed in and took care of it, as though it were the most natural thing in the world for one camper to carry another on a trek."

"Wow."

"Heather, she was incredibly encouraging to me after my incident in the garage on our thirteenth birthday. Then, once we got to high school, I stuck to my plan to put all my energy into my academics. Delaney tried to include me in everything she did, but frankly, I didn't feel up to the task of dealing with the rejections—from slights to outright humiliations. I just wasn't ready. I didn't feel all that deprived in my book-lined cocoon, but she always wanted me to have more of a social life."

"Did you go to college together?"

"Delaney wanted to. But by that time, I knew it wouldn't be right for either of us to keep her attached to me, so I told her I preferred to do it on my own. She went to New York for college and grad school and lives there now. She's an investment banker, of all things."

"Why 'of all things'?"

"She majored in English literature in undergrad, and got her masters in European history."

"Then why banking?"

"I'm not sure. She enjoys her work but says someday she'd like to teach."

"She sounds like an amazing sister."

"I adore her."

"I'm honored you shared that with me, Danni. I assume you'll be telling Marnie."

"I will. But there's a reason I'm letting you know all of this tonight."

"Okay." I hadn't a clue where this was going.

"When Delaney and I were hanging out at Mom's house, I told her I have two new friends, and how much we enjoy spending time together. We got to talking about you guys in some depth, and I shared your idea that we start our own law firm—if we can overcome the hurdles."

"What did she think?"

"She said she might loan us the money to get the firm started."

"What? How?" I jumped up and started pacing.

"Delaney's very frugal, and she's an excellent investor. So, she's already socked away quite a bit of money. There's a big caveat, though."

I stopped in my tracks trying to absorb the news. "What?"

"She wants to meet both of you. Like soon. She said she could fly in Saturday morning and we could talk over dinner at my apartment. I offered to take us all out to eat and arrange for a small private room. But she said she enjoys visiting the gorgeous dining set she gave me for Christmas two years ago."

That explained how Danni could afford to have so many expensive pieces of furniture. Her sister was obviously generous, and I assumed, as vigilant as hell about her twin, whom she intended to protect from Marnie and me. "But we haven't even gotten into the details on the cost side. I'm not sure I can put everything together by then."

"You don't need to, Heather. Delaney understands the status of things. Frankly, I think she just wants to meet you guys to evaluate whether you are people she'd invest in."

"How does she feel about bawdy humor?"

"I guess we'll find out."

"Danni, I don't understand why you kept us in the dark about having a twin sister."

"Now, I'm embarrassed I did. I guess the truth is that she's the most precious thing in the world to me, so I'm very cautious about sharing her. I've been having more fun than I've had in a long time—actually, ever—getting to know you and Marnie. But we just met in person six months ago. I think telling anyone about Delaney feels like letting that person into my heart."

"And now?"

"I'm ready. Whether or not everything falls into place so we can start our own firm, I feel like I know you both well enough to want to share her with you."

"Thanks, Danni. I'm honored. Marnie will be too."

"Wonderful. Good night, Heather."

"Bye, Danni."

I plopped back down on the couch, and let out a long sigh. Now I'd be getting what I'd been hoping for since our first meal at Danni's—a chance to overcome one of the two hurdles. I knew I'd be nervous as hell for the next four days worrying about blowing it. I drank a glass of wine before bed in the hopes I could ease my anxiety enough to get some sleep.

Chapter 7

We were scheduled to arrive at Danni's apartment at 6:00 p.m. on Saturday, and Marnie and I ran into each other in the lobby at 5:55. I suppose we both realized the one thing we could control in this interview scenario was punctuality. Danni and Grizzly greeted us at the door, and we could hear Delaney working on something in the kitchen as we handed our wraps to Danni.

I'd debated between blue jeans, which I decided said I didn't care enough, and a long gray wool skirt, which I worried would come off as too dressy, and settled on a knee-length corduroy skirt and a sweater. Marnie had on a red tunic top over black leggings and flats. Danni looked darling in a perfectly tailored, plaid jumper, silk blouse, and cute, black leather booties.

I said, "Danni, you look fabulous. You must have a great tailor."

"If I did, it would cost a fortune."

"Then how do you get such a great fit?"

"I sew all of my clothes."

"One of many talents," I said. "Where did you learn?"

"The leaders taught us in Girl Scouts. Then when I really started to care about fashion, I made it my hobby out of necessity."

Marnie said, "I wish I knew how to sew, but it would be daunting working with yards and yards of fabric—just to make a simple skirt."

Danni smiled. "Needing a lot of yardage is not a problem I can identify with."

We all laughed, I'd say nervously, since we knew Delaney was probably listening to every word.

Danni called out, "Delaney! Our guests are here."

"So I heard," she said, as she waltzed through the kitchen door in blue jeans and a sweater, drying her hands with a dish towel.

I stepped forward to introduce myself, and while Marnie did the same, I couldn't help staring as I took a half step back. I said, "It's remarkable how much you two look alike."

"Is that a compliment?" asked Delaney.

"Definitely. You have Danni's exact pretty face, and coloring. Danni told me you're fraternal, but you would look like identical twins—"

"If she weren't a dwarf," said Delaney.

Trying to redeem myself, I added, "You are both lovely." I paused. "So, how was your flight, Delaney?"

"I'm here."

I nodded to the woman, who was not acting at all like I'd expected. "Marnie and I are thrilled to meet you."

Marnie said, "What can we do to help in the kitchen?"

"Nothing," said Danni. "It's all under control. Let's sit in the living room."

Marnie and I waited until Danni and Delaney sat down, then Marnie joined Delaney on the couch, and I took one of the small recliners, as had Danni. Apparently, it was important to Delaney that this be a business meeting rather than a cocktail hour, since there was a pitcher of ice water and four glasses on the coffee table. No wine.

Delaney still hadn't cracked a smile, although I assumed it would be as radiant as Danni's if she ever deigned to try it. She said, "Danni's told me a lot about both of you. But I'd love it if you would share a little bit about yourselves." She was looking at Marnie, who didn't miss a beat in responding.

"A very broad question." Marnie laughed and added, "For a very broad person."

Delaney gave her a closed-mouth semi-smile then asked, "Is your immediate response to everything a self-deprecating comment?"

"No. Sometimes I deprecate others. Listen, Delaney, I know you're here to evaluate us for a possible investment in a hypothetical law firm. I think you should know who I am."

"Isn't that what I just asked you?"

"Good point. The truth is that I'm a 'back-office' lawyer who achieves impressive results by virtue of my analysis and strategy, and my writing. I've read transcripts of hundreds of depositions, motions and appellate arguments, all of which I could've handled as well, if not better. Heather thinks I'm being deprived of something I'm more than capable of doing and would enjoy. Maybe she's right that it would fulfill me in some profound and meaningful way. But I will not give up an interesting, well-paying job unless I'm convinced the three of us can make a go of it.

"I admit that I don't control any business, but it's because I've had no opportunity to create a reputation, much less burnish one. The partner I work for signs his name to my letters and briefs—even the appellate briefs which really should include both of our names. I honestly don't know if prospective clients would like me—many people don't. But I guarantee they would like the results I could get for them on their files." Unlike me, Marnie didn't seem the least bit nervous. She was sitting no more than three feet from Delaney and had turned her body so they were face to face.

Delaney kept her eyes on her but didn't say a word. Marnie continued. "I'd love to practice with Heather and Danni because I've never enjoyed anything as much as spending time with the two of them. We worked together by phone for six months as co-counsel on a Lake County matter—the case of the mouse in a cola bottle—and it was obvious they are both especially good lawyers. Since then, we've spent a lot of time together socially, and I've learned that they are also especially good people. Since Heather first shared her idea with us, and I fell off the couch laughing, I've had a lot of time to think about it. I slave away at a firm that keeps me in a closet. I love to work, and as corny as it sounds, I love the law. I'll do everything in my power to make the venture a success if we decide it's a go. But even if we receive your financial backing, we would still need to come up with a business plan that holds a realistic chance of succeeding. As you know, your sister is in pretty much the same position as I am. Only Heather has clients, and the chances they'd all follow her to a new firm are slim. But even if they did, it wouldn't be enough work for three attorneys. I don't require a guarantee, but I won't embark on this without having a realistic business plan in place. I'm pretty sure 'if you build it, they will come' only works for baseball."

"So, you're confident you would keep clients if you were given the opportunity to work on their files, but you don't know how to make that opportunity happen."

"That's it."

Delaney said, "Let me pour," then leaned in to fill each glass and handed them out. She turned to me. "Heather, this venture was your idea. How do you respond to what Marnie said?"

I was having trouble seeing Delaney as Danni's loving sister, because she seemed to be almost antagonistic towards me, but I didn't have time to focus on my feelings. I'd thought about how to answer the question. I just needed to present my answer cogently to a woman who seemed intensely skeptical of me. "There are a number of ways to develop business, the first of which is the one Marnie mentioned. I would divide the files I'm able to take with me among the three of us. I'll probably have to agree to supervise the files—without charging for it—to persuade some of the clients to give Marnie and Danni a chance. Once they've proven themselves, the clients should start sending files directly to them, or asking me to assign certain matters to them. As Marnie said, that's not enough. So, we use the time we're not busy with substantive work to write articles for industry magazines and bar journals to get our names out there. We design and produce informational pamphlets that should be of interest to the clients we target. We volunteer to make presentations to potential clients on legal issues of concern to them. We join bar associations, attend their meetings, and become active on their committees. As more attorneys get to know us, the hope is that they'll recommend us to their clients as conflict counsel—to be hired when the firm the client really wants has a conflict of interest which precludes their retention."

"Anything else?" asked Delaney, as though nothing I'd said yet had been terribly interesting.

Sipping my water kept my mouth from going dry, but I was starting to perspire. "We all three use our contacts, whatever they may be, to seek legal work. For example, if Danni were to let other LPA members know she started a law firm, she might be able to get some opportunities out of that, both in and outside of Illinois. Keep in mind that any of the three of us can generally practice in jurisdictions beyond Illinois by seeking leave of court to appear *pro hac vice*—just for that case—in association with a local counsel from the jurisdiction."

Marnie said, "If I ever hear of a fat people of America group, I'll definitely join and drum up some business."

I ignored her. "We don't worry about billable rates at the beginning. We accept any work, from insurance defense files—which typically pay lower rates—to corporate and contract work. Marnie uses her skill at handling appeals to recruit referrals from other defense firms that don't have the time or inclination to handle their own. Finally, once we've left our current firms and we're all able to contact clients, Marnie and Danni will be free to reach out to those whose files they've been working on for the past six years. They'll explain that they've been doing the majority of the work on those files and bring up some of the strategies they employed on the most notable victories. We don't ask for all the files, we ask for one file. Our point will be that we just want the opportunity to show the client what we can accomplish for them."

Delaney said, "It sounds like you're going fishing, with no idea of what you might catch."

"That's right," I said. "We wouldn't know."

"How will the clients feel about being represented by Danni?"

I took another quick sip, but kept my eyes on Delaney. "I don't know. I hope they'll evaluate her by her work, rather than by her height. One point I will make to prospective clients when I tell them about our new firm is that our attorneys look a bit different. Just being women will get each of us more attention. Marnie and Danni will get an extra dose of it because of their physiques." I leaned in. "Look. Intensive attention can be a disadvantage if the attorney who gets it is ill-prepared, or unable to think quickly on her feet. But if she's the most prepared person in the courtroom, and can respond in the moment to any eventuality, then that attention can be a very good thing, and can ensure that a great reputation is built quickly. What I'm saying is that I don't think we should try to blend."

"Fat chance of that," said Marnie. "Oops, sorry Heather. I used the f-word."

Delaney placed her glass on the table and didn't touch it again. She stared at Marnie for a moment.

I said, "My point is that we should rejoice in who we are—"

"Now that just sounds too biblical," said Marnie.

I ignored that comment as well. "We show the court and the other attorneys that we are top-tier lawyers, who enjoy the hell out of our friendship and have each other's backs come what may. I think we can make it work. Finally, I make sure that Marnie's and Danni's early experiences in the courtroom go well by carefully orchestrating their early days in Lake County. The first or second day we're open, I'll take them around to all the courtrooms and introduce them to the judges, clerks, and bailiffs. They'll accompany me to the county bar association events, join the Women Lawyers' Club, and join me in court so that I can show them where and how we fill out orders after a ruling, and other details of what to expect. It will take some time, but they'll become accepted members of the bar." I took a long sip of my water, then set my glass across from Delaney's on the coffee table. She was looking at me, but didn't speak, so I went on.

"On the client side, we start meeting my current clients as soon as we're up and running. The three of us will take those who are local out to lunch, to introduce them to Marnie and Danni. The others, I'll introduce by phone or facetime. From my standpoint, no reasonable person can get to know Marnie and Danni and not like them. That's how we'll get more files: do excellent legal work, earn great reputations in the courthouse, and let the clients see how interesting and impressive Marnie and Danni are."

" 'Interesting' is a good choice of descriptor," said Marnie.

"Both words are," I said. The whole time I was giving my answer, my eyes never left Delaney's. I wasn't convinced she'd loan us the money, and I wouldn't have been surprised if she didn't. There was so much uncertainty, I wasn't sure I would recommend such an investment if a client of mine asked for advice about it. But I very much wanted to make a good impression on her—because she was my friend's adored sister. Troublingly, I was getting zero positive response.

She looked away for a moment, then said, "I believe that would go reasonably well. And I expect the three of you could attend to all of the minutiae of opening a new business effectively and efficiently. I don't know what to say about the problem of securing clients, but I do trust that you won't jump in without figuring it out. I'll also give it some thought."

Marnie said, "If you think of any good ideas Heather hasn't already mentioned, be sure to let us know."

"No." Delaney shook her head. "I'll keep them to myself." She just stared at Marnie, who burst out laughing. Delaney released a gorgeous, wide smile aimed at Marnie, and looked exactly like a tall version of Danni. But she didn't smile at me. Instead, as she rose from the couch, she said, "Now, I'd like to chat with Heather privately. Shall we grab our coats and check out the balcony?"

I sputtered, "Sure," and I thought, *This should be a barrel of laughs.* I grabbed my glass and took several quick gulps. Danni fetched our jackets, and I readied myself for the interrogation I'd half-expected. Out on the balcony, we stood at the railing and studied the city stretched out before us like a twinkle-lit kingdom.

"Are you warm enough, Delaney?" I asked.

"Yes. You, too?"

I nodded, then said, "Winter nights feel so much cozier when I'm gazing at the soft glow of lights in all the windows and the stream of yellow flashes on the highway, everyone warm in their enclosures."

She didn't comment. Then after what felt like five minutes, she said, "Perhaps you've guessed what I wanted to speak with you about." She was looking straight ahead, but I sensed she'd be listening intently.

I modeled her and fixed my gaze on the most distant buildings. "I've never walked into a meeting unprepared in my life. So yes, I've thought about it quite a bit. I tried to put myself in your position, Delaney. My sister, an accomplished attorney, is content with her current employment, and well-paid for her labors. Along comes a lawyer of average height, who can't possibly understand what Danni has gone through to get where she is. The woman recommends that my sister give up what she has in exchange for an uncertain future which will include at least some opportunities to appear in court—to what reception no one knows. And she recommends that Danni embark on this course with a potentially offensive, definitely overly self-deprecating obese woman attorney, who is also in no position to bring any files with her, who will find opportunities to appear in court—again, to what reception no one knows. All of this leads to one question: why?"

"You're right, Heather. All of that does concern me. But further fueling my curiosity is the fact that you should be up for an offer of partnership from the firm you are with now in the next few months. It's more typical for your firm to make their associates wait until the end of their seventh year, or later, to receive an offer to join the partnership. But you, being considered a star, are to be an exception."

I jerked my head to stare at her profile. "How could you possibly know that?"

"My private investigator told me."

I felt exactly as though I'd been struck in the head. "You had me investigated?"

She turned to look at me. "Marnie too. Listen, Heather, I know this may seem a bit over-the-top, but I've been looking out for Danni since we started kindergarten, and I'm incapable of stopping now. You're right that my question for you comes down to 'why?' A person's motivation is often fairly clear to me. Yours isn't. Sure, you see it as an issue of sexism and bodyism, and you want to stand up for people who are being compartmentalized into oblivion. But nothing in your history tells me you would try to pull off something like this. So, yes. I'd like to understand why." We both resumed staring into the distance.

"It's a reasonable question." I thought, *Although having me investigated was way beyond the pale.* "I've been trying to understand it, myself, and I think I may've gotten to the heart of it. There's this story that seared itself into my memory when I was a child. I had a favorite great aunt, Agatha, my grandmother's sister. From the start, we felt a deep affinity for each other. She would take me to the library, or a movie, or sometimes to a community theatre production. Over the years, I learned her story, which is the tale of countless wives and mothers of the 1950s and 60s." I glanced at Delaney. She continued to look out over the city, but I could tell she was paying attention.

"In 1949, Aunt Agatha married Herb, who had served with the Marines at Guadalcanal. After the war, Herb landed a job in sales at a local men's clothing shop, then following the wedding, the couple started a family. Agatha stayed at home and raised their first son, who was born fifteen months after their wedding, and then their second, who came along two years later. She nursed the babies, changed the diapers, took them for their check-ups, and pasted black and white photographs in the boys' baby books. She cooked, and cleaned, tended the vegetable garden, and ran the PTA for several years. She ironed her husband's dress shirts for his work, darned the holes in his socks, served the meals and cleaned up afterward, got the boys bathed, read to, and into bed, while Herb read the paper and then fell asleep in front of the black and white TV. Then, weary to the bone, she fell into bed." I paused and took a deep breath before getting on with the story which I hoped wasn't taking too long for her.

"One day, Herb developed a splitting headache from which he could get no relief. Agatha got the boys into the station wagon and drove him to the emergency room. After several days of tests, they were told he had a brain tumor, probably malignant, but operable. He survived the first surgery but was not quite the same as before the operation. Herb was sent home to recuperate, but the doctor informed Agatha that the tumor was likely to return, and, although his team could operate again, Herb's chances to beat the cancer were slim.

"They had no savings. Herb's paychecks paid for the mortgage, groceries, clothing, and every other bill that darkened their mailbox. Circumstances dictated that Agatha, who had worked as a licensed practical nurse before her marriage, get into an RN program as soon as possible. Caring for her husband, keeping up with her sons, managing the household, and studying for her classes demanded more energy than Agatha even knew she possessed. But it only took the first class in the nursing program for her to realize how much she'd missed that world. She thrived on studying, but she also loved being with other adults, and doing work that was meaningful to more than just her immediate family. Agatha felt guilty that she found such joy, while Herb was home in bed, bandages plastered all over his skull. It was as though, somehow, her happiness came at his expense. But there were few extra moments to worry herself over it."

I pulled my coat tightly around me and folded my arms over my chest for warmth. "Are you still warm enough, Delaney?"

"I'm fine. Go on."

"Herb had a second surgery, and nine months later, a third. Agatha completed her course and took the licensing exam. A state official let her know on the sly that she'd earned the highest score he'd ever seen on the test. Agatha took a part-time position with a hospital within walking distance of her home, while Herb's body tried to recuperate. A week after Herb passed away, she went to full-time status as a nurse. Within two years, she was named Director of Nursing, a position she held until her retirement, thirty-five years later. Fairly early in her nursing career, she came to realize that she longed to attend medical school, but at that time, it wasn't a possibility.

"So, it all adds up to this. She'd been successful as a stay-at-home mom, but she felt smothered by society's expectations. Because her mind wasn't getting enough oxygen, she grew depressed and deflated as she went through the appropriate motions, a smile plastered on her face. Hearing her story as a pre-teen, I thought it was unfair that Uncle Herb got to work from nine to five, but Aunt Agatha worked night and day. But now I see it differently. It was a waste of talent—Agatha should've been a doctor. She was miserable when she was only allowed the homemaker role. She was comfortable working as a nurse, but she never got to taste the forbidden fruit—to pursue her dream of something she was perfectly capable of doing."

Delaney said nothing, so I kept talking. "Of course, I'm a feminist. I don't want any special privileges for women—just equal opportunity." I turned to look at Delaney, but she didn't look at me. "Marnie and Danni aren't being given the same opportunities their firms give the other associates. While in their case, it's bodyism, it reeks of the same stink as racism and sexism, and frankly, it pisses me off. When it hit me that Agatha's story was playing out all over again in Danni and Marnie's lives, I thought maybe I could do something about it."

"Is that all?"

Embarrassed for talking so much, and defeated, I sighed softly. But I tried to give honest consideration to her question. "Almost. I also have a purely selfish motive. I love spending time with Marnie and Danni, and I can't imagine a more satisfying work life than one we would share." I figured if she said, "Is that all?" again, I'd jump off the balcony.

Fortunately, what she said was, "I see." She also turned to me and favored me with the barest hint of a closed-mouth smile—or maybe it was a grimace. She motioned for me to step ahead of her through the sliding door, back into the apartment.

As we both shrugged off our coats, Danni said, "Did you two have a nice visit?"

"I did," I said.

Danni looked at her sister and said, "More importantly, was it satisfactory to you?"

"Let's just say I have what I came for. I'll let you know my decision in a few days. Shall we have some dinner? And maybe you three ladies can tell me what sights not to miss. My flight home isn't until Monday morning, so Danni and I have all day tomorrow to play tourists together."

I couldn't help imagining all the double-takes they'd get walking together down Michigan Avenue, but I'd be damned if I'd say a word about it. I crossed my fingers that Marnie wouldn't mention it either. She was busy muttering to Grizzly while rubbing his belly, and didn't make any comment, so she must not have been paying attention to our conversation. I had zero faith Marnie could resist making a quip if one came to mind, and one definitely would've come to mind.

Chapter 8

There was really no point in spending time planning how to launch a new law firm, since Delaney might very well decline to finance us, but I couldn't help myself. I filled several pages of a legal pad with business development ideas. I didn't know if Marnie and Danni were doing the same thing because we didn't discuss it. Marnie invited us to her apartment for the Saturday night after our visit with Delaney. I assumed Danni would've heard from her sister, and would share the news with us then.

Because we all enjoyed meeting at restaurants so much, we'd never had a meal at Marnie's before. She lived in an old brick building on Wells Street, just a mile or so from Danni's place. I arrived first, got buzzed in, sprinted up to her third-floor walk-up, and knocked lightly. Marnie flung open the door, and said, "Welcome!"

We hugged, and I stupidly said, "I don't know why, but I assumed you lived in a building with an elevator."

"You don't know why?" asked Marnie.

I realized my mistake, didn't reply, and braced for a barb. Marnie just laughed. Then she grabbed my hand and pulled me the twenty feet or so into her kitchen. "Look what I got for us." A bottle of Dom Perignon sat in a silver ice bucket beside three elegant champagne flutes.

"Is this uncharacteristic optimism, or do you know something I don't know?"

"I'm sure I know a lot of things you don't know. But Danni hasn't confided in me about her sister's response."

"Then why the champagne?"

"Because Delaney's answer is obvious."

"It is?"

"She loves her sister. We love her sister. Danni is happy when we're together. We'll be a huge success. Her sister can afford it. Do I need to go on?"

"I love your confidence."

The buzzer sounded and Marnie hurried to the front door to press a button to unlock the front door of the building. She and I stepped out into the hall to greet Danni, and Marnie yelled, "There's no one in the stairwell. Send him up!"

We heard, "Okay," and Grizzly bounded up the last flight, three stairs at a time.

As she leaned over to stroke the dog, Marnie said to me, "I asked her to bring him."

Once we were all standing in the living room, Marnie said, "I'm not going to offer a tour, but I cleaned what's in plain view." Her modern glass, chrome, and black leather furniture, and white woven rugs looked stunning against the blond oak floors and interior brick dining room wall. Like Danni, she had a balcony, but hers faced west and gave us a completely different view of the city—a few odd skyscrapers and mid-rise structures in the distance, and near-by low-rise apartment buildings and shops. The evening sky was already dark, and the glow of lights poured out of windows, near and distant. It was too cold to hang out on the balcony, and a roaring gas log fire beckoned to us to gather in the living room.

"Lovely place, Marnie," I said.

"Yes. It's really stunning," said Danni.

"Thanks, guys. I'm partial to clean lines and simple, almost invisible tables and chairs."

"Well, it really works," I said. "Where's the little guy?"

Marnie said, "If there were a guy of any size here, I think I'd know."

"Igor. The ceramic statue."

Marnie looked at me like she'd never seen me before. "Imagine you remembering that." She led us to her corner, steel bookcase, where Igor sat on a middle shelf. Marnie handed the small porcelain figure to me. His cream-colored glaze shimmered in the light. Fat tummy, truncated arms and legs, with a shock of red hair sticking straight up out of his head, he reminded me of a plastic version I'd once had.

"He's charming," I said.

"Rescued him from a garage sale. I'm pretty sure he's been faithful to me, which makes exactly one." She replaced Igor, and said, "You guys take a seat, and I'll bring some drinks in." She walked to the doorway to the kitchen and stopped. Danni sat on the couch and I chose one of the love-seat-length pieces. Marnie asked, "Chardonnay, Cab, Dom Perignon?"

Danni laughed hard. "How did you know?"

Marnie hurried back into the living room.

"Oh, my god! What did she say?" I asked.

"My sister loved you guys."

"I can't believe it. She never even smiled at me," I said.

"Sorry about that. She was testing you, Heather. She

wanted to see how persuasive you could be to someone who didn't want to hear what you had to say."

In spite of Danni's assurances, I was flat-out shocked. I swallowed. "Wow. She did a good job."

"It was an important decision for her," said Danni.

"Eek!" I screamed and the others couldn't help but join in while we all hugged.

"You guys sit. I'll bring the champagne," said Marnie.

Once she popped the cork, poured, and served the flutes, we toasted ourselves. "To success," I said.

"To our new venture," said Danni.

"To friends," said Marnie, who then did something I hadn't seen her do before, and didn't see again for two years. She cried. That, of course, made Danni and me join in the waterworks, and we all got up and hugged again.

After a few minutes, I said, "Shit. Now we have to focus on the other tiny, little hurdle."

"Not tonight," said Marnie. "Let's just relish this moment, and tomorrow we'll take the next step." She turned to Grizzly and said, "What do you think of that?" The dog glanced at Danni, then nodded his head up and down—twice.

Marnie served trout almondine, and had a small, off-the-bone, cooked steak for Grizzly.

I said, "You really did guess the good news, didn't you?"

"There was no guessing involved," said Marnie, as we all dug in.

****

The next day, we got together at my apartment to divide up assignments for analyzing client opportunities and fleshing out specifics on the article-writing and pamphlet creation. The truth was, no new firm could be sure it would receive any business for the simple reason that it was a violation of the Code of Ethics to ask a current client to direct your old firm to allow you to take files with you when you left. The logic behind the rule was fairly obvious. Each of us had a responsibility to promote the interests of our current employer, and certainly not to undermine them, while we were being paid by them, and practicing law with them.

So, we discussed the details of how we would go about recruiting clients starting the day we'd open, basically along the lines of how I'd laid it out for Delaney. We created a detailed list of assignments to be undertaken, some before, and some only after we'd resigned our old positions and announced our law firm. In fairness to my friends, I reluctantly reminded them that they'd agreed to at least ask their bosses for the opportunity to handle their own courtroom work. There was no harm in giving that approach one last chance, although none of us was optimistic about their prospects. We agreed they'd both make their request of the partners they worked for on Monday, and then report back after work.

We didn't have any extra time to travel for a meeting, so the next evening we had a conference call so Marnie and Danni could share how the partners they worked for responded to their requests. I took the call sitting on my couch, with Chica-the-Brave next to me for moral support. I knew it was flat-out selfish, but I prayed their old firms wouldn't surprise us all by agreeing to their requests. "Hi, guys. Who wants to go first?"

"I'll go," said Marnie. "His speech was so inspiring

that I can't wait to share it with you." She lowered her voice, and did an impression of her boss.

"Him: 'Marnie, Marnie, Marnie.'

"Me: 'Yes. That's my name.'

"Him: 'I think you know how much we value you.'

"Me: (nothing).

"Him: 'Is this about money?'

"Me: 'Did I mention money?'

"Him: 'To get to the heart of it, you are too good behind the scenes to waste your talents in court.'

"Me: 'I think you can do better?'

"Him: 'Excuse me.'

"Me: 'You're excused. Why? Did you burp or fart?'

"Him: 'I'm not sure you're being respectful, young lady.'

"Me: 'Are you?'

"Him: 'What are you saying?'

"Me: 'I'm saying that there is no legitimate reason that I'm not being given the same opportunities as other associates at my level. So you are the one being disrespectful.'

"Him: 'But you are so good where you are.'

"Me: 'That's true. I am good. And I would be good in a courtroom.'

"Him: (Sigh).

"Me: 'So, what is it? What's the real reason?'

"Him: 'I'm afraid your appearance isn't consistent with the firm's image.'

"Me: 'What about my appearance?'

"Him: 'This conversation is over. You should be glad you have this job, considering—'

"Me: 'Considering what?'

"Him: 'Let's just say you wouldn't be the first

choice of any law firm looking to hire…if you had an in-person interview.'

"Me: 'Because?'

"Him: 'Because you don't meet the ideal, or even the average appearance of a young woman lawyer.'

"Me: 'I understand. You are prejudiced against me because of my weight.'

"Him: 'I didn't say that.'

"Me: 'Actually, you did. But you won't have to try to remember every word you uttered because I've got it all on tape.' I tapped a spot between my breasts.

"Him: 'I want that tape.'

"Me: 'You try to take it and I'll call 9-1-1. The proof of the assault will also be on the video I'm taking. But thanks for explaining things to me. I'm going back to my cave to finish an appellate brief I'm working on so that you can leave my name off when you file it.' I left the room."

"Oh, Marnie, I'm so sorry," said Danni.

Having caught onto Marnie's sense of humor by then, I asked, "You really said all that?"

Marnie burst out laughing. "Of course not! I wasn't in a bridge-burning mood. I just asked, and he said courtroom work isn't in the plan for me. I thanked him for being frank, although his name isn't Frank."

Danni said, "Damn it, Marnie. I believed you." After a moment, she added, "I'm glad it didn't really happen."

I released a long sigh. "What about you, Danni?"

"Sorry I haven't prepared a made-up story. And the partner I work for reports to my uncle, so I knew it wouldn't be a terrible conversation."

"What did the guy say?" asked Marnie.

"He acted like he was trying to protect me from

being bullied in court." She lowered her voice impressively, like Marnie had done, which was pretty funny. "He said something like, 'Danni, I have no doubt you'd be very strong at oral argument. But your opposing counsel is likely to be rude and/or condescending. Just walking into the courthouse will attract pointing and stares, which would undermine anyone's confidence. Also, I hate to say it, but many of our clients would be unhappy if we assigned a little person to represent them in court.' So, I asked, 'Do all the partners feel that way?' His response was, 'We do. We discussed it at a partnership meeting when your uncle brought you in, and it comes up every year when we evaluate your progress. Everyone thinks you do a fine job, and we very much enjoy working with you. But your role was never intended to include courthouse work—' I interrupted, 'Or depositions.' He said, 'Yes. Or depositions.' I said, 'Or client meetings.'

"'Right. I hope you can understand that this is for your protection.' So, I said, 'I can take care of myself, thank you. And I'm way past worrying about what rude and ignorant people say or do. I'd hoped you would support me on this.' Then he just said, 'I'm sorry, Danni.' "

I took a moment. "Okay. So, they both blew their last chance. I'm sorry they were Neanderthals with you guys, but I'm actually glad they didn't agree." I felt a big smile creep across my face. "We're on."

"We are," said Marnie. "Let's all work on our assignments and meet again next Saturday for an all-day planning session?"

"I'm on it," said Danni. "I'll just take some of my many accrued vacation days to get my part ready."

"As will I," said Marnie.

"Me too," I said. "This will be much more fun than a vacation, anyway."

****

It was a beautiful, crystal-clear day when we next met at my place in Evanston. Danni was giddy because she thought she'd seen the man who had saved her on the windy day. He was walking a curly-haired, black standard poodle not far from my building, and when he saw Danni from a block away, he'd tipped his baseball cap to her, like in an old movie. Marnie confirmed that it looked like the same guy, and definitely attractive. I said, "Good. Another argument in favor of having our meetings in Evanston."

I made a coffee cake and threw together a bowl of fresh fruit so we could have breakfast while we got down to business. We ate and sipped coffees as we talked. The results of our research confirmed there was no way to guarantee success. We debated whether it was unavoidable that the only way to find out was to launch.

I said, "I think we should just jump in—and sink or swim."

"I'm pretty buoyant," said Marnie. "I'm not sure if I could sink if I wanted to—well, maybe if I tie concrete blocks to my feet."

"I'm ready," said Danni. "Let's go ahead and pull the plugs on our old jobs."

"Don't anyone suggest that we roll the dice," said Marnie. "One more cliché and I'm out."

"So, if I mentioned a flag pole and saluting?" asked Danni.

She turned to me. "I'd have to kill you. There's no way I'm going through Grizzly to kill Danni."

By mid-afternoon, I'd been assigned to find office space, furniture, file cabinets for our back-up paper files, and an office manager. I was also charged with enlisting him or her to arrange for the phones and computer hook-ups so we could be up and running on Day One. We all did our own typing, so the office manager would be freed up to do all the administrative, billing, and reception work, as well as copying and filing what the three of us would type up.

Marnie agreed to take care of ordering the computers, printers, office supplies, stationery, and find a good billing program. Danni would open our bank account and be responsible for the financial aspects, including creating an LLC, securing insurance, and finding an accountant/tax specialist to periodically look over our records.

Danni was staring at her "to do" list, when she looked up and said, "Guys, there's one little, bitty thing we're forgetting."

Tension rushed through my body that I could've missed something important. "What?"

"Marnie can't order stationery, and I can't start an LLC without a firm name."

Marnie laughed, then said, "Good catch, Danni." She turned to me. "What are our choices?"

I shook my head. "I believe we're limited to our actual three names, Ms. Ames."

"So you're not thinking *Heather Hightower Law Offices*?"

"Of course not. In fact, I wonder if we shouldn't go with your name, Marnie. At least it would get us to the top of alphabetical listings."

Marnie put her hand up to her chin and took a

moment to reply. "There are a lot of Irish judges, especially in Cook. Maybe we should go with Dooley." She paused. "Plus, Danni's sister is financing us."

"I don't think that's relevant," said Danni. "After all, only Heather will bring work with her."

"I agree with Danni," I said. "Those things don't matter."

"Right," said Danni. "Shouldn't the choice be based on which order somehow shows us to best advantage?"

"You mean, which order of names has the best ring to it?" I asked.

"We're not naming a pop group," said Marnie. She scratched her head, then added, "But I do agree we need the most memorable name to go first."

"Why?" I asked.

"Because, once we're established, everyone will refer to us just by the first name."

"True," I said.

"You're right," said Danni. "So which name is the most memorable?"

"Sadly for my little four-letter name, I have to admit it's Hightower," said Marnie.

"I agree," said Danni. "Moving on, which sounds better: Hightower, Dooley and Ames, or Hightower, Ames and Dooley?"

"I don't see much difference," I said.

"Me neither," said Marnie. "So, unless Danni strenuously disagrees, we should call ourselves Hightower, Dooley, and Ames, LLC."

"Is it really okay with you for your name to be last?" I asked Marnie.

"Sure. But I get first dibs on choosing an office."

"Fine with me," said Danni.

"Suits me, too," I said.

"And one other thing," said Marnie.

"What?" I asked.

"My names goes first if we form a pop group."

"It goes without saying," said Danni. She looked over her "to do" list again, then said, "Do we need to choose a managing partner?"

"Already done," said Marnie.

"How?" asked Danni.

"Heather's personality means she'll manage us."

"Is that an insult?" I asked.

"Not entirely," said Marnie. "I'm just being realistic. You know the legal community in Lake County, you have the client contacts, and you've pushed us to where we are today."

I thought for a moment and had to admit she had a point. My stomach started to churn. "Shit. I guess I have been pretty aggressive. I'm sorry, guys."

"Heather, you pushed me right out of my cave, for which I'm thrilled. I agree with Marnie that you're the logical choice for managing partner. Okay with you?"

I laughed, mainly from embarrassment. "Sure. Hopefully I'll push us in a generally successful direction."

Our quick agreement on those things was not emblematic of the speed of the other decisions we would make over the next several months. Because we were all three planners and worriers, we agonized over everything, and the stress took some of the fun out of it. Fortunately, we'd all survived challenging situations before, and we remained confident we would come out the other end in reasonably good shape.

Eventually, everything was lined up. On launch day,

we would each announce our departure, go live on our website, and run an advertisement in the law reports and the local Lake County papers. I would call the clients with whom I had files and ask them to advise my old firm to allow me to take those matters with me to Hightower, Dooley and Ames. Our office manager would officially start that day and would ensure that the furniture was all delivered and set up, computers in place, and phones operating.

Marnie and Danni would also call the clients they'd worked with and request that their active files be transferred to our new firm. No one was optimistic this would yield much, but there was no reason not to make the request. Late in the day, or early the next morning, we'd do the tour of the courthouse and I'd make introductions.

Chapter 9

We launched on Monday, May 7th, and everything went wrong. If it had been D-Day, we'd all be speaking German today. The office manager I'd hired, a twenty-something recent secretarial school graduate, arrived at our new office twenty minutes after her scheduled start time. Later, when Marnie and Danni made it from Chicago, after announcing their respective departures to the partners for whom they'd worked and saying goodbye to their friends, our new office manager barely made it through introductions before grabbing her purse, explaining that she was sorry but just not the right person for the job, and hightailed it out the door. Our office space, in one of the renovated complexes near the courthouse, had been freshly painted, but the furniture arrived finished in a shiny black lacquer, rather than being the blond oak we'd ordered. We needed to get to work right away, so we decided not to insist that the desks be exchanged. Then the man who delivered the file cabinets said his order didn't include anything beyond getting them inside our front door, where they consumed most of the floor space of our reception area. So, Marnie and I shuffled the five-foot-high cabinets into the file room, with only a couple of bruised toes. Danni offered to help, but we feared a catastrophe if one of the things should escape her grip. The two of us were both pouring sweat by the time we got them all lined up in place.

Thankfully, the phone company guy and the computer store woman arrived as scheduled and got our offices and the office manager's desk set up, everything functioning. Unfortunately, we had no one to occupy the swivel chair behind the desk.

We stood around in the reception area taking a cardiac break. Danni asked, "Heather, did you interview anyone else for the office manager position? Maybe one of the other candidates is still available."

I sighed. "Yeah. I did three in-person interviews during my lunch breaks. There was only one other applicant who has all of the skills we need, Jeanne Coopersmith. But, honestly, she looks like she's in her mid-seventies, if not older."

"I'm surprised at you," said Marnie, who was still wearing a patina of perspiration from all the pushing. "Here, you're all over sexism and bodyism, but you're an ageist."

I opened my mouth to respond but nothing came out. Then I stammered, "I…" and then, "Well…" and finally, "It's just that we'll be demanding an awful lot from our office manager, so it seems reasonable to choose someone with a lot of energy."

"Marnie's correct," said Danni. "That's ageism."

"Well, damn. I guess you guys are right." Embarrassed at my failure to catch myself on this, I added, "Other than the age thing, I really liked her a lot. She has decades of experience, but she's also up to date on procedures."

"Good," said Marnie, as she dabbed at her face and neck with a tissue.

"I'll call Jeanne and see if she's still interested."

"Oh, and be sure to mention that one of us is a little

person, and one is an obese person," she added.

I stared, not sure if she was kidding.

"Well, we don't have time to parade before a viewing stand of office managers who reject us once they get a good look at us. We have to be efficient."

"Fine. I'll call her from my office." My new black desk and ergonomic chair were still wrapped in plastic, so I sat atop my credenza, which I'd already liberated, to make the call. When I returned to the reception area, I said, "Good news, guys! When I told Jeanne what you asked me to say, she said, 'Lovely. I look forward to meeting them.'"

"So, she took the job?" asked Danni.

"Yep. She's on her way here right now."

We all plopped down on the two reception area couches, both also encased in plastic, and Marnie said, "We're dying to know how your calls went this morning. Will your clients let you take your files?"

"First of all, they were all shocked I'm leaving the firm I've been with since I started practicing."

"How did you explain your decision to move?" asked Danni.

"There was no way I'd bad-mouth that firm since those folks are all friends of mine—and good lawyers. So, I just said I had a strong interest in starting an all-woman partnership and that I think the time is right."

"What did you tell them about us?" asked Danni.

"Just that you are both my age—my level. And that the three of us are ready to be our own bosses."

"How many files are we keeping, Heather?" asked Danni.

"As you guys know, I had fifty active files. Of those, thirty-five will move to our firm. Frankly, my clients were all terribly supportive. It's just that a couple of them have limits on the number of firms they can spread their Lake County files among. So, they can't add our firm to their list without removing some other firm, which could happen someday, but not overnight. Another client likes me and my work, but is a personal friend of one of the partners in my old firm." I paused to pull a loose piece of plastic off the couch, feeling bad that I'd disappointed my partners. "I did my best."

"Oh, no, Heather," said Danni. "You did great."

Marnie said, "Frankly, I'm surprised you were able to run off with thirty-five. I'm impressed."

"Thanks. But we need more files."

"Heather, we were always going to need more work. We have to relax about it and stick to our plan," said Danni, who did look almost serene, sitting on one of the couches with her ankles crossed.

"I know. How did your calls go?"

"Pleasant," said Marnie. "But the bottom lines all went something like: 'You've been a great support on our files. But, of course, they'll remain with the partner to whom they were originally assigned.'"

"Did you squeeze in the fact that it was actually you who planned the strategies and secured the results?" I asked.

"Of course, I had to do that delicately. I said something like, 'Just give me a call if you're ever in another situation like the Smith case, and I can share with you how I went about finding our hook, or the flaw in the opponent's argument.' So, I slipped it in—but no one bit."

"It's a good foundation though, Marnie," I said. "Maybe someday they'll realize they could really use your help."

"No doubt," she deadpanned.

I turned to Danni. "How did yours go?"

"Like Marnie's, without a pitch about being a brilliant strategist. Everyone was kind and said the right things. But I've been so back-officed, it's not realistic to think my clients will wake up one day, and think, 'We need Danielle Dooley!'"

"That's okay," said Marnie. "We're right where we wanted to be today—well, with our second-choice office manager, with the wrong furniture, and with hernias from moving the file cabinets."

Danni laughed, and I shook my head. "Actually, Jeanne said she was only five minutes away. She should be here soon." No sooner had I finished my sentence than the front door to our suite opened. In walked a short, fair, older woman wearing a tailored peach skirt suit and three-inch heels, with her short dark hair tightly curled in a neat perm. She had on a matching necklace and earrings, and her elegance almost masked her stooped shoulders and hump neck.

She said, "Good afternoon, ladies. I'm Jeanne Coopersmith. Congratulations on your new law firm."

We all stood to welcome her, and Marnie and Danni introduced themselves. Even in heels, Jeanne was short enough that she didn't have to lean over to shake hands with Danni, and she showed no reaction at all to their shapes. Then she turned to me and said, "It's so nice to see you again, Ms. Hightower." She stashed her handbag behind the desk. "I'll just leave my purse here. Then, if one of you will give me a quick tour, I'll know which office each of you will be in."

"Absolutely," said Marnie.

Jeanne gave her a big smile and followed her down the hallway, walking surprisingly quickly on her high heels, Danni and me trailing behind. As we made our way back to the reception area, Jeanne said, "It's all charming." She flung off her suit jacket and reached into her large purse. "I have a nice sharp box-cutter in here that should make quick work of all the plastic. It's almost one o'clock, and I'll wager none of you has had lunch. Why don't you leave me to it, and go out for a nice celebratory meal?"

"We have so much to do," I said.

"Of course, you do, Ms. Hightower. But even a quick repast can be celebratory."

"Oh, Jeanne," I said. "You really must call us Heather, Marnie, and Danielle."

"Make that 'Danni,' " said our shortest partner.

"Very well," said Jeanne. "I believe we girls are going to get along quite well."

The three of us were all stifling giggles as we stepped out of our office space and closed the door behind us. Marnie said, " 'We girls.' She's a riot!"

"I adore her already," said Danni. "I have that feeling about her—the same one I got about you two. That's why I asked her to call me Danni."

I said, "She is different...in some way I can't quite put my finger on. Anyway, she should fit right in." I led my friends—my law partners—to a small café only a block from our building. Surprisingly, no one I knew was present, so I didn't get to make any introductions, but we were all in good spirits as we snarfed our sandwiches, all dying to get back and start our first day of work.

When we re-entered our reception area, all of the plastic had been removed and disposed of, and our offices were similarly readied for us. I looked at Jeanne "How—?"

"Don't you worry about the office management, Heather. Now, do you have the list of files you need to have brought over from your old firm? I can give their office manager a call and arrange for the client paperwork to be done right away. I'll insist that the files be delivered by five o'clock, so you can prepare your substitutions, and get started on your work."

I nodded and said, "Thank you." I walked into Marnie's office, the first one down the hallway, and the largest, where she sat behind her new, shiny desk, and Danni was sitting in one of the visitor chairs. I grabbed the other. "It seems that Jeanne will have all of our files here by five o'clock. We should stay and get them organized in the file cabinets, and make sure we have the complete electronic files."

"Maybe," said Marnie. "But why do I get the feeling Jeanne will magically have that done for us if we so much as step out for a breath of air?"

"I know," said Danni.

"Anyway, I have a list of our files, and a short description of each case, which I made a couple of weeks ago. If you guys give me twenty minutes, I'll divide up the files we're keeping and give you each a list of your eleven or twelve. Then I'll get on the phone and start scheduling client lunches and conference call introductions for this week and next."

"Great," said Danni.

"And tomorrow morning, since there are no court appearances scheduled on any of our files, we'll go over to court early, before the call begins, so that I can introduce you guys to the judges in the civil courtrooms."

"I'm so excited," said Danni. "I've never been introduced to a judge."

"Come to think of it, neither have I," said Marnie. "But I have no illusions they will go better than any other introductions I've had."

"I think you'll be pleasantly surprised, Marnie. Our judges are big on decorum. Whatever they may think about our law firm being different, you're not likely to hear a disrespectful word."

"Maybe," said Marnie. "But you're not claiming that all the other attorneys are also angels, are you?"

"Certainly not. Most are fine, some are sexist, some specialize in misleading the court, and a few are outright scoundrels. But it's nothing we can't handle, girls." Of course, Marnie and Danni caught the Jeannesque reference. I headed to my office to divvy up what we had.

We received the boxes containing our files, all the electronic files, and the pertinent docket sheets by four-thirty. By five, Jeanne had all the paper files secured in the file cabinets, and had arranged to have all of the empty bankers' boxes removed. At 5:45 she stopped by my office to let me know the status of things, including the fact that she now had her docket system in place. I walked with her back to the reception area. As she grabbed her purse and suit jacket, Jeanne said, "Shall I plan to work from 8:30 to 5:30, with a one-hour lunch break?"

I said, "That sounds great. And Jeanne, thanks for joining us."

She had started for the door, but turned to look at me, and said, "Joy and harmony will abound in this place."

Having no idea how to respond to that, I simply

smiled and nodded. We all took a seven thirtyish train toward Chicago, and I hopped off at the Evanston stop, half-way to Marnie and Danni's downtown destination. As I'd told them, I had absolutely no concern about the reception they'd receive from the judges. But we would also run into many attorneys, and I had little confidence they'd be universally welcoming. I planned to keep in mind that I, too, had been nonplussed the first time I saw my partners. Our goal to break down stereotypes would take months and years, not seconds and minutes. I kept reminding myself that we mustn't be discouraged by initial reactions.

Still, I had a lot of trouble getting to sleep that night, worrying about the reception my friends would get at the courthouse in the morning, and desperately wishing there were some way I could insulate them.

Chapter 10

Launch-day-plus-one presented us with a gorgeous, clear, fifty-degree May morning. We had only from 8:00 to 9:00 a.m. to make our way to as many as possible of the courtrooms on my list, so I could make the introductions. We walked into the first at 8:05, and I explained to the bailiff that I was hoping to visit the judge in chambers to introduce my new law partners. It wasn't a random choice. I got along well with the judge, who was an especially genteel elderly man, and with his bailiff, with whom I often chatted before and after court was in session. Marnie had followed me into the courtroom with her chin lifted in a way that suggested she owned the place—or soon would. Danni looked more like the proverbial deer-in-the-headlights, but must've intuited that her smile would go a long way. I was feeling pretty confident, since I knew to expect a kind reception from the judge.

The bailiff slipped back to inquire of the judge, and returned quickly to escort the three of us into chambers, which was located directly behind the courtroom. We all stood in front of his cluttered desk, as he didn't invite us to sit. I introduced Marnie and Danni, and handed the judge one of our new business cards. He asked them what firms they'd been with before, and welcomed them to Lake County. Of course he noticed their unconventional shapes, but he certainly didn't let on.

When we turned to leave, he asked that we stop by again once we got through the initial crush of work and would have more time to visit.

Marnie said, "You bet we will, your honor."

Danni said, "I'd be honored."

Marnie and Danni were both smiling as we walked out of chambers and down the hall. Our second visit was with a woman judge in her early sixties who had been a state's attorney on the civil side before she was appointed to the bench. We had to wait while she finished a phone conversation and were then warmly welcomed. In fact, she should've been our first stop as it turned out, because she was impressively effusive in her enthusiasm for our venture.

"Heather, I had no idea you were thinking of opening your own shop."

"Actually, it was getting to know Marnie and Danielle that got me thinking about it."

She looked them over, and said, "I see. Well, what a wonderful idea! Marnie and Danielle, I don't believe I've seen either of you in my courtroom."

Marnie said, "That's true. You would've remembered us."

I tried to catch Marnie's eye to get her to tread lightly, but the judge seemed to stifle a laugh. Wisely though, she didn't take the bait to refer to their shapes. "Yes. Women attorneys are still in the minority here."

She asked them where they'd practiced before, and urged them to be sure to join the Women Lawyers' Club. Then she said the words I'll never forget. "I can tell you are all brave women. You'll need your courage the way I needed mine when I was one of the few women practicing in the courtrooms of this building a hundred years ago. But you have something I didn't—each other. Enjoy your journey, counsel. I have to get out to the bench now, but let me just say that meeting you has absolutely made my day."

Once out in the hallway that ran the length of all of the judges' chambers, Marnie whispered, "Damn. We're a hit. We should've done this years ago."

"But we've only known each other for a year," whispered Danni.

"That was amazing," I said. "But the only way out of here is through one of the courtrooms, and they're all full of lawyers by this time."

"So?" asked Marnie.

"So, brace yourselves," I said.

Our experience promenading from the hall, through the center of the courtroom, between the two large counsel tables, through the swinging wooden gates, past the spectator pews, to the large double doors, was the most humiliating walk of my life. Because the judge was about to enter, I couldn't stop to make any introductions. Marnie and Danni just followed my path to the door. As we stepped through it, I heard the bailiff say, "All rise."

Before that, I'd heard a lot of other phrases: "Oh my god," "Those can't be Heather's new partners," "Jeez," and "—a circus...the midget... fat lady." But what I saw hurt even more than what I heard. Every head was turned our way. Mouths literally hung open. Lawyers nudged others who had been studying their paperwork. The eyes of the entire room full of attorneys followed our parade to the main door. The judge had to have noticed as she approached the bench. I wondered if she still felt we'd "made her day".

I couldn't imagine that Marnie and Danni weren't

devastated. Once we were out in the hallway, which was almost empty, Marnie snorted out a chuckle. "I think I've just been whipsawed."

"I'm so sorry, guys. That was hideous."

"What was?" asked Danni.

I looked from one of them to the other, my jaw gone slack.

Danni laughed. "Heather, this moment was always going to be like this. We'll get where we want to be."

Marnie said, "Remember, we're all 'brave women.' "

"It's true," said Danni. "You can't let that kind of shit bother you."

It was the first time I'd heard Danni swear. I said, "You two are even cooler than I thought."

Marnie said, "Exactly what the lawyers in that room are now whispering to each other."

"Let's go meet some clients by conference call," said Danni. "Then, when do we need to leave for our lunch meeting?"

I was incredibly relieved, and also enormously impressed with my partners' resilience. Also, I couldn't help wondering whether it might be an act, or whether they really were that self-possessed. I said, "Twelve-fifteen would be fine. The client's just in North Chicago."

"Good," said Marnie. "That'll also give us some time to get acquainted with our files before lunch."

Marnie and Danni needed to read the file materials for the twelve matters I'd assigned to each of them in the hope that my clients would agree they could take over those files. Of course, they wouldn't be able to bill the clients for the review time since it was duplicative of the work I'd already done. But they were both efficient, and they'd be doing productive, billable work in short order.

Jeanne greeted us with, "What a beautiful day for your court visit. How did it go?"

"As we expected," said Danni.

"Well, whoever got to meet you should've been honored. I hope they appreciated you."

"Not so much," said Marnie, as she headed toward her office.

"Ah, but they will," said Jeanne, who then resumed typing.

At ten o'clock, Marnie and Danni joined me in my office so I could introduce them by telephone to a client of mine located in Nebraska. It was one of my favorite insurance company clients because the company handled high-risk insureds, which led to lots of interesting and complex lawsuits. They were both standing at my desk, leaning over the speakerphone to be sure she could hear them clearly. She picked up on the first ring.

"Linda Steevers here."

"Hi, Linda! It's Heather. I want to introduce you to my two law partners, Marnie Ames and Danielle Dooley. They are both at my level of practice—six years or so— and have been handling casualty cases, contract disputes, and appeals at their Chicago firms. As we discussed briefly yesterday, I've been giving some thought to the five files I've been working on. My suggestion is that I keep the three oldest ones for myself, and assign one of each of the newer filings to Marnie and Danielle. Of course, we won't bill you any time for them to get up to speed."

"That sounds fine, Heather. Hello, Marnie and Danielle. I'd love to hear each of you tell me a bit about yourselves."

"It's Marnie here. I've been handling the types of files Heather described, all with the same Chicago firm, Brown and Rogers, for over six years. I really look forward to working with you, Linda. I'll get a comprehensive assessment of my file out to you early next week, so you can let me know if you agree with my strategy."

"That sounds good, Marnie. We can get to know each other through your work on the file. And can you tell me how many cases you've taken to trial?"

"Unfortunately, my files tended to end with a summary judgment in my client's favor or a settlement. As a result, I've not yet had the opportunity to take one to trial."

"I see. Listen, Heather, if my file with Marnie should go to trial, I'll need you to be the lead trial attorney. Marnie is welcome to assist, but I'll only pay associate rates for her work in that capacity—at least to start off."

I shrugged to Marnie. "That's fine with us. I'll make a note of it."

"Good. And Danielle, what is your experience?"

"The same as Marnie's—casualty defense and contract disputes—but I was with a different Chicago firm, Watson and Reed."

"So, also no jury trials?"

"That's right. But I look forward to the opportunity."

"Okay. So, Heather, same deal here."

This time, I looked at Danni and shrugged. "Of course."

"Danielle, give me a call once you review your file

so we can chat a bit about it."

"Absolutely."

"Is there anything else I should know about you all?"

I said, "I'd like to introduce Marnie and Danielle to you in person as soon as possible. If you don't get out our way in the near future, we'll plan a trip to see you."

"Really?"

"Definitely. I'd like to get our visit in before we get too busy for the three of us to be able to be out of the office for a day at the same time."

"I'm glad to hear it, Heather. You see, one of the associates from your former firm gave me a call this morning to say he'd seen the three of you in court."

"How nice of him," I said, through clenched teeth, feeling the anger well up.

"Yes. My thought exactly. Anyway, I really would like to meet Marnie and Danielle. Please make that happen in the next couple of months."

"We would love that," I said.

"I look forward to working with all three of you. And congratulations on the new firm."

"Thanks, Linda."

By the time I hung up, I was furious. Marnie and Danni plopped down into the chairs. "I know who he is. I saw him in the courtroom with a sinister grin on his face. Actually, I just thought it looked weird, but now I know it was sinister."

"What an asshole," said Marnie.

"He works fast," said Danni.

"So, he's probably called all of our clients by now," said Marnie.

"That's a good point. Listen, we still have time

before we need to leave for our lunch. I'll just make a quick preliminary call to our other clients. I'll let them know up-front that Danni has a form of dwarfism. Of course, I won't mention that you are plus-size, Marnie. A decent percentage of women are, and that includes some of our clients. Then, we'll get through all of the conference calls by the end of the week."

"I think you should call Linda back, as well," said Danni. "Tell her more about my dwarfism. She already knows we're not trying to hide it since you told her we'll be visiting. But give her some more detail—privately, so you don't hurt my feelings."

"Wait—"

"No, Heather. I'm not saying it's possible for you to do that. What I'm saying is that you could tell Linda the details about me more extensively if I'm not on the call."

"It's a good thought. I'll make her my first call." Marnie and Danni left to get to work on the files we all hoped the clients would agree to let them handle.

After calling Linda back, I reached out to my remaining three clients. Based on what they'd said in conversations I'd had with them in the hours immediately after I walked out the door of my old firm the day before, I knew exactly which of their files remained in my inventory. There were six with Julie Davidson, who was with an insurance company in Missouri, seven with Mike Huntsman, a claim department manager with an insurance company based in Indiana, and nine with Irene Baldwin, from an insurance claim department in Ohio. Knowing they'd certainly been told about Danni's dwarfism, and possibly Marnie's weight, by my snarky former friend, I started the calls without my partners on the line. Since I'd already secured the files, the sole purpose of my calls was to get their agreements to allow me to assign some of the matters to Marnie and Danni. If they would agree, I'd set up a separate call to introduce them and discuss specific files.

My next call was to Julie.

"Hi, Heather. I'm so happy for you that you've opened your own shop. Congratulations!"

"Thanks so much. And I want to tell you about my two wonderful partners, Marnie Ames and Danielle Dooley."

"I've already heard about them."

"From someone at my old firm?"

"He was among several."

"I see. I guess we made a big splash."

"I, for one, was moved by how kind your competitors were to call me and let me know about your partners' appearances."

"Seriously? More than one lawyer called you about my partners' looks?"

"Of course. The dear boys thought I should know."

"Well, since that's been covered, I'd like to fill you in on their experience and how impressive they both are."

"No need, Heather. I have to run into a meeting in a minute. If you chose them as your partners, I know they must be excellent lawyers. I've looked through the files, and I'd like you to continue to work on the two oldest matters. Feel free to assign the remaining four as you see fit, but I hope I'll get to work with both of them."

"Thank you, Julie. I think you'll be pleased to have them on your files."

"I have no doubt. So, I'll get to know them through

working with them. No need for a visit or anything like that. Well, I gotta go. Again, congratulations!"

My remaining two calls also went well in that my clients didn't admit to being put off by what they'd heard from my helpful competitors. Nevertheless, they both decided not to have me reassign any of my existing files to Marnie or Danni. They shared the concern that since I'd worked up the files, I was best positioned to take them to their conclusions. I explained that neither Marnie nor Danni would charge anything to review the files to bring themselves up to date. Neither client bit. They weren't really being unreasonable since some little something could be left out in the translation. If that was really the concern. The only way to find out was to watch to see if new files would come in with instructions that I could assign them as I would see fit.

At that point, I had approval to move just three files each to Marnie and Danni, and that wouldn't cut it. In spite of the fact that I knew full well that the development of work for them would take time, I was starting to feel nauseated with worry. It was never far from the front of my mind that I had enticed them to give up good jobs for whatever was about to play out. Just before heading out of my office for our luncheon, I took an antacid and swallowed hard.

I'd rented a car in Evanston for the day because none of us city mice owned one. We arrived at the restaurant at 12:50 p.m., ten minutes before our client Don Peale, who had agreed to move all eight of the files I had with him to the new firm. He owned a large printing business and I handled all of his contract matters, as well as any tort cases, which he had to arrange to have defended since his business was self-insured. I'd had a steady stream of files with him for several years and we enjoyed a good working relationship. Probably in his late forties, he lived in Libertyville with his wife and three daughters, and was active in the large Catholic Church there. Several people I knew who were in his parish told me they thought highly of him. Somehow, I assumed that would bode well for his retention of Marnie and Danni.

We were already seated at our table when he walked in with a big smile on his suntanned face. He wore a sports coat and slacks, had on a tie, and moved with the assurance of someone who is the boss of something. He walked around the table to shake hands with each of us, and then took his seat, ordered an unsweet iced tea, and looked at Danni, who was directly across the table from him. "Achondroplasia?" he said.

Danni gave him one of her thousand-watt smiles and nodded her head. "How did you know?"

"I read a lot. So, Danielle, it's a pleasure to meet you. I can't imagine getting to where you are today was easy."

Marnie said, "Actually, it was a straight shot down Green Bay Road."

I was shocked. He was clearly trying to give Danni a compliment. But Don roared. Then he turned to Marnie and said, "I like you." He smiled. "And I have a deep admiration for people like Danielle who overcome disabilities. I'd like you to tell me about yourselves, ladies, but know in advance that if Heather vouches for you, I already know you must be something special."

Marnie and Danni kept it to the things they'd said on the conference call meeting, but Don pressed them to explain why they wanted to participate in something as risky as starting a new law firm.

"Frankly," said Marnie, "we want the opportunity to try cases. It's something we were both told we'd never be doing at our old firms. I've read plenty of trial transcripts as part of my appellate work, and I'm confident I'd be effective in front of a jury. Plus, Heather bullied us into this."

Don laughed, then turned to Danni.

She said, "There's really no reason Marnie and I can't be as, or more, persuasive to a judge or jury as any other lawyer. If we get the opportunity, I'm sure we'll do well."

Our soup and sandwich specials arrived and we took some time to enjoy the food, and chat about the weather, his kids, our dogs, and other non-controversial subjects. After the server removed our plates, Don looked at me and said, "I agreed you should take all eight of the files we have together, and presumably, they're already sitting in your office."

"Yes. Thanks, Don."

He nodded. "I wanted this meeting to assess Marnie and Danielle, to make a decision as to whether I want them also to be the face of my company." He turned to them, "I like you both very much. And I believe you will do great things in the future, including winning jury trials. But the truth is, a lot of people are prejudiced, and I believe your appearance could disadvantage me, whether you are addressing a judge or a jury. As owner of my business, I have to do everything in my power to ensure the success of our legal matters. So, I'm afraid I won't be one of the clients Heather can bring either of you in to represent."

We glanced at each other, but none of us responded.

"Look," said Don, "I know this isn't what you

wanted to hear, and I admit it's not fair. I'm really sorry to have to go this direction, and I genuinely hope your other clients see it differently."

"I understand," said Danni. "One day, I expect our reputations will persuade you to give us a try."

I held my breath as to how Marnie might react. But as she'd said earlier about her request at her old firm, she wasn't a bridge-burner. She said, "Don, I wish you great success in your business, and I guarantee you, we'll have great success in ours. Would you care for any dessert?"

"Thanks, all of you, but I have to run. Heather, I appreciate that you introduced me to your partners. Best of luck, ladies." With that, he was up and out the revolving door of the restaurant, on his way to his next appointment.

"So," said Marnie. "Hell of a productive lunch!"

Danni smiled, then said, "Thank goodness we're brave women." But she looked deflated.

I paid the check and we headed back to the office. Jeanne greeted us with, "Nice lunch?"

I didn't have the heart to go into it, and just said, "It was fine."

Marnie and Danni got to work reviewing the files they'd each been approved to handle. I'd contacted all of the clients on our thirty-five files, and the shift of only three each to my new partners left me with twenty-nine. We'd never counted on my thirty-five being the entirety of our inventory, and I knew it was ridiculous to get discouraged on the second day we were in business. But I continued to fight off a fear of failure that was boiling up within me—since I was the one who had talked my friends into it.

I'd had a few minutes to think things through while

driving back from the lunch, since Marnie and Danni were discussing some new trick Grizzly had mastered. When we met in my office to plan the next morning, I said, "I'd like to put the judge visits on the back burner for a day or two. After what happened in the courtroom this morning, we can't let the other lawyers think we're anything but proud as hell of our new firm. I'll check the court call lists this afternoon, then tomorrow, we'll waltz into the busiest court room at 8:15 a.m. As the lawyers arrive, I'll introduce you to all of the attorneys I know, including the little fiend from my old firm. I'll introduce myself, and you guys, to any lawyers I don't already know. Then we'll move on to the next most crowded courtroom and do the same thing. We keep moving until court calls begin at 9:00 a.m."

"So, you plan to shove us in their faces," said Marnie.

"Damn right, I do."

"Cool," said Danni.

Marnie said, "I'll wear my best navy lawyer skirt suit. The pinstripes are vertical, so no one will notice I'm fat."

Danni said, "How could no one have told me that's how I'll look taller? Damn."

I just sighed as they headed for their offices to dig into their respective three files.

****

The next morning presented us with another pleasant spring day, the loveliness of which was reinforced by the vases of daffodils from Jeanne's garden that she'd placed on each of our desks before we arrived. If I could have found the key to her *joie de vivre*, I'd have made a duplicate for myself.

Marnie, Danni, and I were stationed outside the door of another courtroom at eight fifteen. When the elderly bailiff opened the door, I explained to him that I wanted to introduce my new partners to the other attorneys, but we'd be out of the courtroom by nine o'clock. When I introduced Marnie and Danni to him, he whispered, "Good luck," and gave them a wink.

The first couple of lawyers, both of whom I knew well, walked through the door, and I pulled them aside to make the introductions. They shook hands with Marnie and Danni, and pleasantly welcomed them to Lake County. The same thing happened with each of the lawyers as they entered through the double doors. Even the young skunk from my old firm acted polite and friendly. It was evident that people would only stab you in the back—never in the front. As the arrivals slowed to a trickle, we slipped into the second courtroom, where a number of attorneys were already seated at counsel tables, and in the pews. I took my partners up to each one, or cluster of lawyers, and made the introductions. To a person, the attorneys were respectful and welcoming—even encouraging. The same thing happened in a third courtroom. When we stepped out of the last one at 9:00, and into the lonely hallway, Danni said, "What a difference a day makes."

"What a difference an introduction makes," I said. "You guys are no longer the dwarf and the plus-size woman. Now you're Danielle and Marnie. Of course, some of them are two-faced jerks who can't wait until we're out of sight to take pot-shots at us—"

Marnie interrupted, "How can they shoot at a target that's out of sight?"

"Right. But what I was going to say is that a lot of

them were truly taken off guard yesterday and will try to act like decent people around you, and possibly, not even gossip about us too much."

" 'Possibly' being the operative word," said Marnie.

"It's a beginning," I said.

Danni excused herself to visit the ladies' room, and returned a few minutes later trying to stifle her laughter.

"What happened?" I asked.

Marnie and I leaned in so we could hear her without anyone passing by listening in to her story. "So, I was in one of the little toilet enclosures, and I heard two women come in, talking at normal volume."

"This will be good," said Marnie.

"Woman number one said, 'Did you see Heather's new partners yesterday?' Woman number two: 'How could I miss them? They caused quite a stir.' Woman one: 'If Heather doesn't introduce them to us soon, let's walk over to their office.' Then I could only hear toilets flushing as I stepped up to the sink to wash my hands. There I stood, drying my little dwarf hands when they both stepped out of their enclosures. Woman one: 'Oh my god! You're one of Heather's partners.' She started to shake my hand but, when I withdrew my arm, she remembered she hadn't yet washed her hands, and laughed as she went about it. I said, 'I'm Danielle.' Woman one: 'I'm Natalie. You probably heard we are both dying to meet you.' I said, 'I heard. Why?' Woman two: 'Are you kidding? You two are a breath of fresh air around here.' 'Really?' I said. 'In what way?' Natalie: 'In the way that most of the lawyers are middle-aged or old White guys. What's the other new partner's name?' 'Marnie.' Woman two: 'By the way, I'm Kim. Natalie and I are both active in the Women Lawyers' Club, so we'd like to put together a luncheon so the others can meet you. Just brown bag in my office's conference room. Danielle, here's my card. Please check with Heather and Marnie, then let me know some dates that would work for you guys.' I will. Natalie, breathlessly: 'I'm so glad we got to meet you.' Kim, effusively: 'Me too.' "

"Honestly, guys, it was as though those two had just been killing time for ages, anxiously awaiting our arrival at the court house."

"That's not terribly surprising," I said. "The women lawyers up here are generally good at sticking together and standing up for each other." As we headed back to our office, I said, "Are you both feeling a little better about Lake County than yesterday?"

"Definitely," said Danni.

"It's odd though," said Marnie. "Going from being so encouraged by the two judges yesterday, to being gaped at minutes later like we were Tasmanian Devils who had been set loose in the courtroom, to being heralded as the second coming in the ladies' room just now. It's just a big shift. Well, a person could get whiplash up here."

I said, "If you do, I know a good law firm."

****

We made time for the Women Lawyers' Club lunch the next week, and the experience was the opposite of our first day walking through the courtroom. Only eight of their members were available, and six of them were from the state's attorney's office. The other two were the enthusiastic Natalie and Kim from Danni's ladies' room encounter. They'd all brought their own lunches, and had kindly purchased three deli sandwich and chips combos and soft drinks for us. They had also thoughtfully arranged to have a pillow on Danni's chair. Sitting around the rectangular table, talking and laughing, reminded me of the high school cafeteria in the carefree good ole days.

Marnie said, "Our first experience with the Lake County bar wasn't exactly a dream scenario—more of a nightmare." When she described our parade through the courtroom, she had the women in hysterics, which I knew she and Danni strongly preferred to pity.

"The boys' club guys are such toads," said one of them.

Another waved her hand and said, "Forget about them. Here's what our group has to offer. We meet once a month, like this, at lunch time, and whoever is available shows up. So, you'll eventually meet everyone. But you can also check us out on our website. If you decide to join us, we'll need a picture and a little blurb about your backgrounds. At this point, all of our extra events are purely social, but there's no limitation on what we might do in the future since we have no mission statement or charter or anything like that to limit us. Last year, we did an outing to Ravinia, a ski-day at Wilmot, and a trip to a comedy club in Northbrook."

Danni said, "That sounds like fun."

Another woman threw in, "And last Christmas, we had a cookie/recipe exchange. Each confection had to be named in honor of one of the judges up here, and it was up to us to decipher the reason. My favorite was one called 'No nuts chocolate squares.'"

I raised my eyebrows, and she went on, "The lawyers on the civil side knew immediately who it was because we have a judge up here who never grants summary judgment motions. One dessert was called 'As Bitter as it Looks Sugarless Lemon Bars,' and another, 'Too Sweet to be Believed Peach Kuchen.' Of course, we never disclosed or confirmed guesses as to the actual judge names associated with the recipes, since none of us wants to be disbarred." The others laughed.

We were almost finished with our lunches and small talk when one of the two women from the rest room meeting spoke up. "If any of you has children, you might be interested to know that a group of us is working up an initial assessment of possibly starting a child-care co-op. Our idea is that it would eventually be for the babies and pre-K children of all the lawyers, secretaries, paralegals, clerks and courthouse employees. Obviously, that would be a huge undertaking, so our thought is to start with a smaller cohort—probably just our club members—and, if it works, slowly build it up."

Danni said, "None of us has children. But it's great to know you are working on this in case we do some day."

"Unlikely," said Marnie.

Danni jumped right back in. "You never know."

Watching them interact with those women temporarily relieved my anxiety. Maybe I wasn't ruining my friends' lives after all.

Chapter 11

In those first few weeks, I spent more time than I should've checking my computer and voicemail messages for new case referrals that didn't materialize. Then some started to trickle in from a couple of my usual sources, Mike Huntsman and Irene Baldwin, but I was specifically asked to handle each one, although having an associate on the file with me would be fine. I pressed both clients to within an inch of pissing them off, but neither would allow me to assign their files to Marnie or Danni. Nearing the middle of our second month in business, I had thirty-two files, and Marnie and Danni still had a whopping three each.

I was desperate for the two of them to develop their own business, but they were already doing everything any of us could think of. There was so much to take care of in addition to file work that my need to hire an associate became pressing. We needed to have a serious conversation about whether my partners should start assisting on my files, basically as my associates. No one would know they were being billed out at associate rates except us and the client, but the last thing in the world I wanted to do was supervise my friends. Nevertheless, the fact was that they were sitting in their offices with no billable work to do, while I was swamped with things an associate could easily help me with.

I asked them into my office to talk it out. Once I

explained the problem, Danni said, "I'm willing to do it. At least I'd be bringing in money. And I'd get a chance to present and defend motions in court. I see it as a temporary phase. How could it hurt?"

Marnie cleared her throat, then said, "It's not like I haven't been humiliated before. I can take that. But if we're working on your files, Heather, instead of doing business development, how will we ever get past this phase? It's not acceptable as a permanent arrangement."

"Of course it isn't," I said. "I'd like to leave the decision up to you two."

"In that case," said Danni, "I'm happy to work on your files as though I were your associate."

I nodded.

Marnie said, "I think I'll keep pumping out articles and attending bar meetings until new files start to roll in."

"That's fine with me," I said.

"The thing is, Heather," said Marnie, "and I know I may sound like a prima donna—"

"What?"

She hesitated for a moment. "It's just that the first time I stand up in court to say, 'Marnie Ames for the defendant,' I want it to be on a file I'm running."

"That's more than fair, Marnie. Both of you guys deserve to run your own defenses." I paused to think through what we were doing. "So, Danni, I'll select a number of files that need work so you can get at it."

"Cool," she said.

"Go get 'em, Danni," said Marnie, as the two of them walked out.

Danni's first court appearance was on a simple motion to compel discovery from the opponent whose answers to interrogatories and production of documents were a month overdue. Since the other lawyer was bound to lose the motion, he didn't even bother to appear, which I, personally, considered bad form. Nevertheless, when her case was called, Danni had the opportunity to approach the bench with her folding stepstool in hand, climb up, and utter the words all of this was designed to make possible: "Good morning, Your Honor, Danielle Dooley for the defendant."

I'd stopped by the gallery to watch and felt proud to know her. What most impressed me was that Danni had thought of everything. She'd gotten the permission of the bailiff to rest her stool against a wall near the front of the courtroom, so she wouldn't have to lug it between the two swinging gates when her case was called. And she'd already filled out the order, having assumed she'd prevail, so she was able to hand it up to the judge to sign, the moment he ruled.

After her "Thank you, Your Honor," she got her stamped copy of the order from the clerk, and placed her stepstool back in the position against the wall, so she could retrieve it after the call was over. In that way, there was no chance she'd disrupt the proceeding. Afterwards, she and I stepped out into the hall.

"Danni, how did it feel?"

"Like I was born to be in a courtroom." She gave me one of her bright smiles.

"I'm really happy for you. But now that you're out here in the hallway, and your stool is still in the courtroom, aren't you stuck hanging around here?"

"Of course. That's why I brought file materials to review while I sit and wait on one of these visitor benches."

"I can see you're all over this thing, Danni. So, the backpack is to keep your arms free so you can lug the stool?"

"Exactly."

"Brilliant. You looked great up there, partner."

"Thanks, Heather."

I turned to leave as she pulled papers out of her backpack and settled herself on the bench. I said, "I'll see you later back at the office."

One routine motion and Danni was hooked on appearing in court. She pestered me to let her handle anything that I didn't absolutely need to attend to myself. Fortunately for her, one of her three cases had been almost ready for a summary judgment motion when she took it over. She secured the last affidavits needed, prepared the motion and supporting memorandum, and filed. At the scheduling hearing, she asked for a short date for her reply brief, which she had plenty of time to work on. It was as though Danni had been thirsting for the past six years, and then found herself on an oasis, with a fountain spouting fresh, cool, spring water.

Marnie and I walked over to court to watch her argue her first dispositive motion. The hearing had been specially set for the afternoon, so only Danni and her opposing counsel were with us in the courtroom when their case was called. She set up her stool before the judge's bench, and her opponent stood to her right. With the stool, they were almost the same height. Her initial presentation of the motion went smoothly. She had notes sitting on the ledge in front of the judge's bench, but never needed to look at them. When she started talking about the case law, she did something I'd never before seen a lawyer do. She pointed out to the court that there were a couple of cases that supported her opponent's position, which he had not cited. She laid out the facts, law, and the decision the court reached in each, and then explained convincingly why those rulings had been erroneous, or didn't control her case. She said something like, "It's important that this court know the full range of arguments, and why, taking all of them into consideration, the defendant is entitled to judgment as a matter of law."

The judge didn't comment on her approach, but his lips curled up at the corners in a hint of a smile. He put his hand up to cover his mouth, elbow on his desk, and I got the impression he was stifling a much larger grin.

In any event, Danni's opponent was clearly unprepared to comment on the two cases his research had missed. He stuck to his notes, and woodenly completed his argument as though Danni had never mentioned them. The judge reserved ruling and promised an order within a week. I caught a glimpse of the judge watching Danni as she folded up her stepstool and walked toward the door. Marnie stood and held open the swinging gate for her partner to pass.

Once we were out in the hall, I said, "You were fabulous, Danni."

"You really were," said Marnie. "I have to admit it. I'm jealous."

I wasn't sure what to say to Marnie, so I basically ignored her comment as the three of us left together for our offices. But the fact that I didn't say anything to her didn't mean I wasn't thinking about her situation frequently every day, and non-stop when I was at home. I'd lost six pounds since launch day. I had to put safety pins in the waistbands of several of my skirts. I hid them with a knit top or a jacket, and imagined I was hiding my weight loss pretty well.

Chapter 12

It was in the third week of June that the three of us made good on our promise to visit Linda Steevers in Omaha, so she could meet Marnie and Danni. We'd agreed to rendezvous at the gate for our 7:15 a.m. nonstop flight, O'Hare to Eppley. I arrived first, and from my seat at the gate, spotted them heading my way from the direction of security, with their briefcases in hand. I suppose it was the fact that I was watching, rather than walking with them, that allowed me to fully appreciate how the wall of people actually separated to give them space. I wondered whether folks suspected Danni might be contagious, or simply didn't want to get in her way, lest she break out in circus acrobatics, but the sea definitely parted.

Once they reached me, Danni was chipper, as always. "Good morning, Heather. Isn't it a lovely day to fly?"

I decided not to mention the parting of the Red Sea. "Absolutely beautiful."

Marnie took one of the seats beside me. She sighed. "I hate morning people."

Danni sat down at my other side. "What do you mean? You always get into the office at least as early as we do."

"That's because I need to get busy on my non-productive business development efforts, not because I relish the time of day."

"I'm with Danni," I said. "I love mornings. In fact, if I accidentally oversleep on the weekend, it irritates me all day that I missed my favorite part."

"Sleeping through it isn't the same thing as missing it," said Marnie. "To my mind, it's the best way to enjoy it."

"How can you savor something you're not conscious of?" asked Danni.

"Now you guys are just ganging up on me. I'm going to get some coffee. Anyone want anything?"

"No thanks," we both said.

We'd each brought work with us to review in our free minutes—which turned out to be hours, in light of our schedule. I was engrossed in some case law on the Statute of Repose when Danni nudged me and said, "We're boarding."

I stuffed my papers into the slim briefcase I use for day-trips, grabbed my purse, and eyed my pass for my boarding group number. For some reason, I was in Group 2, while Marnie and Danni were in 4, and they insisted I go on ahead. As it turned out, I had an aisle seat near the middle of the airplane, so I had a good view of the parade of passengers. I assumed someone was assigned to sit beside me, so I glanced up at each person who paused near my row, at the ready to step out into the aisle to allow access to their window seat. I didn't have to wait long. A slender, elderly man arrived and took the spot.

A few minutes later, I heard a loud sigh from the middle-aged woman in the seat directly across the aisle from me. I glanced up and caught her scowling at whoever was coming down the aisle. She stepped out to allow access to the window seat, vigorously shaking her head, tight-lipped, and obviously unhappy. The person who was waiting to slide into the seat was Marnie. I held my breath.

Marnie feigned deep concern. "Are you all right, ma'am? You don't look well."

The lady stammered, "It's just that I need to have my full allotted space."

"And?"

"These damn seats are so small these days."

"So?"

The woman didn't take the bait. "So, nothing. I'm up. Go on." She waved Marnie in.

Marnie said, "I would. But I fear that I need to have my allotted peace of mind." She turned to the gentleman sitting beside me. "Sir, would you be willing to sit beside this pleasant woman so I can take the seat by my friend?"

He smiled kindly and rose. I'm not sure he'd heard the earlier exchange since he was wearing hearing aids, and he appeared to be completely unperturbed. Once Marnie was situated beside me, my body blocked the view of her offender, and I thought she seemed to relax. When she placed her elbow on the armrest, I said, "My allotted space, please," then embarrassed myself by snorting. But she didn't crack a smile. My stomach started to churn.

Minutes later, a flight attendant reached up above a seat a few rows ahead of us to turn off the call button, and said to someone, "Yes?"

A young man's voice responded, "Would it be possible to re-seat me?"

"There are a couple of window seats in the back row."

"Great!" He bounced up, opened the overhead

compartment to retrieve his duffle bag, and hurried to the back of the plane. I couldn't see a thing as to the source of his discomfort with his assigned seat, but somehow, I knew.

I spent the remainder of the flight alternating between actually focusing on the words in the cases I was reading, and staring blankly at them while I ruminated over the overt prejudice against Marnie and Danni. But what could I do? Was being a witness and a confidant enough? Were these micro-aggressions or life-sucking insults? Or both? Worse still, hadn't I sometimes done what the woman across the aisle did to Marnie? Certainly not so dramatically. I can only hope not even visibly. But, in my heart, hadn't I been exactly that clueless and selfish?

How could my two closest friends, who suffered the real trauma of everyday indignities, ever accept me? How could an oppressor ever be a true friend with one who is oppressed? I tried to imagine how I would feel if people visibly grimaced at my arrival, or actively sought to avoid physical proximity to me. I couldn't do it. I could witness it all day, every day, but I was incapable of imagining what it would feel like. I had not the faintest idea what my reaction would be—to the first insult, the hundredth, or the thousandth.

How could the holder of the privilege of acceptable appearance ever understand what it was like not to hold it? And did we truly have to understand to be intimates? I feared the answer was yes, and that I'd be forever locked out of the deepest parts of my friends' hearts. Because I spent the flight agonizing over it, I had to call upon all the self-control I possessed not to cry.

Once we'd landed, Danni waited to leave her seat

until Marnie and I made it down the aisle to her row, and the three of us entered the concourse together.

"That was a smooth flight," said Danni.

"Depends on your definition of smooth. If it includes 'without incident,' I'll have to beg to differ," said Marnie.

"Oh, no. What happened?"

We stopped walking, and Marnie and I grabbed nearby seats so we could be at Danni's eye level. I recounted the episode. Danni said, "I'm so sorry, Marnie. That was wrong."

Marnie kind of squinted her eyes at Danni. "And the young man who couldn't abide sitting next to you?"

"I understood. Of course, I knew it was my presence that made him uncomfortable. But I don't blame him."

"You should," said Marnie. "There's such a thing as decency. Why set the bar for it so damn low? Seriously. How would either of you have felt about that fool if he'd refused to sit beside a Black person?"

"Intolerable," I said.

"That would be unacceptable," said Danni. "But don't I get to decide for myself what pisses me off?"

"Of course," said Marnie. "But you might want to consider raising your standards."

"You're missing my point. If I let every slight put me in a bad mood, I'd pretty much live my life in a bad mood. I don't forgive their ignorance for them—I do it for me."

I waited to see if Marnie wanted to pursue it further. She looked away. I said, "Let's freshen up and grab a cab for Linda's office. It's probably a forty-five-minute ride, so we wouldn't be terribly early if we head there in the next fifteen minutes or so."

The insurance company offices were part of a large, modern business compound, and I directed the cab driver to the front entrance of our client's space. Once inside, I noted they'd redecorated since my last visit a couple of years before. Now everything was bright and contemporary, with lots of chrome, glass, and light-gray leather in the reception area. We were each handed a visitor pass to stick on our lapels, and told that Ms. Steevers would be down to see us directly.

Five minutes later, she stepped out of the elevator, and I was reminded of how much I enjoyed her loud, raspy voice and effervescent personality. She wore a well-fitted navy pantsuit, two-inch heels, and had her gray hair up in a bun, with a fringe of loose strands around her face, which somehow reminded me of a lion's mane. "Heather! It's been much too long." She gave me a hug before turning to Marnie and Danni.

I introduced them and Linda said, "I've been dying to meet both of you. Let's get comfortable in a conference room, and you can tell me all about how the new firm is doing."

We followed her into the mirrored elevator, and all looked straight down. As we got off on the third floor, we found ourselves facing a wall of small conference rooms. She led us to one at the end of the aisle, where the lights were on and a carafe of coffee and four black mugs emblazoned with the company name awaited us.

"I like the new décor," I said.

"Just having new carpeting and paint thrilled me. The paintings on the walls are on loan from a local art gallery. They rotate them in, so we have something fresh to look at every quarter. The art was my idea."

"What a lovely way to get to experience art during

your regular workday," said Danni. Turning to me, she added, "Maybe we could arrange for something like that."

I smiled and nodded to her.

"I hope you can, Danielle. But my pitch was that we have over 150 employees, some of whom may be coaxed into actually visiting the gallery by seeing the display."

Marnie said, "We'll have to come up with a different pitch."

Linda had placed a cushion on one of the chairs, and Danni thanked her before taking her seat. Once we were all arranged around the table, with coffee cups full, Linda inquired about Marnie and Danni's legal experience, and how each of them had come to practice with me in Lake County. After they filled her in, she turned to me. "How are things going?"

The three of us had discussed how to answer this likely question, and agreed it would be best to exaggerate a bit to accentuate the positive. "Really well."

"I'm glad to hear it. Peeling off from an old, established firm doesn't always go that well. And with your competitors calling the clients to gossip about Danni and Marnie, I just wondered how everyone would react."

"Actually, Linda," said Marnie, "I suspect those really may be negatives in the eyes of some of Heather's clients. But there's nothing we can do about our bodies. What we do offer is excellent work on the files. We'll just have to wait for the reality of our talents to catch up to the prejudice."

"You and Danielle are certainly making that happen on my files, Marnie. Even though the matters you two have now are not terribly complex, your Comprehensive

File Reviews were thorough, creative, practical, and particularly well-written. And, ladies, I don't say that to many of our lawyers. Honestly, I'd love to be able to give you more assignments as we sit here today."

"Is there a *but* coming?" asked Marnie.

Linda smiled. "But I can't because I have nothing new in Cook or Lake to assign. As Heather probably told you, we cover high-risk insureds on a nation-wide basis. The bulk of them are nursing homes, amusement parks and carnivals, zoos, and trucking companies. Some of the truck accident cases are relatively small matters, like the two you are taking care of for me, Marnie, and Danni. But the majority of the claims I see involve severe injuries or death and fairly novel, often complex, fact patterns. The verdict potential is frequently astronomical."

"We could handle those for you," said Marnie.

"I know. And the next one that comes in from Cook or Lake is yours. It'll be a lot of work for your firm. I'm sorry I have nothing to give you today."

"We understand," I said. "And we really look forward to working with you a lot more in the future."

Linda leaned toward me conspiratorially. "Say, Heather, have you told Marnie and Danielle about the fact patterns in any of our cases?"

"I haven't." I turned to my partners. "I should probably tell you that several of Linda's cases I defended involved incidents set at carnies, circuses, and amusement parks. One, a case involving a tiger with a grudge, took place at a zoo. The others settled, but I got to take the tiger case to trial."

Marnie said, "Heather, you're much more interesting than I thought you were."

I laughed. "I'm really not. But my cases with Linda have been fascinating. Most of her assignments are intriguing factually, and often legally, as well." I turned to my client. "That's one of many reasons I enjoy handling your files so much."

"Thank you. It's always been a pleasure working with you, and I know the same will be true with Marnie and Danielle. Are you ladies ready for lunch? I've reserved a table at a terrific little steak joint."

Marnie said, "I never say no to a meal—as you can see."

Linda laughed. Thank goodness.

When we arrived at the restaurant, Linda led us into the small log structure. The inside was as charming as the outside. Native American-looking throw rugs softened the wide-plank pine flooring with dark pegs. The log walls, which made for a fairly dark interior, were warmed to a glow by the soft light emanating from numerous mission-style bronze chandeliers. Rectangular sconces hanging on the walls also helped create a cozy ambiance.

Linda had reserved a table, and just like in her conference room, a chair had been readied with a cushion for Danni. Each of us had a glass of wine with the appetizer, which may have accounted for the relaxed atmosphere at our table. Linda, who was divorced, told us about life in Omaha, and how thrilled she was her daughter and son-in-law had decided to remain in town to raise her two grandchildren.

Immediately after we'd placed our orders, a child in pigtails, probably eight or nine years old, approached our table. The little girl walked up to Danni, with a pencil and a piece of paper in her hand. "Excuse me."

"Hello."

"Ma'am, would you make an autograph for my little brother?"

Danni looked puzzled, as we all were. I checked out the table from which the child had evidently come, and saw a little boy, several years younger than the girl, looking at Danni through the slats in the back of his chair, hiding as best he could. Danni said, "Why does he want it?"

"He thinks you're one of Santa's elves."

"Oh, my."

"I know that's stupid. But Mom took our baby to the bathroom to change her, and Toby won't quit pestering me about getting your autograph."

"What's your name?"

"Stella."

"Mine's Danielle. And I'm not really an elf. I'm just a woman with a medical condition called dwarfism. But you don't have to tell Toby that." She signed the piece of paper, and drew a little picture of Santa beside her signature. "Just tell your brother I'll put in a good word for him with Santa."

"Thanks, Miss. As my mom would say, you're a good sport."

"You're welcome, Stella."

Linda, Marnie and I were all riveted by the exchange. Linda said, "Does that happen often?"

"The truth is, comments about my dwarfism are fairly frequent, but not usually so benign—and never before about being an elf."

"That was pretty sweet," I said.

"But most are totally devoid of sweet," said Marnie.

"I was just discussing the issue with Marnie and

Heather at the airport," said Danni. "You see, my approach is not to let any of it bother me. Otherwise, I'd be bothered all the time."

"So, you're able to just let it go?"

Danni lifted her hands, as though releasing a butterfly, and said, "Poof."

"That works?"

Danni looked at Linda for a moment, then said, "Maybe."

I hoped Marnie wouldn't launch into a debate about it in front of Linda. To her credit, she just said, "I think some rude behavior needs to be called out. But Danni's pointed out that the choice on how to respond belongs to the victim of the rudeness. As the sometimes recipient of unwelcome comments, my approach is just different from Danni's."

"It's interesting," said Linda. "I really can see the merit in both approaches. You three must have some interesting discussions."

I looked back and forth between my partners. "Linda, you have no idea."

She laughed. Our server placed a basket of bread and a plate of olive oil on the table. The topic of our appearances didn't come up again.

Chapter 13

Two months had passed since we'd opened for business, and I spent the July 4th weekend worrying about our future. It held true that each of the new files arrived with instructions that I was to handle it. With everything else we were trying to do, I certainly could've used an actual associate to assist with my work. Of course, Danni was doing a lot of associate-level work for me, but at her pay rate, it wasn't sustainable. Poor Marnie was sitting in her office dreaming up and executing on non-billable projects that might attract some work—someday. I was reading through one of my new files when my phone rang.

"Heather, it's Julie Davidson."

"Hi Julie. How are you?"

"That depends on your answer. This is about Danielle Dooley."

I wondered how there could be some problem with Danni already, since she only had a couple of Julie's files. "Danielle?"

"As you know, I agreed to have her handle two of my files, *Maddox* and *Johnston*, in spite of the issue of her small stature."

"Of course. I'm familiar with the cases. So, what's going on?" I tried to keep my breathing level, although I was panicking.

"It's not about the files, per se."

My chest was starting to tighten. "What's the problem, Julie?"

"A few days ago, I had to attend a meeting at our home office in New York of all the claim department managers from all over the country."

"I remember you mentioning you'd be going." I was nervously tapping my pen against a legal pad.

"The Senior Vice President of Claims gave us a stern talking-to about our need for diversity in our defense counsel. He made it clear that our bonuses will reflect our success in hiring law firms that comport with the company's goals."

"Oh, I see. So the problem is that we don't have any attorneys of color."

"No. The focus of his presentation was hiring attorneys with disabilities. Of course, I had to be sure, so when he encouraged questions, I asked if dwarfism would be considered a disability in furtherance of the company's goals. He smiled and said it certainly would, although an attorney with dwarfism, especially one who is a litigator, would probably be hard to find."

"What are you saying, Julie?"

"I'm saying I'm going to send all of my new Lake County and Cook County files to Danielle. You guys are still handling Cook, as well. Right?

"Absolutely."

"Good. And since I'd really like to earn a bonus this year, I'm also in the process of making a list of probably twenty fairly recent filings which I'll have transferred to Danielle from the firms currently handling them. I need you to be honest with me, Heather. I know she must already have a full plate. Could you possibly move all of my files to her and maybe move her cases with other clients to yourself or Marnie? It would be a huge favor if I could have her full time."

"I think I can make that happen. When would you plan to have the files delivered?"

"I'll finalize my list, then get on the phone right away to instruct that the twenty be delivered. I'll ask those firms to have them in your office within forty-eight hours."

"Great. I think you'll enjoy working with Danielle."

"I know I will. Thanks so much for helping me out on this."

"My pleasure, Julie."

I got up to corral Danni and Marnie with the news, but my knees actually buckled. I knelt on my floor, trying to calm myself down with deep breathing. Marnie happened by my office door and said, "You're either on your prayer mat or you lost a contact."

"Marnie! Grab Danni." I made a little gasp. "I have news."

"Are you okay?"

"Yeah."

Marnie stepped down the hall to the next door to fetch Danni. By the time they made it to my office, I was standing behind my desk, and they made themselves comfortable in my two chairs. As I started to speak, I realized I was still wobbly, and clumsily rolled out my desk chair to sit.

"What's up?" asked Danni.

"You guys aren't going to believe this." I told them everything Julie Davidson said.

Danni looked stunned.

Marnie said, "Not only is that amazing, but it reveals the big hole in our business development plan. Danni, you have to join the disabled lawyers' society, or whatever they would call such a thing. And, instead of headshots, we commission full-body photos of the three of us for all our advertising. I'll admit I was starting to worry about us, but this is a huge break. Congratulations, Danni!"

I hurried around the side of my desk for a group hug. Danni still hadn't said anything. I stepped back and said, "How do you feel?"

"Ready. I can't wait to receive the files. Honestly, I've never been really happy at work unless I'm super-busy, so this means the world to me." She paused, then added, "I'm so excited to tell Delaney."

Tears glistened in Danni's eyes, which gave me shivers. But as thrilled as I was for her, I knew this development must have felt like a mixed blessing to Marnie. She was now the only one of us who wasn't bringing in business.

She commented on it before I could. "So now as the only dead weight—and that's a lot of weight—I'll have to figure out how to conjure up some files for me to work on."

"First of all," I said, "I'll move the file Danni has with a client other than Julie to you."

"Great! All one of them."

"Hey! Your inventory just went up by twenty-five percent," I said.

"No. I believe you said Julie wants the two files I have with her moved to Danni. So, my count actually went down by a third. Plus, it adds another file review that I can't bill for."

"No one cares about that," I said. "We're at the beginning, just building a foundation."

She made no more wisecracks. "I know. I'm in the middle of an article that the journal doesn't even realize it needs—so I'd better get back to it."

I would've loved to go out to celebrate Danni's breakthrough, but it was too much to ask of Marnie. We'd celebrate like mad once she also brought in a few matters. After they'd both left, I let out a long breath. This was a huge break for us, but the circumstances were unique, to say the least. Marnie wasn't going to receive a whole book of business because of her appearance. She'd have to build her inventory client by client, file by file. Based on the past two months, I had no reason to believe that would happen anytime soon.

There was another issue, as well. Once Danni would have a full inventory of Julie's files, she wouldn't be able to assist me on my matters that needed associate-level help. Marnie hadn't brought it up, but I hoped she would soon. I'd continue to have an antacid for dessert every night.

Chapter 14

Several months after Danni stumbled upon the mother lode of files, she got a chance to take one of her cases to trial. In the process, she learned about a phenomenon none of us even knew existed. She was representing an electrical contractor who had installed a new switch box in a large barn just outside of Round Lake Beach. The stable caught fire a couple of days after the electrical work was done. All of the horses made it out without injury, but one of the stable hands suffered third-degree burns on his arms while rescuing the animals, and the injured man's lawyer sued the electrical contractor for bodily injury.

Danni's investigation revealed that a number of bales of hay had been delivered, and were being stored in the stable, piled high against one wall of the structure. The building burned to the ground, with nothing left of the electrical parts, the hay, or anything else. Danni hired a fire expert who explained to her that hay which is baled with a moisture content of over twenty-two percent can spontaneously combust, especially when stacked in a barn. In the depositions she took, she focused on how the hay came to be at the barn. She studied articles on the science of the processes involved with hot hay, which led her to the conclusion that the hay in the Round Lake Beach stable could well have been the cause of the fire.

When the day arrived for her first jury trial, Danni

was beside herself with excitement. Marnie and I walked over to the courthouse with her each day of the three-day trial. I sat at counsel table with her and her client, Mr. Quinn, as back-up in case she might need help with anything. She didn't. In addition to her other pre-trial motions, Danni asked the judge if she could use her stool behind the lectern when she addressed the jury, so she could be sure everyone could see her. Of course, there was no objection, so her motion was granted, and we toted her stepstool with us to court each morning.

When the first group of twelve people took their seats in the jury box for *voir dire*, Danni was seated at the defense table, and her appearance didn't cause any discernible stir. But when it was her turn to question the prospective jurors and she walked to the lectern, their expressions were memorable. At first, the jury reminded me of a litter of puppies, since so many heads cocked the moment she rose from her chair. Eyebrows ascended, chins dropped, and a couple of women raised their hands to their mouths—none of which seemed to phase Danni. She used the lectern to ask her questions of the potential jurors, and was, from my biased point of view, charming. There were a number of recesses, as the judge was required to attend to other matters, but by the end of the day, the twelve-person jury had been empaneled.

As the trial got underway the next morning, Danni soon ditched the podium so she could walk around while she questioned witnesses. The owner of the barn admitted that a large number of hay bales had been dropped off about three weeks before the fire and were being stored against a wall of the building. They'd been delivered and stacked by a farmer, whom he had not quizzed on their moisture content. He also admitted that he had never tested the interior temperature of the bales with a hay probe thermometer.

Next, the farmer testified that he'd cut the hay within two weeks of making the delivery and believed the moisture count was less than twenty-two percent, which he thought meant that the hay wouldn't combust. However, he also conceded he had tested only a couple of the bales, and the specific percentages on the others were unknown.

The injured young man who was the plaintiff testified that he didn't know anything about the hay, or the electrical work, because he had just returned from a month-long-vacation. When he saw the fire, he rushed to the barn. He was trying to let the last horse out of its stall when blazing material from above fell on his arms and he suffered the burns. Danni was sympathetic but got him to agree that he really didn't know what caused the fire.

After the plaintiff's attorney presented his medical evidence and then rested, Danni had her client, the electrical contractor, explain that his work replacing an old switchbox was straightforward and that he had done hundreds, if not thousands of such projects, all without incident, in his twenty years as an electrician. Danni put her expert witness on the stand to testify in some detail about hot hay. The jury learned that when hay is cut and baled with a high moisture content, spontaneous combustion is a hazard for approximately three to six weeks. The reason is that when warm temperature types of bacteria grow, they can cause a chemical reaction producing flammable gases that can ignite. That was why at-risk hay should be checked twice a day using a hay thermometer. This should be done for a minimum of three weeks after baling, depending upon what the results show.

After Danni rested, plaintiff's attorney recalled the owner of the barn to again emphasize the proximity in time between the electrical work and the fire. He asked nothing about the hay. On cross, Danni simply confirmed with him that he'd done no testing with a hay thermometer.

At the end of the case, after the jurors had been removed from the courtroom, Danni made a motion for a directed verdict, which I actually thought might be granted. Her argument was basically that plaintiff had the burden of proof. Even giving plaintiff the benefit of the doubt, the most the trial evidence established was that the fire might have been caused by the electrical work, and might have been caused by hot hay. It wasn't the defendant's burden to prove the electrical work did not cause the fire; it was plaintiff's burden to prove that it actually was, at least in part, the cause. Since plaintiff had not done that, she asked the judge to direct the verdict in favor of her client.

The judge said he thought it was a fairly persuasive argument, but he would let the question go to the jury. Marnie leaned over to me and whispered, "More *no-nuts brownies* at the recipe exchange this year." Danni and the plaintiff's lawyer went off to debate the instructions which would be read to the jury after closing arguments.

Once everyone returned to the courtroom, closing arguments began. Plaintiff's attorney seemed uninspired. He contended that proximity in time is tantamount to causation. He dismissed Danni's fire expert as a paid testifier. And he made more than one pitch for sympathy for his client, who'd been injured while he was simply trying to save a terrified horse.

Danni gave her closing argument from the stool behind the podium, because, as she told me, she didn't want her appearance to distract. Basically, the jury could see only her upper body and head. She said, "Mr. Quinn has been working as an electrician, his own local business, for over twenty years. He testified that the replacement of the old switch box he did at the barn was a simple matter, no different from the hundreds and hundreds he's done throughout his career. Plaintiff hasn't presented one iota of evidence that Mr. Quinn did anything wrong." She paused. "He did have the bad fortune that he completed his work just a few days before the barn burned to the ground. But the nearness in time of two events doesn't mean that one caused the other. If proximity in time equals cause, then every time you feed your guests a meal, and one of them develops stomach pains the next day, it would be your fault. Every time you wash your car, and it rains the next day, you caused the rain. And when you decide to leave work early, and get into a car wreck, it was leaving work early that caused the accident. Of course, it doesn't work that way.

"As the judge will instruct you, the defendant does not need to prove he *did not* cause the fire—plaintiff must prove that Mr. Quinn *did* cause it. The law does not require the defendant to show you what actually caused the fire. But, in this case, there happens to be another explanation. According to the fire expert, the fresh hay, stacked high against the wall of the barn, with plenty of air flow to allow ignition, could have spontaneously combusted. So, the question for you is simply whether plaintiff has proven to you that Mr. Quinn's electrical work was the cause. But, of course, there is no evidence of that."

I could only see Danni's back, but she appeared to be relaxed and confident from the sound of her voice and her arm movements. She concluded by directly addressing the issue of sympathy.

"Mr. Barns is a pleasant young man, and it appears, a brave one. He has medical bills from his injuries, some pain, and some residual scarring. Any person would feel sympathy for him. But, as the judge will instruct you, you must set aside your natural sympathy to do your duty as a juror. It is your job to answer one question, and one question only: did plaintiff prove to you that it is more likely than not that the electrician, Mr. Quinn, caused the fire? Really, there can only be one answer. On behalf of Mr. Quinn and myself, thank you very much for your consideration."

The jury came back with its verdict in less than two hours, barely time for them to have read the instructions, selected a foreperson, and voted. Danni's client had left for a job, and Marnie, Danni and I had just gotten back to work in our office when Jeanne received the call from the courthouse that the verdict was in.

As we hurried back down the street, Danni asked me, "What does a quick verdict usually mean?"

The answer was that it generally signified a defense verdict, because no time was needed to calculate damages for the various injuries and losses. But there was no way I'd get Danni's hopes up with that, in case it had gone the other way. I said, "In my experience, juries are unpredictable. I don't like to guess. We'll know in a few minutes."

When we arrived in the courtroom, only opposing counsel and Mr. Barns were there, sitting at their table. I joined Danni at the defense table, and Marnie sat, alone, in a spectator pew. The judge appeared and took his seat at the bench. He asked the bailiff to bring in the jury, and the twelve of them paraded past us, back to their seats in the jury box. None of them looked at us, but neither did they glance at plaintiff's table. The judge confirmed with the forewoman that the jury had reached a verdict and asked her to read it.

The middle-aged woman, wearing a turquoise silk blouse and a gray skirt, rose and read from a piece of paper. "We, the jury, find the defendant, Donald Quinn, not guilty."

Danni looked stunned, and tears began to stream down her cheeks. Plaintiff's counsel declined to poll the jury to have each one state that this *was and is* his or her own verdict. The judge thanked the jurors, released them from their service, and left the bench.

Plaintiff's attorney walked over to our table, and said, "Good job, Danielle. But expect post-trial motions."

"Of course," she said. "It was a pleasure trying my first case against you."

Plaintiff asked his lawyer if he could speak to us, and the attorney nodded. Mr. Barns said to Danni, "When I first saw you, ma'am, I made certain assumptions about how this thing would go. I just want to say that you are really good."

"Thanks, Mr. Barns. Take care."

Danni and I were so interested in what Mr. Barns had to say that we didn't notice that five or six jurors had queued up to speak with Danni. The first in line was one of the two women whose hands had flown up to their mouths when they first set eyes on my partner. She leaned in toward Danni, who was still seated at counsel table, and whispered, "I owe you an apology. My first thought was that you don't belong in a courtroom. I'm really sorry, Miss."

Danni said, "Please don't give it another thought. Thank you for speaking to me."

The other person whose initial shock had propelled her hand to her mouth, the only Black juror, an elderly woman, was next. "I've watched one of those little people reality shows on TV, but I've never met anybody like you before. Well, dear, you're just like anybody else, aren't you?"

"I am." Danni gave the woman a big smile and the lady smiled right back, before heading to the door.

A young man, with his arms folded in front of his chest, said loudly, "I was wrong about you. You're good." He then turned to leave before Danni could respond.

A bearded, middle-aged man in jeans and a work shirt was up next. He said, "I'd like your business card in case I ever need a lawyer. I like how you talk so anybody can understand." I pulled one out of my purse to hand to Danni, who gave it to the man as she said, "Thank you. It's kind of you to say so."

The last person in line seemed quite comfortable waiting for her turn to speak with Danni. Stylishly dressed in a cream-colored knit skirt suit, and probably in her early seventies, she walked over to where I was sitting and asked me if she could borrow my chair so she could speak with Danni eye-to-eye. I jumped up and pulled out the chair for her, before stepping back to where Marnie was awaiting us, leaning against the wall. We were still able to hear every word.

The woman said, "I've been thinking about you since the first day we saw you walk out from behind this table. You forced me to face the fact that I'm a prejudiced person, which I truly did not think I was. It's not sexism. What do you call it?"

"Bodyism," said Danni.

"Well that's an appropriate word. Is there some organization I can donate to for the little people?"

"There are several good ones. If you'd like to give me your email address, I can send you some links."

"Good. I'd really appreciate it." She reached inside her purse and pulled out what looked like an old-fashioned calling card in pale pink.

Danni said, "Thanks so much for your interest in dwarfism."

"My dear, I plan to contribute much more than just my interest."

"Wonderful," said Danni, who seemed unsure how to end the conversation, since she didn't want to cut the woman off. But the lady had had her say, rose, nodded to Marnie and me, and walked out of the courtroom.

"Congratulations on your 'not guilty,' " said Marnie.

"And on your fan club," I said. "I've tried over a dozen cases, and the jurors never once responded to me like that."

Danni broke down and cried. After she used the tissue I handed her, she said, "Thanks so much, guys. I'd never have gotten here without you."

"Well, it was mainly Heather," Marnie said.

"No," Danni said. "It always was and always will be equal."

Marnie said, "So then, I suppose you expect us to

grab equally heavy piles of files and your short-lawyer stool, to haul back to the office."

Danni laughed then said, "Of course I do."

I ran smack into the same problem I'd faced when the truckload of work was dropped on Danni—how to celebrate without making Marnie feel worse than she already did. Fortunately, she solved the dilemma for me by suggesting a celebratory dinner the following Saturday. We agreed and decided to meet at a nice place in the city.

We went to Chicago's lovely Drake Hotel, and not a word came up about Marnie's paucity of work or how she was feeling about her lack of contribution to the bottom line. Nevertheless, I feared for her emotional state. When Danni left the table for the restroom, I took the opportunity to ask Marnie if I could take her out for a drink after work one evening, without Danni. She raised her eyebrows at those two last words, but nodded.

****

Two days later, we both simply worked an hour longer than usual. As soon as Danni was on her way to the train station, I grabbed my briefcase, and stopped at Marnie's door. "Ready?"

"I don't know. Am I?"

I put my briefcase down and took a seat in one of the chairs that faced her desk. "Listen, we don't have to go out. I just wanted us to have privacy so we can talk. But since Jeanne and Danni are gone, we could just do it here."

"Fine with me. I don't like to mix pain with pleasure—unless the guy is hot enough to justify SM."

I laughed, but I was perspiring, and my heart was racing. "I hope our conversation won't be too painful for either of us."

"I know what you want to talk with me about. My failure to thrive."

She had her hands folded on her desk, and appeared to be completely relaxed. It struck me that Marnie never seemed to get nervous. Angry, definitely. But not jittery. I said, "No. I just want to make sure that you are still optimistic about our future."

"I'm not sure I ever really was—deep down. But you and Danni have proven me wrong."

"Marnie, I know it must be hard to watch all of the opportunities come in for Danni and me, while you could do the same work as well, or better."

"It is." She paused for several moments, kept her hands clasped, her eyes on mine. She added, "I've been thinking about how pathetic it is that I haven't had the chance to take a case to trial. And as ridiculous as it may be, I've actually been envious of a dwarf."

"It's not ridiculous. It's normal. All litigators crave the chance to take something to verdict. The only thing that's pathetic is that we haven't been able to bring in files for you to work on. But it's not your fault."

"Of course, it's my fault. You guys aren't my mama bird, dropping morsels into my mouth."

"No. It's more like we all plowed the field together, and your crops didn't happen to come in as well as ours. So, we'll all just do more planting."

"That's a terrible analogy, Heather. But if we want to stick with it, you and Danni each had some decent seed, while I've been planting sawdust and wondering why it doesn't sprout."

I smiled. "That's pretty good. So, what are we going to do about it?"

"I don't know what else to do. I think I've saturated the market with in-depth articles on cutting-edge legal topics."

I was starting to think about asking her to assist with my files so she'd at least be doing something billable. But I couldn't go there. All I said was, "I'll push harder to persuade my clients to let me assign some of the new files to you, and I'll take you with me any time I go to meet with a client. I'll ask them what topics they'd like to have pamphlets on, so you can create something of value for them. It will take time, but we'll get there."

"If I knew that, I could better tolerate the dry season."

"So, you really did appreciate my analogy." I smiled, but she didn't return it. "We can't know it, Marnie. We can only have faith in it."

She just rolled her eyes, and said, "You're getting biblical again, Heather."

We agreed to head home, and hadn't said another word about it by the time I got off at my stop. Later, as I lay in bed not sleeping, I realized what had been gnawing at me since my visit with Marnie. It was her eyes. Usually full of light and fire, they'd looked almost flat. So, there it was. One of my two best friends had dead eyes, and I had killed them. Of course, I wondered if I'd imagined it, the illusion fueled by sleep-deprivation. But I didn't think so.

But what was bothering me even more was what I hadn't done. We all knew that, without Danni's assistance, I really needed help on my files. Of course, Marnie's time would be billed at a lower, associate rate, and I'd be responsible to the client for the matter. But at least Marnie would be billing time and bringing in some revenue. If I'd had the guts to be professional, I would've asked her—again—to consider it. More accurately, I would've told her we needed her to do it. The truth was, I was putting our friendship ahead of the business. Worst of all, Marnie knew. She wasn't stupid. She knew what I was doing. I should've suspected then how my dereliction of responsibility would play out.

****

We all expected Danni would receive post-trial motions, especially since plaintiff's counsel told her they'd be coming. But we certainly didn't expect a motion unlike any of us had seen before. Mr. Barns' attorney entitled it, "Motion for Judgment Notwithstanding the Verdict or For a New Trial due to Sympathy." The body of the motion posited that defense counsel's dwarfism resulted in sympathy for her, and prejudice against plaintiff, because "any reasonable juror would conclude that the disfigurement of Mr. Barns' burned arms pales in comparison with the disfigurement of defense counsel's body."

When Danni called us into her office the next day to share with us the gem of legal reasoning, both Marnie and I cracked up. Fortunately, Marnie didn't end up on the floor. We joked about possible responses.

Marnie said, "That's like saying no blind lawyer should be able to defend a lawsuit because there's nothing worse than sightlessness."

"What about an ugly lawyer?" I asked. "There would be much more sympathy for him or her than for a handsome young man with a couple of barely visible arm scars."

"We could go on and on," said Marnie.

"Please don't," said Danni. "I need to get back to

work. I just couldn't resist sharing this with you guys."

As Marnie was walking out the door ahead of me, she turned and said, "What about an elderly lawyer with a cane, or a bad rug, or offensive breath, or—"

"Go!" said Danni.

As I was closing Danni's door behind us, Marnie stuck her head back in and said, "Or morbid obesity—"

Chapter 15

For weeks after that, I could tell Marnie was miserable because her wise cracks had dwindled to almost nothing. In the months since the full inventory of work had fallen into Danni's lap, she'd taken scores of depositions, argued dozens of routine motions, won two motions for summary judgment, and prevailed in the three-day jury trial. All the while, Marnie was working on some non-billable project or other, which failed to translate into new files. She wrote, and succeeded in having published, two major articles, was awaiting word on the publication of a third, and had a fourth in the works. She created a handful of brochures on topics the clients were interested in, attended bar association meetings in Waukegan and Chicago, and volunteered for a couple of committees of a national defense counsel organization. I'd never thought of Marnie as an introvert, but all of the socializing seemed to be taking a toll on her. Danni and I were too busy with work to join her, so I imagined her marching into the meetings alone, like a soldier on some dangerous, solitary mission.

I tried to think about how I would've felt in her situation and couldn't avoid the conclusion it would have been intolerable. I'd probably have given it what I would've deemed a reasonable amount of time, and then started interviewing to find a position with a firm that actually had billable, substantive work for me to do. It would only have been my deep affection for my friends that would have allowed me to delay starting the process for more than a few months. I didn't believe that Marnie would be more patient than I would've been, so I assumed similar thoughts were occurring to her. But that wasn't the half of it. I would have been going through all that knowing that my appearance would not cancel out my credentials. Of course, I'd have to fight through different prejudices, but my six years of successful in-court lawyering would've gotten me over that irritating little hump just fine. It wouldn't go so smoothly for Marnie. The situation had to be driving her crazy.

During workdays, I was so occupied I didn't have time to focus on the problem, beyond doing the few things under my control. But alone at night in my apartment, it was all I thought about. No television show, movie, or book was up to the task of distracting me from ruminating on what I'd done. The unvarnished truth was that I'd pried Marnie out of a lucrative job she enjoyed, a position which allowed her to orchestrate the defense of major litigation, and to brief appeals of complex matters at every level of the system. My notion that she needed to get her body into courtrooms was the siren's song I played until she succumbed. This was all my fault. Living on crackers and water to be able to keep functioning, I continued to lose weight. I didn't fail to recognize the irony in that.

Neither Danni nor I ever expressed any disappointment or pessimism about Marnie's business development, nor did we discuss the feelings her failure to prosper surely caused each of us. She continued to receive her monthly paycheck, equal to mine and Danni's. I found it interesting that the person most willing to speak to Marnie about her predicament was Jeanne. Looking back on it, it may well have been our office manager's encouragement that kept Marnie from starting her job search until a full eight months after we'd opened. Jeanne was so kind to each of us that it took me some time to catch on to how sensitive she was to Marnie's plight. I overheard her say, "Marnie, you are going to absolutely dazzle when you command the courtrooms that are your destiny." Of course, I knew Jeanne tended toward hyperbole, but every word she spoke seemed to come directly from her heart, and with marked assurance.

I learned later that it was in January that she began her search for a job. It was on the first Tuesday of February around 11:00 a.m. that Marnie rang Danni and me and asked us to come by her office. She was sitting at her desk, which looked unusually tidy. Danni and I sat across from her.

"What's happening, Marnie?" I said. "Wait. Let me guess. The lawyer's journal's going to print another of your articles."

She gave me a half-smile and said, "Actually, they are. But that's not what I wanted to talk with you guys about."

I suspected Marnie wanted to argue for her salary to be reduced, or her equal ownership of the firm to be suspended for a while, so she'd receive just her paycheck, and no share of the profits. In spite of the fact I'd spent every evening of the past six months or so thinking it would happen, what she said next floored me.

Marnie leaned back in her desk chair and clasped her hands on her lap. "I've decided to move on. I'm very unhappy in this limbo situation, and I miss being busy working on files more than I would've guessed."

"Oh no, Marnie," said Danni. "It's only been eight months. These things take time. You can't leave us."

"She's right," I said. "Remember, Danni didn't have her own files for the first two months, and now she's happily swamped with work."

"Thanks for reminding me." She rolled her eyes.

"You know I didn't mean it like that. I'm saying that all the contacts you're making will pay off." At that point, I was mouthing the right words, but the reality of what Marnie was telling us hadn't yet fully penetrated.

"They may, Heather. But I can't wait any longer. It's not your fault, guys. For that matter, it's not really my fault. But as much as I'd love to practice law with both of you, that's not what I'm doing here."

"But we don't care!" said Danni, tears starting down her cheeks.

"Thanks. I know you support me—emotionally. But I draw the line at your supporting me financially."

I said, "It's not like that. We're in this together. We cover for each other. None of us is measuring contributions, and we never will." I meant every word I said, but unlike Danni, I spilled no tears. It was as though none of the conversation was fully penetrating.

Marnie said, "Actually, I am. I'm being unfair to you guys. Say, I just thought of a positive to this. It's a good thing we put my name last on the firm—easier to chop it off. Seriously, Jeanne can just take the business cards to the paper cutter to trim them. Also, Hightower and Dooley has a nice ring to it."

"Stop!" I said. "Can't you hear what we're saying? Marnie, we don't want you to leave us."

She leaned in, rested her elbows on the desk, her

chin atop her folded hands, and spoke calmly. "I'm not leaving you. Circumstances are evicting me. Listen, we'll still be best friends, and we'll see each other just like before the seventh of May. But I'll always remember these months with you two. We were great together. It was the rest of the world that wasn't." She paused. "Typical, isn't it?"

"I can't believe you are giving up on your dream to be an in-court lawyer," said Danni.

"Oh, Danni, I didn't give up on the dream. The dream gave up on me."

"I see." I let out a long sigh. "Wait. Was it because you were already job-hunting that you didn't volunteer to help on my files?"

"Of course, Heather. Think about it. If I'd played your associate, someone would have to duplicate my non-billable review of your files after my departure with *another* non-billable review."

"Is there anything we can say to change your mind?" I said. At that moment, I would've promised her my firstborn in a heartbeat.

She shook her head slowly. "Nope."

The shake of her head and the finality of the word did the trick. In that instant, it was real. My head fell into my hands. I couldn't look at either of them, as the truth spilled out of me. "This is all my fault. I pushed you into giving up a job that challenged you. You were happy, and I've made you unhappy. I've been horribly selfish— wanting to practice law with you so much that I ruined your career. I'll never forgive myself. I don't expect you ever to really forgive me, Marnie. But please believe me when I say I am just so sorry." The last words unleashed a torrent of tears.

Danni handed me a couple of tissues from her pocket, then patted my shoulder.

"Jesus, Heather," said Marnie. "Look at me."

I raised my head, still blotting at my eyes. Marnie looked perfectly unperturbed. She said, "Is that what you think happened? Do I look upset? Do I look like a person who thinks her career has been ruined?"

I shook my head.

"That's right, Heather, because that's the farthest thing from my mind. I'm glad we did what we did, and I wouldn't give up the memory of these past months with you and Danni for anything."

"Honestly?"

"Listen, Heather. I don't know how you saw yourself, but I never viewed you as the pretty woman who swooped in to save the fatty."

My chin dropped, but I had no words.

"You haven't been the puppet-master of this show. I'm a big girl—obviously. I'm fairly intelligent, and I have a reasonable amount of judgment. Everything I did was because it was what I chose to do. I don't want to sound mean, because I really do love you, but you need to dial down your ego a bit."

My stomach had been hurting for weeks, but now I felt exactly as though I'd been stabbed in it. I leaned forward from the pain.

Danni said, "That's not fair, Marnie. I can see why Heather feels responsible. Of course, you made your own decisions, but this was her plan from the start. I think she's just trying to own that."

"No," said Marnie. "Heather has completely misapprehended the situation, and her cockeyed idea of what's what has been making her sick."

"What?" asked Danni.

Marnie turned to me. "How much weight have you lost worrying about me?"

There was no use lying, since she'd obviously noticed. "Ten pounds."

Marnie shook her head dramatically. "You didn't lose them, Heather, they just migrated to me. Seriously. While your worry eviscerated pounds, my concern just translated into nervous eating. The world is manifestly unfair." She chuckled. "As always."

It wasn't clear to me whether she hated me for what she saw as my "ego" problem. But then she came around her desk, squatted down in front of me, and took my hands. "Heather, you have to stop feeling guilty. It's wrong-headed, and you are hurting yourself. I'm going to be just fine." She glanced at Danni and added, "I really do love you guys." She took one of Danni's hands and then squeezed gently before rising and walking back to her desk chair. I bit my lower lip, trying hard not to burst into tears again, this time in gratitude for her absolution.

"So, where will you go?" asked Danni.

"Ha. That's a funny thing. It turns out that the partner I worked for who said no law firm would hire me was actually right."

"Marnie, that whole conversation was just a story you made up. Wasn't it?" I said, still working to compose myself.

She laughed. "Now that you mention it, it was. Nevertheless, it was true."

"So, where are you going?" Danni asked again.

"In-house with a company in Schaumberg."

"That's not even on our train line," I said.

"True. But you know what they say, 'Go west,

young man!'"

"Have you already accepted the position?" asked Danni.

"No. I got the offer this morning. I've been looking since the first of the year. Of course, I can't prove it, but the personal interviews seemed to be my downfall for the litigation positions. I wonder why?" She paused. "I've put memos in my files—all two of them—explaining the status, strategy, and everything you need to know. I want to go home and call Schaumburg from there. I don't know why, but I just do. I've packed up my cartoon piggy coffee mug and my research for my next article— which I guess I'll finish on weekends at some point." She rose for a group hug.

As we sniffled away, Marnie said, "Guys, it's not like I'm dying. Let's have another dinner at my place next Saturday." She hesitated and then added, "Unless I've moved closer to Schaumberg by then, in which case I nominate Danni's apartment."

"You won't have moved in a week," I said.

"Good point."

Danni said, "I can't wait to relax over a meal and wine with you guys."

Marnie grabbed her briefcase, and we followed her out into the hallway, both of us pressing tissues to our eyes to keep from crying. She walked around the reception desk and into Jeanne's area. Jeanne stood, and Marnie gave her a long hug. Marnie told her she'd decided to become an in-house lawyer, so she could boss around all the attorneys for a change. Jeanne was facing Marnie and put her hands on both of her elbows, like one soldier giving important intelligence to another. "Marnie, you are going to be a phenomenal success. You will prosper beyond your wildest dreams, and you will find true love."

I shot my gaze over to Danni, who looked as shocked as I was by what could only be called Jeanne's weird statement.

Marnie placed her hands onto Jeanne's arms and said, "If I'd known you'd say that to me on my last day, I would've left months ago." Then she took a deep breath, walked through the reception area, and reached out to open the door.

The phone rang and we all heard Jeanne say, "Hightower, Dooley and Ames," which was unbearably poignant. Jeanne said, "I'm afraid she's just on her way out." Marnie slipped through the door. A moment later, Jeanne covered the speaker on the phone with her hand, and said to me, "This man insists on speaking with her."

I ran out into the hallway and grabbed Marnie's arm just as the elevator door opened. "Jeanne says some guy insists on talking to you. Would you do me a huge favor and take the call? I don't have a clue what's going on with your files."

Marnie sighed dramatically. "So much for my grand exit." As she entered the reception area, she said, "Jeanne, just put it through to my old office."

I thrust a yellow legal pad and a pen at her as she hurried to the space she'd vacated only minutes before.

Forty-five minutes later, Marnie walked out into the hallway, carrying her briefcase. Danni and I were standing there discussing what kind of client call could possibly take that long. Since Marnie didn't say a word, we followed her back toward the reception area. Jeanne looked up from her typing as Marnie walked toward the door. Then she spun around, kicked off her heels, and broke into an exuberant dance, while singing a song I'd never heard before, which seemed to be about cake. It segued into one with a similar beat as she shimmied and shook and did bits of the song as rap. She finished with a moon walk.

We all stared at her, chins on the floor. She probably couldn't hear me over her vocals, but I'd said, "What?" at least three times before she finally plopped down on the floor, panting through laughter.

"Something good, then?" I asked, which caused her to burst into more hysterics.

"Marnie, you have to tell us," said Danni.

Marnie rose from the floor and pulled herself up to take a seat on one of the reception couches, still breathing rapidly from the cardio workout. Danni, Jeanne and I sat across from her on the other couch. "I got it all."

"What all?" asked Danni.

"Remember when I left my old firm and, Heather, you told me to subtly mention that I'd planned the strategies and done all the writing?"

"Yeah."

"Well, you won't believe this, but that firm's biggest client started to notice the decline in the quality of the work coming from the partner I used to work for. Apparently, the appellate briefs were especially uninspired. The man I'd spoken with at the time I left remembered what I'd hinted at and told his boss, who was trying to understand why the work had become so unimpressive. The boss ordered a comprehensive audit done, which showed that ninety percent of the billable time on those difficult matters we'd managed to win for him was mine. So first, he quizzed me about some of the complex matters. Of course, I remembered my strategies like I'd thought them up yesterday. Then he said, 'That's what I thought.'

"Guys, he's sending all of his company's new matters, Lake County and Cook County, to me. And he's pulling from that firm most of his especially complex cases, which will be around twenty, and *all* seven of his appeals. They're all coming to me."

"Oh, my God!" I jumped up and started clapping, then sat back down to hear the rest, my smile about to explode.

"He's making his call to my old firm today. He wants all of the files to be here within seventy-two hours. Then he said, 'We'll pay you the same rate we were paying the partner you used to work for.' So, I stupidly said, 'Our rates aren't quite that high.' He tsk-tsked me and said, 'I'll pretend I didn't hear that. Look, Marnie, never undervalue yourself.' And best of all, he said there's one case that's been fully briefed and is set for hearing before the Seventh Circuit next month. He wants me to do the oral argument.

"He ended by saying he hoped I'd say I could make the time to accept all of the work. I said, 'I'll have to move some things to other partners, but I can make it happen.' Then he said he knows it's a lot of work and it's perfectly acceptable with him for me to use associate help, as long as I keep tight reins on the strategy and do all the major briefs and oral arguments."

Jeanne nodded and raised her elegantly drawn-on eyebrows, clearly giving us a big, fat, "I told you so."

Marnie, Danni, and I all jumped around screaming for a full minute before Jeanne stood and joined us for a long group hug. Then Danni and Marnie said, at the same time, "We need to hire an associate."

"We do," I said. "But first, we have to go out to lunch to celebrate."

Jeanne headed for her desk and asked, "What time shall I expect you girls back?"

"Oh, no," I said. "You're coming with us."

As Marnie headed for her office, she said, "Just give me a minute to make a quick call to Schaumberg. I'll be right out."

Since Jeanne was the only one of us who drove to work, she agreed to drive us to a restaurant she suggested in downtown Lake Forest called Magellan's, a twenty-five-minute drive. It wore an elegant façade of red brick with white peeling paint, and had a stone sidewalk and entry-way, and large potted topiaries standing guard at the entrance. We were seated in the solarium, and in spite of a fierce February wind outside, we were toasty warm beside the blaze pretending to devour several gas logs in a large fireplace.

Jeanne ordered champagne and a cheese tray, and instructed the waiter to put it on her bill.

I said, "Thank you, Jeanne. That's so kind of you. But please let us…"

She waved her hand at me, and said, emphatically, "No. I really do insist."

When the drinks arrived, we toasted Marnie, who then made her own toast. "Finally—full plates all around." For once, she didn't make a joke about her weight.

I said, "This place is so charming, Jeanne. How did you happen to know of it?"

"I like to read the restaurant reviews for all the North suburbs."

"Have you been here before?" asked Danni.

She cocked her head slightly. "Maybe. I can't recall." Then she took a sip of her champagne.

It was an innocuous enough comment, but it struck me as odd because, from what I'd witnessed, Jeanne had an excellent memory.

"But you live here in Lake Forest, right?" I asked.

"I do, Heather. I have a very old home which requires constant repairs just to keep it habitable."

Marnie said, "I've noticed you wear a gold band. If you don't mind my asking, are you married?"

"I was. But my husband passed away a couple of years ago."

"I'm so sorry," said Marnie.

"Me, too," said Danni. They both put down their drinks, and looked intently at Jeanne.

"How are you doing dealing with your loss?" I asked.

Jeanne looked down for a moment before answering. "I'm dealing. But girls, I prefer not to talk about it."

"Of course," said Danni.

"But if you ever want to, Jeanne, we're here for you," I said.

The waiter presented the cheese tray with warm flatbread. We all tried a bite of each of the cheeses, all of which were creamy and delicious. Marnie moved the conversation along. "What does everyone think we should look for in a new associate?"

I said, "It has to be someone willing to zip between Waukegan and Chicago."

"A year or two of litigation experience is essential," said Danni. "But I don't think we can afford anyone with more than that."

I said, "I think the person needs to be special—like us."

"God help the poor thing if she's like us," said Marnie. "What would that even look like, Heather? A fat dwarf with big boobs?"

Danni and I laughed as we usually did. What surprised me was Jeanne's reaction. She didn't exactly spit out her champagne—but she came close. "Marnie, I haven't seen this side of you before." Jeanne raised her eyebrows as she smiled at her.

"Oh, it's always there, Jeanne. My lack of files just depressed me so much that I haven't felt like saying out loud the goofy things that came to my mind at the office."

"So, you're sitting on several months'-worth?" asked Danni.

"It's not like I store it up. My reactions are more like hot hay. When they're ready to spontaneously combust, I can't control them, and would get burned if I tried."

"But you just said you've been stifling them," I said.

"Exactly. And I have the third-degree heartburn to prove it."

Danni laughed and I just shook my head and took another bite of cheese.

"I see," said Jeanne. "Well, never stifle on my account, Marnie. A good laugh goes a long way to calm the crew as we navigate the shoals and tempests of life."

I said, "I love how poetically you speak, Jeanne. Were you an English major, by any chance?"

"Ah, the old days," said Jeanne. "I prefer to focus on the future, girls."

"Understood," I said. "Where were we with the list

of qualifications?"

"I don't care so much about GPA and awards and that sort of thing," said Danni. "I'm more interested in creativity and work ethic."

"Exactly," I said. "And we should try to find someone who will be as excited about our law firm as we are."

"I'd like it to be a young lawyer with excellent research and writing skills, and dare I say it, at least some degree of charm," said Marnie.

"Wait. Is there such a thing as *charmism*?" I asked.

Danni wrinkled her forehead, then said, "I don't think so."

I turned to Jeanne. "What do you think?"

She looked at each of us briefly before she spoke. "Go with your intuitions, girls. You'll know when someone feels right. Wait for that person. She'll be with you for many, many years to come, so you must be as discerning as you would be in choosing a mate. True friendships are every bit as important as marriage."

"You're saying we should look for a future close friend?" asked Danni.

Jeanne nodded slowly and deliberately.

"You think our new associate will become our soul mate?" I asked.

"Yes."

"And you believe it will be a woman?" asked Danni.

"It will."

"How do you know all of this, Jeanne?" asked Marnie, as she placed her elbow on the table and rested her chin on her hand, looking intently at Jeanne.

Jeanne avoided Marnie's gaze, and looked at me. She shook her head and laughed softly. "Of course, I don't *know* it. These are just my guesses, girls."

It was weird, but it almost looked as if the shake of her head somehow brought her back to us from somewhere she'd gone.

"I hope it's true," said Danni. "I'd love to have another close friend." She finished off her glass of champagne.

"I'm skeptical of everyone I don't already know," said Marnie. "You three are my friends, and I'm not looking for more—unless, of course, it's a male, with marriage and lots of sex on his mind."

Jeanne slowly closed her eyes, but didn't say a word.

A waiter arrived to offer more champagne, tell us about the lunch specials, and hand us one-page menus.

Danni said, "I volunteer to take a stab at drafting an advertisement for the position. You three can offer your input, then I'll finalize it and get it out."

I thought it was kind of her to include Jeanne in what would typically be a partnership project.

"Thanks, Danni," I said. "Shall we take a look at the menus?"

We had a delicious meal of piping hot split pea soup, crusty bread, salads, and sea bass. Surprisingly, my stomach felt just fine. By the time we got back to the office, we were all ready to get back into our work projects. But since Marnie's files had yet to arrive, she headed home for a rare weekday walk and a nap, neither of which she was likely to have time for again for quite a while. Because she winked at me when she mentioned the nap, it seemed likely to be a two-person nap. I didn't care if it was a three-person nap, since I was beyond elated that we all now had more than enough work to keep us and an associate busy.

Chapter 16

By the time Marnie's oral argument before the Seventh Circuit rolled around, she had totally immersed herself in her new files. She was getting in early, and still sitting at her desk reading when Danni and I said good night and headed for our train.

On the morning of the hearing, I met Marnie and Danni at the federal courthouse in Chicago. I'd never had the chance to do a federal appeals court argument myself, and my heart was pounding rapidly as though I were the one about to be grilled by three judges, in an intimidating wood-paneled room, packed with spectators. Marnie had already checked in, and she and Danni had deposited their coats in the little room just adjacent to the courtroom. They were sitting in the gallery where I joined them. Just before the first session of cases was to be called, I leaned over to Marnie and asked, "How do you feel?"

She was looking at the podium, rather than at me, as she whispered in a fake, breathless voice, "Mr. DeMille, I'm ready for my close-up."

Shortly before the proceedings began, a clerk entered the room and stacked piles of papers in front of each of the three chairs. Court was called to order and a little procession of three male judges made their way from a door at the very front on the left, and on to their respective chairs. Marnie's case was to be the last among those in the first session.

When it was called, she moved toward the counsel table with an ease and a grace I hadn't associated with her before that moment. As the appellant, she seated herself at the table to the left, between the visitors' gallery and the bench. She basically faced directly toward her opponent, a fifty-something, nondescript sort of man. Three younger people, presumably lawyers with his firm, joined him at the appellee's table. One of them fished a pile of documents out of her large briefcase, and set them before the man. It was then that I noticed Marnie had no papers whatsoever with her—just a blank yellow legal pad and a pen.

Since Marnie's client was the one who had filed the appeal, she went first. I got deep chills when, after stepping up to the podium, she said, "Marnie Ames of Hightower, Dooley and Ames, for the appellant, Benevolent Insurance Company." Then she was off and running—obviously a thoroughbred. I saw it as running because of the rapid-fire questions from the judges, and the quick, pointed responses she returned. Not only did she have a persuasive response to every factual reference and point of law they raised, but it was like she'd been possessed by an orator. Her tones were deep and melodic, her targeted points delivered without hesitation. On top of all of that, she knew the case law on each legal issue as though the text of each reported case was right in front of her, the page turned to the exact highlighted passage of some invisible book. When one of the judges would say something like, "But what about judge so-and-so's comment in the such-and-such case?" Marnie not only incisively answered the question posed, but also referenced the page number and paragraph where it was discussed in the opinion. She did this throughout her argument, and during her second opportunity to speak, after her opponent had his chance at the lectern. But, unlike him, she had no papers or note cards spread out on the little table beside the podium.

Marnie's back was to me, but I could see the judges' upper bodies, and they were obviously practiced at not betraying their impressions. It was only slight movements that suggested to me that they were reacting positively: sitting up straighter, nodding barely perceptibly in understanding or agreement, or hinting at a smile.

The court adjourned for a break after her argument, and Marnie walked up to Danni and me, obviously thrilled with how it had gone. We met her in the aisle. "You were incredible," said Danni.

"Fabulous, Marnie. Congratulations!"

"Thanks, guys. I think it went well."

I said, "You have a photographic memory, don't you?"

"And photogenic mammaries," said Marnie.

I put my hand on her arm and stared at her. "Will you be serious for a minute? Why didn't you tell us?"

"Heather, neither my memory nor my mammaries are achievements. They are gifts, like any other— nothing a refined woman should boast about."

Danni laughed, then said, "I'm so happy for you."

"Thanks. But you two know that a good oral argument does not a victory make. So, let's not celebrate until the ruling comes out, and I win."

"Fair enough," I said.

A middle-aged, bald man in a dark business suit approached our little group. Danni and I took the hint and took a step back so he could speak with Marnie.

"Phil Stewart of Benevolent," he said.

"Marnie Ames of Hightower, Dooley and Ames," she said as they shook hands.

"That was very impressive, Ms. Ames. The company asked me to stop by and observe your argument. I must say, I've never seen one as good as yours—and I've seen a lot."

"Thank you."

Mr. Stewart seemed to notice that there was another gentleman standing to his side, apparently also waiting to speak with Marnie. "Well, congratulations on an excellent job. I'll let home office know about it right away."

"Thank you. I'd appreciate that."

He faded away and the second man, also in a charcoal business suit, approached her. "John Phillips with Citadel Corporation," he said, as he reached out to shake her hand.

"Marnie Ames with Hightower, Dooley and Ames." Marnie must've enjoyed repeating the firm name, because it certainly wasn't necessary.

"I'm here to watch the argument in one of my company's cases—after the adjournment. But I have to say, you were extraordinary. May I have your business card?"

"I'm sorry but—"

Danni thrust one into Marnie's hand. "Oh, it seems I do have one. Thank you for your kind words, Mr. Phillips. Good luck on your lawyer's argument." The man nodded his head, clearly appreciative of his new find, and walked away, presumably to join his soon-to-be former attorney.

As we headed for the courtroom door, I said, "Obviously, you were a hit. So, now are you glad you escaped your cave?"

Marnie asked, "Do hummingbirds hum?"

"I have no idea," said Danni.

I just laughed, and we continued walking. They reclaimed their wraps in the coatroom. As we headed for the elevator bank, I asked, "Shall we grab an early lunch before we head back up to Waukegan?"

"I'm not really hungry yet, Heather," said Marnie. "Anyway, I'd like to include Jeanne."

"Even better!" I said.

"Perfect," said Danni.

As we exited the elevator, she added, "Like I said, I don't want to take a victory lap until the decision comes down in my favor. But I'd love to share the details of today with Jeanne. It's strange, but she's starting to feel like a proper mother—not like the one I actually had—and it hit me yesterday, when I was knee-deep in case law, how much I care about pleasing her."

I said, "I get that." Danni nodded in agreement.

Danni and I worked, and Marnie snoozed peacefully on the train ride back up north. When we arrived at our office, Jeanne had her purse in her hand as she greeted us at the door, almost an hour and a half later.

Marnie said, "You have to join us for lunch, Jeanne. I want you to hear about my first appellate argument."

"Of course, dear. I've been awaiting your arrival." Her excessively formal manner of speech never failed to tickle me.

We all still had a lot to do that day, so we simply went to the nearby café and grabbed a booth. Danni and I breathlessly regaled Jeanne with the details of Marnie's triumph, as we all chowed down on sandwiches.

Marnie said, "It really did go well, Jeanne."

"Of course it did, Marnie." She briefly looked at each of us. "All of you girls are extraordinary. I knew it the moment I met you."

As soon as everyone had finished, she rose, grabbed the check over our strenuous protests, and paid at the counter. Her desire to treat us to meals was a little thing that I didn't understand. Of course, I knew how much we paid Jeanne, and how it compared to what we earned. But I think we all appreciated that her insistence meant it was important to her. So, we gave in—again—and thanked her. As we walked out the door of the restaurant, she said, "On to the next!"

We were all four flying high as we got back into our offices, Jeanne to finish up the billings she'd been working on, and the rest of us to resume work on our hard-earned files. For me, that morning marked more than Marnie's impressive oral argument. In the span of a month, she had ascended from the depths of disappointment to a place of validation and success. I knew instinctively I'd never again have to worry that we had too little business. From then on, the worry would be how to grow our law firm without diminishing what made us unique.

Chapter 17

We'd received a dozen resumes in response to the notice we posted in late February that we were looking for a one-to-two-year lawyer with civil litigation experience. All of us reviewed each applicant's submission, and we agreed that only three had the qualifications we needed and the appropriate number of years of experience. Each of us was to conduct an in-person first interview with one of the top three candidates, then we would compare notes.

Late on a Friday afternoon a week after Marnie's Seventh Circuit argument, we met in Danni's office to share our thoughts. Marnie and I sat in the visitor chairs, each with a small pile of resumes on our lap. Marnie said, "My guy has two years of experience at a small plaintiff's shop in Chicago. He's presented routine motions, but the partners held onto all of the meaty stuff. Of course, he hasn't done any kind of business development. I'd say he's trainable, but nothing to write home about."

"Meaning?" I asked.

"Let's just say if he has an actual personality, he kept it under wraps during the interview."

"Ah. So, Danni, how did yours go?"

"A pleasant enough young lady from a DuPage County defense firm. But she said she prefers court time and depositions to paperwork, and said that 'research isn't my forte.' "

"That's too bad," I said. "My candidate won't cut it either. She said she'd be happy to do anything in Lake County, but she's not comfortable going to Cook because she's never appeared there, and it's too far away for a commute, in any event."

Marnie looked past Danni, out her window toward the courthouse. After a moment, she said, "Damn. Let's think back. Were there any others in these piles we could reconsider?"

"Just one," said Danni. She rifled through the short stack of paper on her desk and pulled out a couple of pieces of paper. "The woman was a Cook County State's Attorney in the criminal division and handled a number of misdemeanor jury trials. She wants to move over to the civil side in the private sector. She has more years of experience than we need—it's just not the right experience. She's never done discovery in a civil case, so we'd need to do a lot of training. Finally, she's four years out, guys. So she's probably looking for more salary than we can responsibly offer."

"I think we should check her out," I said. "Maybe she's flexible on the pay. And at least she already knows what the inside of a courtroom looks like."

"A high bar," said Marnie. "Where did she go to school?"

"Loyola. Her name is Angelina Lockhart."

"How were her grades?" I asked, as I dug through the pile of resumes on my lap for my copy of Angelina's.

"We don't have the transcript, but her resume says 2.8. So, not impressive, but she may deserve some special consideration on that. She grew up in a Chicago housing project. And she does have a high LSAT score," said Marnie.

"Yeah," said Danni. "And her resume lists membership in the Black Students' Union."

"So, she's Black," said Marnie.

"We don't care about that," I said.

"I do," said Marnie. "It's a huge plus."

"Do you mean it would be one more front in our war against prejudice?" asked Danni.

"Do hummingbirds hum?"

She put down the papers and stared at Marnie. "I already told you, I have no idea."

"Let's ask her in for an interview," I said. I glanced at her resume and circled a few points I was curious about. "And not a two-step. I think we may as well all meet her at the same time since she's the last possible hire."

"And if she isn't a good fit?" asked Marnie.

"We wait a couple of months and go fishing again," said Danni.

****

Four days later, I was sitting in our conference room when Jeanne walked her in. "Heather Hightower, this is the candidate for our associate position, Ms. Angelina Lockhart."

I rose and shook hands with Angelina, an attractive, lithesome Black woman, who wore a brightly colored garment that reminded me of a sari. Her hair was covered in a colorful scarf, in shades that coordinated with the caftan, or whatever it was called. Not a strand escaped the head covering. She looked like an African princess, rather than a girl who had grown up in an urban jungle.

"It's nice to meet you, Angelina. Please call me Heather. Have a seat, and my partners will be here in a minute." I turned to Jeanne, "Would you mind letting Marnie and Danni know Ms. Lockhart has arrived?"

"My pleasure, Heather," said Jeanne, who looked so pleased that I thought she might regale Angelina with a bit of poetry about how we were all destined to meet.

When Danni walked into the room, Angelina rose to meet her, got down on one knee as they shook hands, then released a slow-motion dazzling smile, which Danni responded to with its twin. Danni took the chair with the cushion, directly across from Angelina.

A moment later, Marnie entered the room, closing the door behind her. Once she turned to face Angelina, our candidate was already standing. They looked at one another, and Angelina's smile blossomed again as they shook hands.

We all had Angelina's resume in front of us. I said, "We'd like to let you know a bit about us, before we turn to you."

"I've seen enough," she said.

"I beg your pardon?"

"Heather, when I met you, I feared this might not be the right place for me. I've worked for beautiful White people before, and it hasn't tended to give me the sense of camaraderie and inclusion I require in order to do my most confident and creative work. But then Danni and Marnie introduced themselves, and a warm summer breeze swept over me. Of course, I already knew the basics—that the firm is owned by three women and has been in business serving both Cook and Lake Counties, for almost a year."

I was gobsmacked. We were supposed to be assessing her, not the other way around. And if Danni and Marnie were a warm summer breeze, what did that make me? Half of the summer breeze took over. "Okay," said Danni. "Then why don't you tell us about yourself."

She nodded to each of us before she began. "I was an excellent student in a terrible high school on the south side of Chicago. I was so confident in my scholastic abilities that I was dumbfounded when I started college at SIU and it became clear in the first semester that my college preparation lagged behind that of my classmates. I sought tutoring, and basically worked night and day just to keep up. I was able to graduate, a psychology major, in four years—and three summers."

"Did you go straight to law school?" asked Danni.

"I took off a year to work and save some money before applying to law schools. I suspected I'd be admitted somewhere because my LSAT score was very good. But I was surprised to learn I'd been awarded a full scholarship to attend Loyola. I think I would've done very well there, since I'd eventually learned how to study properly at SIU. But my grades were marginal. What is it they say, 'Man plans, God laughs'? She certainly had a good yuk on me. I delivered my daughter a month before law school started. Of course, caring for Eloise took a big bite out of the time I thought I'd have to study."

"Oh, my," said Danni. "So, unplanned?"

"My husband and I intended to wait until I'd finished school to start our family."

"Then you're married," I said, to my great regret.

"Black, pregnant, *and* married."

"I just meant that he was able to help out with the baby while you began your classes." It was the best I could come up with to try to mitigate my insensitive comment.

"He would've loved that, Heather. Unfortunately, he was shipped back to Afghanistan right after Eloise was born." She smiled ruefully at me, which I took as an indication she forgave my stupid remark.

"That must've been hard," said Danni.

"As it turned out, that was nothing compared with the next eight years."

"How so?" asked Marnie.

Angelina nodded. It seemed she had a habit of giving a little nod to the person who asked her a question, before responding. It was actually pretty charming. "Cornell never came home. I mean, some of him is here—at Arlington. But some bits are surely still blowing about in dust storms in the Middle East."

"Oh, my god," I said. "I'm so sorry."

"That's horrible," said Danni. "Are you okay?"

"I don't know if you've ever lost someone you love, Danni. But I'll never be whole again."

Marnie said, "Angelina, you seem like an especially decent person. I'm sorry for your horrible loss, which I honestly can't begin to comprehend. But I have to ask, why are you volunteering all of this?"

"Because even if I meet all your requirements, I don't want you to hire me without knowing who I am. I'm not interested in job-hopping. I'm looking for stability for myself and my daughter."

"That's reasonable," said Marnie. "Then, let me ask you some more questions. For starters, why are you wearing that stunning African-inspired outfit rather than a traditional business suit? Do you always dress like that?"

"Today is the first day I've worn anything like this." She glanced down at her outfit. "Although I do rather like it."

"I don't understand," said Danni. "Why?"

"I was testing you."

"You were testing us?" I asked.

"Right. I don't appreciate requirements to conform to cultural dress norms, or feminine beauty standards."

"Nor do we," I said.

"I see that. That's why I'm so encouraged about all of you."

The meeting wasn't going remotely like I'd assumed it would since we seemed to be the ones being evaluated. I endeavored to get it back on track. "Angelina, let's talk about your work experience."

"Certainly." She gave me a little nod. "I went straight out of law school to the Cook County State's Attorney's office. I've worked up hundreds of misdemeanor cases, and I took a couple dozen to jury trials. I haven't done any civil discovery, no long briefs, and no appellate briefing or argument. I realize these are things you're looking for. But I'm a fast learner, quick on my feet, and I'm quite good at research and writing, according to my law school professors. I did win honorable mention in a statewide legal writing competition for attorneys and law students. It was while I was a second year, and my article was published in the Illinois lawyer's journal. I have a copy for each of you." She pulled the small pack of papers from her slim briefcase, and passed them around. Her article was entitled *A Survey of Illinois Banking Law, 1818 to present."*

"Sexy title," said Marnie.

Throughout the interview, Angelina had appeared perfectly relaxed, which was unusual, and a point in her favor. It was also a way in which she reminded me of Marnie. I could tell Marnie and Danni were fairly enthralled with her, but we needed to be practical about whether she could work out. I said, "In order to have the amount of work we've been able to cobble together, we've needed to accept assignments in both Lake and Cook Counties. Our associate will need to handle Chicago court calls some days, and be up here on others. The same applies to taking depositions. As you know, it's a good hour on the train between the two."

"I don't mind. Actually, I got a lot of work done on my trip up here today. I live with my mother, who takes Eloise to and from school, so I'm free to leave my home whenever I need to in order to handle my work."

"That's good to hear." I paused. "But there is one other issue. We're prepared to pay the going rate in Lake County for a second-year associate. You have four years of experience. But even as a quick study, you would probably take a while to be able to do what a two-year lawyer from the civil side could do on Day One."

"How do you all feel about needing to train me?"

Marnie said, "Any of the three of us could do it with our hands tied behind our backs, but it would be hard to write orders like that."

"I'd love to train someone," said Danni.

"I would too," I said. "My point is that you're a square peg in a round hole in terms of knowing what a fair salary would be."

"That's not a problem. If you all decide to extend an offer, I will assume it will be a fair amount in light of all of the considerations."

"You will?" asked Danni.

She looked intently from one of us to the other, and

we each received a quick nod. "Listen, I'm interested in a long-term relationship with a law firm. If I don't trust the partners implicitly, I won't accept an offer. I'll just stay with the State's Attorney's office a while longer. I'm comfortable with the three of you and Jeanne, but if I'm not the right fit from your perspective, I'll just stay where I am. I go with my intuition. I'm perfectly willing to wait until the situation feels right."

I was impressed she'd included Jeanne in her assessment of the work environment, and with pretty much everything else she had to say, as well as the self-assured manner in which she'd said it. But I wasn't enthralled. I wondered about her comment that she was "testing" us, and what it might bode for the future. Also, she'd carved me out of the warm summer breeze. I needed to discuss this possible hire with my partners.

"Do you have any other questions for us?"

"Just your timeframe, Heather. If I were hired, I would need to give two weeks' notice."

"That would be acceptable. This isn't an emergency situation, although the sooner the better. Now, if you'll excuse us for a few minutes, we'll step out. Would you care for anything to drink?"

"No, thank you. I have my water bottle with me."

We adjourned to Marnie's office, which was directly across the hall. Marnie sat at her desk and we took seats in the chairs.

"I adore her," said Marnie.

"It's no wonder since she reminds me of you," I said.

"I think she'd be good," said Danni.

"I like her too, but I wonder if she might be a bit combative," I said. "She basically turned the interview on its head, assessing us before we could get into her credentials."

Marnie started to rise from her desk chair, and said, "Do you want me to dash back in and ask her if she's an angry Black woman?"

"I thought what she did was reasonable," said Danni, as Marnie sat back down. "More efficient than sitting through an interview, just to decline our offer. She has a raw honesty. I admire that."

"I suppose that's all it was. I guess I was just wondering—if she's that aggressive with us, how might she conduct herself with her opponents and the court?"

"She'd be a dynamo," said Marnie, as she leaned back in her chair.

"What do you think, Danni?"

"Heather, the judge you introduced us to on our courtroom tour told us we are brave women…or that we'd have to be brave. Something along those lines. Angelina seems especially courageous to me and I like her a lot. Jeanne told us to go with our instincts, and mine is saying, in Jeanne-parlance: the day we hire Angelina will be marked with joy in the heavens, will insure success and harmony for years to come, and will fulfill our destinies."

"And secure world peace," said Marnie.

I laughed. "Okay. I admit it. She'll be terrific. But I would like to check out her references and take a peek at her transcripts—in an abundance of caution."

"That's just because you weren't included in the warm summer breeze," said Marnie.

"You noticed, too."

"But she did call you a beautiful White person," said Marnie. "That should count for something."

"You guys want to make an offer today, don't you?"

"I do," said Danni.

"Ditto," said Marnie.

"So, I'll settle for the beautiful White person thing. But let's make it contingent on her references panning out, we get her law school transcript, and one of us reads her banking article."

Marnie raised her hand like a schoolgirl. "Yes. Ms. Ames?" I asked.

"I volunteer to call all of her references and study the transcript. But please don't make me read an article on banking."

"I have an idea," said Danni. "Let's ask Delaney to read it and give us her assessment."

"You don't think she'd mind?" I asked.

"Of course not. She'd love to be able to help out."

"I'd say she's already helping out," said Marnie.

"I promise you guys. She'd be thrilled to be asked."

We walked back into the conference room and made the contingent offer, which Angelina accepted. She said she'd prefer to be called Annie among us. "Angelina" was for the court, and people who aren't us.

"Danni handles it the same way," I said. "Danielle Dooley for legal matters, and with people who aren't close friends. Is there a reason you both guard your nicknames?"

"My mother," said Annie and Danni at the same time.

Danni explained, "Mom chose my name, so I like to honor her by using it in a professional capacity. Of course, I could do that and still be 'Danni' to everyone I meet. I suppose it's just a way to have a smidge of control over my identity."

Annie said, "I also think of it as a way to demand a modicum of respect through formality, something I don't require with people I trust."

Marnie said, "Now Heather and I are jealous we don't have nicknames to differentiate people. I mean, what could they be?" She paused. "Two candy bars?"

Annie got her transcript to us the next day, and there were no surprises. Marnie made the calls to the three references, a Cook County judge, a Loyola professor, and the woman who had been Annie's boss at the bookshop where she worked between college and law school. She reported to Danni and me that they'd all had a drink from the same pitcher—Annie got glowing evaluations from each of them.

Delaney read the journal article on banks right away. She emailed all of us:

"I wanted to accept Danni's explanation for why you all decided to hire an attorney with a less than stellar GPA, and I wasn't expecting all that much from the article. After all, Angelina was just a second-year law student when she wrote it. But the truth is, it was outstanding. It wasn't just well researched and foot-noted, it cogently identified themes and trends, and how those fit with the national banking policy at the time—and why. It was so engaging that folks not the least interested in banking law would find it a digestible and even enjoyable read. Congrats on finding this gem of a young lawyer."

****

Annie started two weeks later. When she walked into our office on her first day, she was wearing a tan skirt suit, pumps of the same color, and she had her slim briefcase in her hand. The head covering was gone, and in its place was a full head of gray dreadlocks. We had all walked out to the reception area to greet her. Marnie said, "Cool dreads."

Annie said, "Do you really like it?" Before Marnie could answer, Annie pulled the wig from her head, tossed it at Marnie, and said, "Here, you can borrow it."

Marnie convulsed with laughter.

Annie said, "I thought it would be funny to see your reactions." Her actual hair was jet black, and very short. The style looked sensational on her.

The three of us and Jeanne gave her welcome hugs and Danni took Annie to her small, interior office to begin her instruction in civil discovery.

I was having a hard time believing she'd just done what she did, but not because I found it objectionable. I just wondered how she could feel so comfortable on her first day that she had the guts to do something like that. It confirmed what I'd said to Marnie. By all appearances, our new hire was probably going to be a lot like her.

****

A few days later, Annie had her first appearance at the Lake County courthouse. It simply involved her presenting a routine motion to compel discovery, but she was gone for over an hour. When she returned from Court, she walked into my office. I assumed it was Marnie who taught her not to knock.

"Heather, do you have a minute?"

"Any time."

She pulled out of her briefcase a yellow legal pad, covered with scribblings. "Should I accept criminal defense matters?"

"Why do you ask?"

"This morning, eight people approached me after I

had drawn up my order and was heading back here. I asked them to line up since we were clogging up the hallway."

"I don't understand."

"You probably don't remember me telling you this, but I'm Black. They were all folks with cases on the criminal calendar who wanted me to represent them."

"But how did they know you have criminal court experience?"

"Heather, they were Black, and I looked like a lawyer. I took down their names and phone numbers. I told each of them to advise the court that they would like a continuance, because they were looking into hiring a lawyer."

"I see. And you want to know if you may call them back and agree to represent them."

"Right. And what would I charge?"

"Okay. Have a seat, Annie. I need to ask Marnie and Danni to step in."

When Marnie arrived, she saw that we were one chair short, and dragged one in from her office while Danni came in and took a seat. I explained Annie's situation.

Marnie said, "What are these folks charged with, walking down the street while Black?"

"Yeah. Things like that. Possession of small amounts of drugs, shoplifting, assault and battery for a bar fight. That type of thing. Not a death penalty matter among them."

Danni asked, "Is criminal defense work billed as an hourly or on a flat fee?"

"I'm not sure, since I only prosecuted," said Annie. "I think it depends on the type of case."

Marnie said, "We would have no idea how to price it as a flat fee. Annie, do you think you could handle these efficiently enough that these folks could afford our hourly charge for you? It doesn't make any sense for you to spend your time on work that pays less per hour than the work you already have on your plate."

I said, "Let's back up a minute. None of the three of us has any experience handling criminal cases, so we can't really supervise your work. Our last exposures to this were our constitutional law classes in law school."

Annie said, "Fortunately, the Constitution hasn't changed since then."

"How comfortable are you defending these cases without partner supervision, Annie?" asked Danni.

"In the immortal words of Marnie, I could do it with both hands tied behind my back—but it would be hard to take notes."

I said, "I propose we let Annie call these folks back, tell them her representation would have to be on an hourly fee basis, with a refundable retainer for the first three hours. Annie, I think we'd need you to keep your criminal defense work down to no more than twenty percent of your time. Come to us with any problems." I looked at Marnie and Danni. "What do you guys think?"

"Sure. Let's give it a try," said Marnie.

"I agree. But let's calendar it for ninety days and look at it again then," said Danni.

"Okay, Annie," I said. "It looks like you've broken some kind of record—bringing in new clients on your first day in court. Once you get all the information you need to open the files, let Jeanne know what you're up to. She'll get all the new files docketed and keep an eye on the billables."

Annie stood to leave. "Thanks a lot. I'm excited to have the chance to do this work. People who don't know the system get kicked around, which just pisses me off."

"Us, too," said Marnie. She smiled as she started dragging the extra chair back to her office.

Chapter 18

A month or so after Annie joined us, Marnie, Danni, and I recognized the logic of living together, since raising our new baby business still demanded 24/7 vigilance and near-constant accessibility. Plus, living in Evanston, halfway between the Lake County and the Cook County courthouses, made the most sense. Frugality pointed us toward a three-bedroom to share, but there were other considerations. Danni was hoping for a modifiable kitchen and needed a pet-friendly environment for Grizzly. Marnie insisted on superior sound protection because she didn't want to annoy any neighbors as a result of her crusade to bed a wide variety and great number of men. For my part, I demanded nothing in particular, but thought a view of a park, Northwestern's manicured lawns, or the lake would be nice. Since Chica-the-Brave was trained to use the pads I laid out on my bathroom floor, my shadow and I didn't require access to a quick spot for a walk.

After a month of searching, it was May by the time we signed leases for three one-bedroom apartments in a charming old colonial-style red brick building near the intersection of Hinman and Lee. The upkeep of the place was convincingly advertised by the freshly painted white wood trim, and the neighborhood vibe was a combination of college cool and family friendly. While the landlord wasn't amenable to changing the appliances, he approved Danni's plans to raise the kitchen floor with hardwood platforms in strategic spots, since the modifications could easily be reversed when she moved out. Marnie was pleased with her corner apartment, after insisting the property manager admit us to the rooms above, below, and adjacent to her bedroom, to test whether Danni and I could hear whatever she was yelling in order to evaluate the soundproofing. The deal was sealed for me when I stepped out onto a tiny fourth-floor balcony that presented a quietly elegant park to the east, beyond which lay Lake Michigan.

On our first night in the new digs, we had a progressive dinner of carry-out, starting in Danni's apartment, where, famished, we dug into the shrimp cocktails she'd persuaded a local restaurant to deliver. Thanks to her movers, her beautiful furniture was roughly in place, but much of the floor and every other surface had sprouted boxes and trash bags labelled with intriguing descriptions such as "for my eyes only," and "secret stuff." Chica-the-Brave was soundly snoozing in my apartment, so I'd left her there to recover from the stress of move-in day. We lounged on Danni's floor to eat and share a bottle of chardonnay.

I said, "Do you guys think we'll have any interesting neighbors?" Just as the last word parted my lips, there was a sharp rapping on the door. I sprang to make my way through the obstacle course of boxes, and slowly opened up a few inches to three thirty-something guys carrying a six-pack of beer, and the odor of having imbibed before their arrival. I smiled and said, "Hi," holding the knob at my hip, keeping the door half-closed.

The best-looking and shortest of the three said, "Hi. I'm Sam. These are my friends, Morrison and Jeff. I saw your moving van out front and thought we'd welcome you to the building."

I glanced behind me at Marnie and Danni, both of whom gave me unenthusiastic shrugs of, "Okay." I reached out to shake Sam's hand. "I'm Heather. My two friends and I moved into our apartments today, so we're kinda beat. But you're welcome to come in and say hi."

Only Marnie's lovely face was visible over one of the boxes until the guys made their ways to the little circle we had carved out on the floor. I introduced Sam to Marnie and Danni, since the other two were lagging behind. He leaned over to shake hands with my friends without a beat of hesitation. After he greeted them, he slid down against a box to sit beside Danni. Once Morrison and Jeff reached us, they took one look at Danni and laughed out loud. Morrison turned to me and asked, "What is it? A midget?"

I looked between the two goofballs. "It was so nice to meet you. I think we'll ask Grizzly to see you out."

"Wait. The midget's name is Grizzly?" asked Morrison, between spurts of laughter.

Jeff, also blubbering, nodded at his buddy, and spat out, "It's perfect."

Danni said, "Grizzly's my dog." Without word or whistle, Grizzly bounded around the side of one of the tall boxes, bared his teeth, and let out a long, low growl.

"Holy shit!" said Morrison, as he and Jeff bolted for the door.

Marnie called out after them, "He only growls at guys with tiny dicks."

Sam stood and spoke to Danni. "My friends are idiots, and a little drunk. I'm so sorry."

"Yeah," said Danni. "But you brought them into my

home."

"Right. I'm really sorry." Sam placed the six-pack beside Danni. "Here. Please keep the beer." Grizzly snarled and Sam backed out of the room, red-faced and awkward as he tried to avoid the various boxes and bags, his eyes pasted to Grizzly's bared teeth.

"Well, that was fun," said Marnie.

Danni said, "The short one looked really familiar."

Marnie said, "I'm uncorking another bottle of wine," as Danni and I went back to our shrimp cocktails.

Chapter 19

By the end of her second month with us, Annie was beating everyone else into the office each morning. I didn't know what she did in her office with her door closed but walking down the hallway or looking through the file cabinets, she was always conspicuously humming or whistling. I'd thought we were a pretty happy crew before that, but Annie raised the exuberance level several notches. I half expected her to break into *Hi-ho, Hi-ho, Off to Court We Go,* when she headed out the door to cover a motion. One day it dawned on me. Maybe she wasn't just blessed with a sunny disposition. She did have all the symptoms.

I shared my theory with Marnie and Danni one evening on our train ride home. The next morning, Marnie stood in Annie's doorway, and we could all hear the conversation. Without a word of preamble, she said, "Are you in love?"

Annie burst out laughing. "How did you know?"

"Heather thinks you are showing the indicia, but Danni and I, never having tasted of that particular fruit, just thought of you as spectacularly—and almost annoyingly—happy."

"Believe me, Marnie, I haven't been demonstrably happy, annoyingly so or not, for a long time. No." She shook her head to emphasize the point. "But I did meet someone, thanks to being up here in Lake County."

Jeanne had now joined Danni and me just outside Annie's door.

"Another lawyer?" I asked.

"Good heavens, no. He's a high school teacher. I met him at court that day I was surrounded by potential clients."

"He's a defendant?" asked Danni.

"No. Although I wouldn't hold that against him if he were, since Black men are arrested for breathing while Black. He took off from work to be with his nephew in court."

"When did you start seeing him?" I asked.

Annie was positively beaming as she answered our questions. "I thought it best to wait until the nephew's matter was concluded. Extra incentive to have the charges dismissed, which is what I did. It's been almost six weeks. His name is Bradley."

"Has Eloise met him?" asked Danni.

"She adores him."

I said, "Congratulations, Annie. I hope it goes well for you guys. Now, if we've solved the mystery of Annie's good humor, shall we all get back to work?"

"You all go ahead," said Marnie. "I want to talk with Annie for a few minutes about Bradley."

Danni said, "I'm really happy for you, Annie." Then she and I headed for our offices.

****

It was on a Friday, about a month later, that Annie brought her daughter with her to work. I glimpsed the little girl sitting in the conference room, drawing pictures, when I arrived. I tapped on Annie's door. "Good morning. Is it 'bring your daughters to work day'?"

"I don't think so. But Eloise's school is having an in-service day for the teachers, and my mom is out of town visiting her sister. Marnie said it would be okay."

"Of course, it is."

"Thanks. I have to run to court, but I'll introduce you as soon as I get back."

"Great. I'll just peek in and say a quick hi since I can't wait to meet her." Annie left, and I knocked on the conference room door before entering. As I did, Eloise rose from her seat. The child was a miniature Annie, slender and lovely, with the same gorgeous coal-black skin. Her hair was in four neat rows of tight braids with a yellow ribbon tied at the end of each. She put out her arm to shake, and her hand in mine felt as delicate as a baby bird. She said, "You must be Heather Hightower. My mom told me all about you. It's nice to meet you."

"It's my pleasure, Eloise. I see you're hard at work, so I'll leave you to it. I'll stop by again in a bit."

"Okay."

It was almost two hours later when Annie and I stepped into the conference room together. Annie said, "Eloise told me you two have met."

"Yes. But just for a moment."

"Good." Annie stepped back to allow me to talk with her daughter.

Eloise said, "Hi, again," and raised her hand to make a little wave. She had papers, pencils and markers spread out before her.

"What have you been working on, Eloise?"

"I'm making pictures of each of you. Jeanne told me she thinks it's a really good idea." Eloise ripped a page from the pad and handed it to me. "Ms. Hightower" was written in neat cursive across the top. The figure actually looked a lot like me, which was surprising since she'd never set eyes on me before that morning. She had drawn a little girl standing next to me, who I assumed represented Eloise.

"It's very good. I think you have a talent for drawing."

She smiled. "Thank you, Ms. Hightower."

I started to hand the portrait back, but Eloise said, "It's for you to keep."

"Thanks very much. It's really quite good."

"Thank you."

"Make yourself at home today. There are soft drinks in the fridge, and you are welcome to any of the pens and paper in the supply room."

"Thanks." She looked up at Annie. "But Mama doesn't like me to drink soft drinks."

"Of course. Good rule. We also have a water fountain—just next to the restroom."

"Great! Thanks."

I excused myself and left mother and daughter to have their little visit. I returned to my office, shut my door, leaned against the nearest wall, and closed my eyes. I couldn't remember when I'd last spoken with a child. I got a flashback to a day at a theme park, where I'd gone with a law school friend after my engagement was broken off. She and I were sitting in a car, floating through a simple, meandering ride, and I fell apart. I'd gotten so close to realizing my plan for marriage, children, and happily ever after, when it had all vanished. Five years had passed, and I was doing nothing to move a fraction of an inch toward that goal. In fact, I was still so raw about what had happened, I wasn't at all sure I'd ever want to press forward on that front. I taped Eloise's drawing to my wall and sat down to immerse myself in research. I managed to stay largely absorbed in work for the remainder of the day. Around 5:00, Annie knocked, which she'd never done before, and brought Eloise in to say goodbye. I gave the little girl a pen with the firm name on it and a yellow legal pad, so she could doodle on her long train-ride home.

After mother and daughter left, Marnie and Danni stopped by my office together and plopped down in the visitor chairs. "Eloise is such a sweetheart," said Danni. "When I stopped by to say hi to her, she said, 'Let me know if I can help you reach anything today.'"

"A kind soul," I said.

"Then she asked if people ever make fun of me. So, I said, 'Sometimes.' She responded, 'You mustn't let that bother you. They are just ignorant. You could pray for them.' "

"Wow," I said.

Marnie said, "She asked me the same thing, and gave me the same advice. I asked her if anyone ever teases her for anything."

"Oh, dear," I said.

"Right," said Marnie. "She said, 'Yes, ma'am. Kids are mean about how dark my skin is.' So, I said, 'Ah. Ignorant children.' Then I uttered words I never dreamed would cross my lips. 'You could pray for them.'"

"She really did get to you," I said.

"Yeah. I rolled over like a bowling pin. That's one cool kid."

"Did you hear what Jeanne said to her when she and Annie were leaving?" asked Danni.

"No. I've been sitting at my desk all day."

"Jeanne was sitting in her desk chair, swiveled to

face out, away from her computer. Eloise stood right in front of her. I couldn't hear what the little girl said, but Jeanne's response was along these lines: 'Eloise, don't worry yourself about your future. You will have a long and happy life. You'll contribute to society in ways beyond even your mother's wildest dreams for you. Your children and your children's children will rejoice in your grace.' "

"Goodness. I wonder how Eloise took that?" I said.

"She seemed to accept it pretty matter-of-factly," said Danni. "Then Eloise said to Jeanne, 'Ever since Mama started working here, she's been lots more fun. Thanks so much to you, Ms. Hightower, Ms. Dooley, and Ms. Ames. I'm sooooo grateful.' Then she and her mom headed for the door, but Eloise ran back to give Jeanne a big hug."

Chapter 20

Even with Annie's help, we were all swamped with work and kept at it most Saturdays and some Sundays—something we encouraged Annie not to do, since she had Eloise at home. On a Friday afternoon in late July, Marnie stopped by my office to argue for a day off. Once she convinced me with the outrageous stats on the hours we'd been putting in and the weather forecast for the next day, I relented and we moved on to Danni's office to get her agreement. We walked in without knocking and plopped down in her guest chairs.

After Marnie explained her reasoning, she added, "I think we should rent a car and drive up to the Milwaukee Zoo."

"Why that one rather than one of the Chicago zoos?" asked Danni, clicking her ball-point and laying it atop her pile of papers.

"I've heard it combines beauty with the beasts—lots of wide, wooded paths winding up hills and down vales. Benches are tucked under the trees so you can take a breather—rather than Heather having to carry you piggyback. And refreshment stands are always within a short walk. Best of all, guys, they serve beer."

"Of course they do. It's Wisconsin," I said.

"It was beer that made Milwaukee famous," said Danni.

I squinted at her, uncomprehending.

She added, "I heard that somewhere."

"So, what do you think?" I asked Danni.

"It's brilliant. We should." She shot us one of her bright smiles.

I said, "I'll arrange for a rental car."

"I would, Heather. But as you know, I have no license."

"I would, Heather. But as you know, I'm cheap," said Marnie.

"Not a problem. It's really my pleasure."

We'd planned to meet in the morning at my apartment to combine our water bottles, sunscreen, and snacks in a single backpack we'd share. I heard the knock on my door, and assumed Marnie and Danni were together. I called, "Come in!" wanting to surprise them with my haircut. I'd visited a neighborhood hair salon the night before and had my shoulder-length hair chopped off. What was left was a chin-length bob with long bangs I could brush to the side. As they walked in the door, I twirled so they could see all the angles.

"Oh, my God. I love it!" said Danni.

"Nice try," said Marnie. It sounded like a scoff.

"What?"

"Heather, you're still stunning," said Marnie.

"No." I shook my head. "But it's more professional looking, don't you think?"

"Definitely," said Danni.

"What profession?" asked Marnie.

"What's wrong with you? I just got a haircut. That's all I did. Why are you trying to make me feel bad about it?"

We'd all been standing just inside my door. Marnie walked a few feet and plopped down on one of my couches, then looked at me as she continued what felt like an assault. "I really didn't mean to. You are gorgeous in your new do. I just assumed you were trying to take your appearance in a different direction from the usual blond bombshell look."

"What bombshell look?"

"Whether you had your hair in a ponytail or bun, or you just tucked your luxurious waves behind your ears, it was always bombshell hair."

"What the hell is bombshell hair?"

"You're right, Heather. Your natural golden blond hair on someone else wouldn't necessarily be bombshell hair. It all derives from your exquisite face and statuesque figure."

Danni seemed to be growing impatient with whatever it was Marnie was doing. She walked over to the coffee table and set her bug-screen and sunscreen beside my backpack, then said, "I think we established that the first day we met."

Chica-the-Brave ran up to me, and I lifted her and held her at my chest like a shield. I said, "As I recall, that day you guys said I looked like an airhead and a plastic doll. How did I move on to a bombshell? I mean, doesn't that word imply intentionality?"

"It's the same thing, Heather," said Marnie. "Unless you wear a bag over your head—and your body—you're going to attract the same attention you always have."

I just stared at her, wondering what in the hell was prompting her comments.

"Heather, all I'm saying is that your haircut looks fabulous. But you haven't moved a fraction of an inch toward blending."

I took a moment to think. Then, I said, "It's weird.

The adjectives coming out of your mouth sound like compliments, but the feeling behind them seems distinctly disapproving. I don't get it."

Marnie looked away. When she returned her gaze to me, she said, "Sorry. Chalk it up to the green-eyed monster." She looked away again, then back to me. She said, "I really do appreciate that none of us can change the essence of our looks."

I may have squinted my eyes a bit at that. I must've. I'd never asked Marnie if she'd tried dieting, and I never would. There was no way to ask that question without coming across as judgmental.

She stood with her arms akimbo, and said, "Don't go there, Heather."

"Where?"

"You know where. The idea that I could diet myself down to a size four."

"I didn't say anything."

"But you thought it."

She knew. And it wouldn't be helpful to bullshit her. "Maybe momentarily, and I'm sorry for that. Honestly, Marnie, I think that falls under the heading of 'your business.' "

"Damn right, it does."

"Great. So, we're in violent agreement." I was desperate to get the conversation behind us since my stomach was starting to act up. I stepped up to the coffee table, set down my shield, and began putting Danni's things into my backpack. "Now, I'd like to get all this stuff together so we can get going."

Danni grabbed my hand and then Marnie's. She turned to face us, one at a time. "You're sorry. And you're sorry." She gave my hand a little squeeze.

I turned on the radio and switched on a lamp for Chica, and we walked out my door. Danni kindly lightened the mood by launching into a funny story about something that had happened the night before, while I was out getting my hair cut. I'd let Danni know I'd be out for an appointment, and she'd offered to take Chica-the-Brave along for her evening walk with Grizzly. Of course, we all had the keys to each other's apartments, which made a lot of things much easier. She'd let herself in to mine to round up my pup.

Danni said, "So, Chica-the-Brave was bouncing around like a bunny rabbit as I tried to attach the leash to her collar."

"Oh, yeah," I said. "She gets so excited for a walk that she really can't hold still."

Danni smiled at me as we stepped into the elevator. She said, "We were walking on a path in the park. Everything was going smoothly, Grizzly to my left side, and Chica-the-Brave prancing along just to his left. Then she saw a squirrel and darted in front of Grizzly, who must have stepped on Chica's paw. So, she snarled at him while she jumped straight up and latched onto his left ear. She just hung there, like a dangly earring. Grizzly reacted by standing completely still until Chica decided to drop off. But it took a good minute, and passersby were pointing and laughing."

"I've never seen her do that," I said. "But it's definitely in character."

"Yeah," said Danni. "It was refreshing that all the pointing was clearly directed at the dogs. Of course, I could've pulled Chica-the-Brave off, but she wasn't hurting Grizzly, and it really was hysterical to watch. It was like Grizzly was thinking, 'A fly. Danni, there's a fly hanging onto my ear.' " By the time we got to the rental car, we were all laughing.

The drive west on I-94 was uneventful, but due to traffic, it took us almost an hour and a half to reach the zoo entrance. Perhaps everything looked lovelier on a summer day, but upon entering, I was stunned by the shimmering water in the penguin display that sat right before us, the first exhibit. A cloudless periwinkle sky and a temperature of eighty seemed to accentuate the charm of the wet stone wedges surrounded by pristine blue water and populated by countless penguins in their tuxes. I thought I could've enjoyed spending the whole day watching them effortlessly dive and glide. But of course, we pressed on.

The first thing I noticed—after the penguins and how crowded it was—was that every adult, or adult couple, seemed to be accompanied by one or more children, and many of the women carried the next offspring prominently under clingy maternity tops. The youngest children couldn't help themselves as they stared unabashedly at Danni or Marnie, or both. Those a bit older peeked out of the corner of an eye. The pre-teens and teens simply turned in another direction, evidently too embarrassed for our little group to even look. Or maybe they just weren't ready to admit that people who looked like Danni and Marnie existed in their world. But the adults didn't fit a pattern—just doing whatever they pleased.

My friends acted as though they were completely unaware of the minor stir they were causing, so I kept my mouth shut. But the truth was, they were being studied rather like the animal exhibits. I reminded myself to focus on the gorgeous summer day and my good fortune at having such dear friends with whom to share it.

Because I was dying to see the tigers, I suggested we start our tour to the left of the penguins' display. We skipped the kiddie zoo because we wanted to be sure we'd have time to catch the "Oceans of Fun Seal and Sea Lion Show" a couple of hours later. Just as Marnie had described, our route to big cat country meandered along a wide, tree-lined walkway. We stopped to watch hippos and rhinos in their roomy enclosures, complete with attractive bathing ponds. The camel area was also fairly large, but I wondered if the spaces were really adequate. As we watched the animals standing around for photos, Danni said, "I've always adored zoos. But having watched herds of animals like these on nature shows running gracefully over savannahs..." She paused. "I don't know. I guess it's bittersweet."

"I understand that. I have the same feeling," I said. We walked slowly as we talked.

"Not me," said Marnie. "I'm sure life sucks for them, but it also sucks for most humans. So, basically, life just sucks."

Danni said, "Of course there are sucky parts. But there are also non-sucky parts."

"But mainly sucky for these creatures whose mission in life is to pose for photos by sweaty humans dressed in their finest flip-flops, shorts and tank tops. And that's just the men."

"The animals do live much longer in captivity," I said. "It's a combination of nutrition, medical attention, and the absence of natural predators."

"Great for them," said Marnie. "They have miserable lives, but they get to keep on having them for twice as long."

I just shook my head. I wondered if Marnie was really okay. Her humor seemed even darker than usual.

We finally made our way to the front of the crowd staring at the tiger exhibit. "There's more to it," I said. Just then, a stunning, deep gold and black Amur tiger stood, stretched his mammoth body, and paraded by the viewing window, his coat undulating as he moved. He was close enough that we could've touched him were it not for the pane of glass.

"Fabulous animal," whispered Marnie.

"And in the wild, he has only a fifty percent chance to survive to his second birthday," I said. "I've read a fair amount about tigers. Would you guys like some interesting facts?"

Marnie said, "No." Danni shrugged.

A few minutes later, we pivoted to face the folks waiting to take our spots, and had to take baby steps to make any progress. I turned for one last look at the tiger, then said, "Anyway, it really is a bad situation. Preservation of the species may only be possible by the breeding done at zoos like this. All tiger subspecies are going extinct in the wild because of human development in their habitats. That and poaching."

As we popped out onto a less crowded stretch of sidewalk, Danni said, "That's inexcusable. Have world leaders no consciences at all about wild life preservation?"

Marnie rolled her eyes.

We continued on to the zebras, and had to wait several minutes to find an open spot at the rail so we could all see. The crowds kept moving—slowly—but in an assortment of directions. There was no one-way policy like at an art museum special exhibit. Having spent the time to finally secure a few feet from which we could all watch the animals, we weren't in a hurry to move on. We'd been standing in the blazing sun studying the handsome creatures for several minutes when Danni pulled on my hand. I looked down to see that her other hand was tightly gripped by a curly-haired little girl, cheeks flushed from the heat, maybe five years old, wearing shorts and a blue t-shirt featuring a large unicorn head made of sequins. I leaned down so I could hear what Danni was saying.

"Heather, let's step away from the crowd so I can make out what this child is trying to tell me." I grabbed Marnie by the elbow, and we all headed for a bench, partially shaded by a tree, just across the wide walkway from the zebras. Danni and the child sat down, and I handed the girl my water bottle, hoping her mother wouldn't be angry about my germs.

The child spoke to Danni. "You're a Munchkin. I saw you in a movie."

"My name's Danni. This is my friend Heather."

I smiled at the girl.

"And this is my other friend, Marnie." The child's big blue eyes grew even larger at Marnie's girth, but she set the bottle down and accepted a high-five.

Danni took control. "What's your name?"

"Lola. My mom got lost. With my baby brother." She was staring down at her lap, but shot a quick look at Danni as though she'd just realized something horrifying. "I hope he didn't get lost by himself."

"I'm sure they're together." She patted the child's hand. "So, Lola, what's your mom's name?" Danni was doing a good job with her calm tone.

"Jane."

"That's a nice name. And your little brother is—"

"Jack."

"Do you know your last name?'

"Of course. It's Welton."

"Lola Welton. What a pretty name."

Lola smiled at Danni, then said, "I picked you because you're a Munchkin, and they're good."

"Good choice, Lola. Do you happen to know your mom's cell-phone number?"

"Not all of it. It starts with 8-4-7."

"That narrows it down," Marnie whispered to me.

Danni was intently focused on the child, who was now crying softly. "Lola, you don't have to worry. We'll find your mom and your brother. We'll do it together."

Still crying, and wiping at her chubby cheeks, the girl shrugged her shoulders. "But how?"

"You're a big girl. And I'll bet you're smart. What do *you* think we should do?"

"Not go far from here. Because this is where I noticed she got lost."

"Excellent idea. We'll sit right here. Was your brother in a stroller?"

"Yes."

"How could that help us?"

"We watch for a stroller?"

"Perfect. But since we're both short, how could we see all the strollers better?"

She whispered to Danni, but it was like a stage whisper, and Marnie and I heard clearly. "Ask your tall friend to look?"

"Great idea." Danni looked up at me. "Heather, will you help us by looking for a woman pushing a stroller?"

216

"Of course. But there are a lot of those." I was catching on to Danni's Socratic method. "How could I narrow it down?"

Lola said, "I guess you could ask each lady with a stroller if her name is Jane."

Marnie said, "Or she could ask each baby if his name is Jack."

Lola gazed up at Danni with a look that said, *I'm sorry your friend is so stupid.* She said to Marnie, "He can't talk."

At first, I wondered what it was about Marnie that she could use sarcasm on a lost child. But my brain seemed to be hardwired so my default position was the innocent construction rule—from defamation law. If there was a possible innocuous reading, I'd go with that. So, I assumed Marnie must've thought Lola wouldn't catch the joke.

Danni said, "Lola, I wonder if the zoo has a speaker system, like for important announcements."

The girl grew visibly excited. "If they do, the owner of the zoo could say my mom's name and tell her where I am!"

"That's brilliant. But how can we tell the owner?"

She thought for a moment, then ventured, "Someone should run to the ticket area, where all the buildings are?"

"That sounds good." Danni then pulled a puzzled face. "But should you and I do that?"

"No. Because if Mom is looking for me, she won't see me if we're gone."

"That's true. Well, what about my tall friend?"

"No. Remember, she's looking for strollers."

"Oh, that's right. So, who does that leave?"

Lola timidly pointed her finger at Marnie. Probably trying to redeem herself, Marnie said, "I'm on it." Then she looked at Danni. "Smooth way to unsheathe your swift sword of retribution."

Lola said, "What?" The child was nervously rubbing her little hands together.

But Marnie had turned to me. "Heather, please be here when I get back, or we'll have another missing person situation for Lola to solve." Off she went, not quite running, but walking quickly—for Marnie.

Since I was only a few feet from them, I heard Danni's next suggestion. "While we're waiting for your mom, would you like to practice remembering seven numbers in a row?"

"Why?"

"Just so you can see how easy it will be to learn the rest of your mom's cell number."

"Great! I already know 8-4-7."

They practiced for five minutes or so, and I questioned a half dozen stroller-pushing women about their names. But I didn't have to question Lola's actual mother, a trim, thirty-something woman with brown curly hair, who was racing around with a stroller, a panicked look on her face. When I glimpsed her through the crowd, I fought my way up to her and said, "I'll bet you're Lola's mom."

She grabbed my arm in a vice-grip with one hand, the other tightly holding the stroller handle.

I walked her to the bench where Danni and Lola were laughing and shouting out numbers. Jane squatted without letting go of the stroller handle, and said her daughter's name. As they hugged, the mom cried, but Lola had a big smile on her face. She said, "Mom, my friend Danni and I figured out how to find you!"

Jane looked at Danni, took her hand, and cried again. "How did you do it?"

"What?"

"Keep my daughter calm. I never expected to find her beaming. You must be a teacher."

"No. Lawyer."

"Oh, my."

Danni said, "May we see Jack?"

Lola's mother pulled the stroller closer, and Danni and I admired the rosy, plump little guy wearing a navy-blue sunsuit. He was deeply asleep with his head leaning against his shoulder. "He's beautiful," I said.

"Such a lovely baby," said Danni.

Lola said to her mother, "Would you write down your cell phone number? Danni's super-good at helping me memorize."

Jane said, "Oh, honey, we've taken enough of these ladies' time."

"Please, Mom."

Danni said, "Actually, I'd like to do it. It'll just take a minute."

Jane pulled a piece of paper from her purse and jotted down the number. Lola turned toward Danni and they started whispering. Then she looked up at her mother. "Just give us a minute, Mom."

Jane seemed taken aback at her child's confidence. She and I stepped away, and she asked me if I was also a lawyer. I told her a little about our firm, and she exclaimed that she lived in Lake Forest, Illinois, and would be happy to call us with any legal needs and recommend us to her friends.

Lola bounced up and flawlessly recited the phone

number. I asked Danni if she happened to have a business card with her, and, sure enough, she pulled one out of the pocket of her slacks.

As Lola's family was about to set off to enjoy the rest of their day at the zoo, Danni beckoned the child to return to the bench. She said, "Lola, I just want you to know that I'm not really a Munchkin. I'm just a regular woman with short arms and legs. It's called dwarfism. So I'm called a dwarf."

Lola smiled, then said, "But you are good like a Munchkin."

"Thank you, Lola. You are too."

Lola, Jane and Jack left before Marnie returned. Danni and I were relaxing on the shady half of the bench when Marnie emerged from the crowd, sweat pouring down her face, and judging by her red glow, overheated. She plopped down beside us, grabbed my water bottle out of my hand, and poured what remained over her head. She said, "Where's the kid?"

"I found Lola's mom and brother," I said. "So reunited and grateful, they took off to enjoy their day."

"But not so grateful they'd wait to thank me, when I'm the one who walked seven miles for that urchin."

I stared at her. "In a dust storm, right?"

She wasn't in a mood to laugh.

As Danni and I scooted over so Marnie could sit in the shade, Danni said, "This was never about any of us wanting to be thanked by Lola's mom. But, Marnie, you did a good deed. Isn't knowing that thanks enough?"

Marnie eased herself down on her half of the bench, and said, "Not in a million years."

"What happened with the management?" I asked.

"They couldn't find the right person to ask.

Apparently, the girl misunderstood and thought I wanted to apply for a job. So, after sitting in the office for six or seven hours, I gave up and headed back here."

"It's only been thirty minutes," said Danni.

"That office wasn't air-conditioned by any chance?" I said.

Marnie huffed, then said, "What difference does that make, Heather? Do I look refreshed?"

"Guys," I said. "Let's head to the snack area for one of those cold beers that made Milwaukee famous." Marnie was still giving me the evil eye, so I added, "And burgers with a basket of fries? My treat?"

"Now that's a more appropriate expression of gratitude," said Marnie, as she mopped at her hair with napkins Danni had fished out of our backpack.

For the rest of the day, I couldn't stop thinking about it. Danni had never failed to impress me. But this was different because it had nothing to do with how she tolerated insults. Of course, I'd always known she was a kind soul. But it was more than that. The truth was, she was brilliant with that child. If the girl had come to me, I would've taken over, coddled her, and eventually found her mother. But Danni had included Lola at every step, treating her like an equal, instilling confidence, and at the end, pride. She was a natural. Danni would make a better mother than anyone I knew, but I doubted she'd ever have the opportunity. What a waste.

Chapter 21

We'd been living within yards of one another for just over three months, generally taking the same train to and from work where our offices were separated by a few feet, and our weekend girls' nights out were in each other's company. It was bound to happen. Like blowing up a balloon for a child's birthday party, even though every breath was a measure of love, the thing could only take so much.

It was a Saturday morning in mid-August, and Danni had invited us for brunch because she wanted to try out a new quiche recipe. Danni and I were in the kitchen, where she was pouring a pot of coffee into a carafe for the table when Marnie walked through the front door. As she stepped into the light in the dining area, we saw that her face was bruised, she had a black eye, and her wrists, exposed by her three-quarter length sleeves, were red and raw. Grizzly reacted to Danni's response by moaning softly.

Marnie said, "I didn't bother to try to cover it with concealer because I'm too cheap to spend a fortune on makeup for a breakfast with you guys."

Danni and I hurried to her, and I took her fingertips in mine, so not to cause her any pain.

Looking at her wrists, Danni said, "Are those rope burns?"

I whispered, "What happened?"

Marnie pulled out her customary chair and slowly lowered herself into it, in a way that imparted that her face wasn't all that was bruised. She said, "What's the new recipe, Danni? I'm starving."

"Marnie," said Danni, "what happened to you?"

"Coffee first?"

Danni was still holding the carafe, which she handed to me. I poured Marnie a cup and she took a sip. "Okay. Since you two are bent on finding out, it was one of my dates."

"We should call the police," I said.

Marnie laughed. "I'm sure I don't know his real name. Relax, guys. This is just the result of the chance you take when you're into hook-ups."

Since the food was already on the table, I poured the other two cups of coffee, and Danni and I took our seats.

It was odd, because I never shied away from adversarial exchanges at work, but taking on Marnie about this terrified me. My right hand visibly trembled as I lifted my cup, so I set it back down quickly, hoping the others hadn't noticed. I rested my hands on my lap to hide that they were shaking. "You have to stop. What you're doing is dangerous."

"Drinking coffee?"

I twisted my mouth as I tried to think how best to deal with Marnie.

Danni said, "Inviting strange guys into your apartment."

"They're not all strange. Some just like sex with no strings attached."

"But you don't know them," said Danni. "You could be murdered. Seriously."

"Well, if I were murdered, I'd consider it serious—

but then again, I'd be dead."

"Stop joking around. Danni's right. You can't keep doing this, Marnie. Why not just buy a top-quality vibrator, and slow yourself down on the self-destruction? Maybe start actually dating before bedding."

Marnie's chin had dropped a fraction of an inch just before the barrage began. She looked at me, and then Danni, but she started with me. "You're some expert on dating and true love, aren't you, Heather? You could find a date any day or night of any week, but I haven't known you to go out with a man—or a woman—a single time since we met. You locked your chastity belt and threw away the key. And why? Oh, this is rich. Because you're afraid the reason guys want to date you is that you're hot. That's like saying it's surprising that the reason we eat ice cream is that it tastes good. How do you expect to find your knight on the white stallion if you won't give any man a chance?" She paused for a moment, but she wasn't finished with me.

"But there is some consolation." She gave me an insincere smile. "If you delay dating long enough, you'll get old and wrinkled, so you'll finally be freed of your shackles. But guess what? All the good men will be married with 2.5 kids by then. I don't know what it is with you. Seriously, have you always been so paralyzed by your beauty? Have you ever actually dated, Heather?"

I took a deep breath. "You don't know anything about me, Marnie. But at least I didn't come to brunch wearing the latest in black and blue."

"Of course I know about you. You haven't been out of my sight for more than twelve hours at a time for a year. How am I not right? What do you think I'm missing?"

I was trying to appear calm, but my heart was racing. "If you really want to know, I was in love once. I was with a damn knight—for four years. And since you're so curious, we had plenty of sex. Looking back on it, I suppose it was my compensation for supporting us his last two years of law school, which he did after I'd graduated and was working. Yes. I fell in love with an asshole. I got engaged to an asshole. Of course, I didn't know it until his law school graduation party, when I found him having sex with someone in our guest bedroom."

"Oh, no!" said Danni, with her usual tenderness.

"My former best friend."

Marnie said, "I see. So that's why you chose a dwarf and a fat girl for your new best friends?"

Now it was my chin's turn to drop.

Danni said, "That's too much, Marnie. Heather was hurt badly. She has a good reason she can't trust men. Also, I think you are turning on her because you don't want to focus on what happened to you. Why can't you just stop with the hook-ups? How can sex with a stranger possibly be more important to you than your safety?"

"Danni, I know it's mean to pick on a dwarf, but how could you even remotely understand? From what you've told us, you don't even know what a sex life is. You said you're open to dating little people or tall people. So the hell what? You're not making it happen any more than Heather is. You explained about the social gatherings of little people, but you never go. You could get out there, like anybody else."

"What? Bars?"

"Of course not. Bars are meat markets, and only Heather is Grade A, USDA approved. But you could do volunteer work, join a club, or even, if you really get desperate, become a member of a church. You're doing absolutely nothing to move toward a possible dating scenario. Once you are, then we can talk about me."

"You're doing it again, Marnie," said Danni. "I asked you a question about you, and you turned around and attacked me. But I'm not defending *my* risky behavior. Say anything you want about me, but could you eventually get around to answering my question?"

"Listen, Danni. I've been under a lot more stress about our new firm than you guys. Heather got to keep her clients and her files. Two months after we opened, you had more work than you could handle because of your dwarfism. But I suffered the indignity of bringing nothing to the table for nine months. It's a well-known medical fact that sex relieves tension. Our perspectives are a little different."

I couldn't believe Marnie was dredging that up, as though I hadn't done everything in my power to move files to her. "Can you possibly be so self-absorbed that you've forgotten I pressed every one of my clients to allow you to handle their files? I introduced you to them, I helped you identify issues for articles and handouts, and I urged you to be out of the office for countless hours of business development."

"I'm not saying you didn't. I know you worked yourself sick for me. I haven't forgotten anything. But I am saying that it was especially hard for me. I've been an overachiever my whole life, and all of a sudden, I was a failure. You were upset. I was humiliated."

"Damn it all, Marnie," said Danni. "Do you have attention deficit disorder or something? It was a shitty time. We supported each other, and we prevailed. Let's talk about the real issue. According to what you've told us, you were hooking up before we met. Once you received your deserved load of work, and dazzled the courtroom with your brilliance, you still hooked up. You hooked up last night. Focus, woman! Heather and I are saying one simple thing. We think you should stop the hook-ups. We say it because we care about you. What do you say?"

Marnie grimaced, shook her head, then spoke slowly. Deliberately. "I'm not addicted to drugs, or alcohol, or even sex. I do what I do of my own free will. I'm almost thirty-three years old. I do not need or want an intervention. I think I'm just going to split. If you guys ever decide to treat me with respect—as though I'm actually an adult in full control of my faculties—we can hang out again. I think you both owe me an apology."

With that, Marnie pulled herself up from her seat, using the corner of the table for support, and walked out. Grizzly followed her to the door, then turned to look at Danni. The door slammed. The two of us were still sitting, and we didn't say a word for a moment or two.

I was still trying to process what had just happened when Danni said, "Is she right?"

"I don't know. I have to think it through." I felt completely drained.

"Think it through with me, Heather. Let's get some air with the dogs."

"Good idea. I'm sorry we didn't get to taste your quiche, Danni."

"That's okay. I'll wrap up a slice for you to have later. Let's take a deep breath. I'll meet you in front of the building in a few minutes."

I knew it would help to talk it out with Danni

because she was a wise woman—in spite of her inexperience with men. My old stomachache was starting to come back, but I tried to ignore it. As Danni and I walked down the block toward the park, we came across a tall young woman holding hands with a little boy, probably four or five years old and wearing a t-shirt and shorts. No one else was around to witness it when he pointed at us and said, "Look, Mommy. A big and a little."

Still upset about Marnie, I immediately jumped down the mom's throat. I walked up to her and said, "Ma'am, you really should teach your son not to comment out loud on people's looks."

She leaned toward me and said softly, "He was talking about the dogs."

I looked down at my white *little* standing a couple of feet from Danni's brown and black *big*. "Oh. Sorry." I hurried to escape the scene of my faux pas, requiring poor Danni to practically run to keep up with me. We crossed the street and I fell into the nearest park bench. "I'm so embarrassed, Danni. I just did something I usually try so hard to be mindful not to do. I was judgmental of a stranger. A child, no less!"

"It's okay, Heather. The mom didn't seem to be angry with you. I think she understood it was an innocent mistake."

I shook my head in disbelief at my idiocy. After taking a moment to compose myself, we resumed our walk, Chica-the-Brave prancing happily ahead of me, and handsome Grizzly always right at Danni's side. "Do you think we were unfair to Marnie?" I asked as we slowed to let my *little* do her signature walking-urination.

"She was driving me crazy with how unresponsive she was, but now, I'm trying to look at it from her point of view."

"And?"

"I'm thinking she refused to engage on the topic because she really thinks it's none of our business."

"Yeah. You know, Danni, I think we were both responding to her bruises, while she was trying to tell us it's just part of the package. And that she's old enough to make up her own mind about whether she wants that particular package."

"Plus, Marnie's not the type of person who likes to be told what to do," said Danni.

"Understatement."

"I'm not saying she's automatically oppositional, like she has a DSM-level mental disorder. Her first reaction to being corrected is just to get her back up. And that's exactly what we were doing—correcting her. I'm pretty sure the reason we didn't handle it very well is that we were both horrified by what happened to her last night."

"You think we owe her an apology?" I asked.

"About the way we handled it, yes."

"Me too. We were out of line. Also, the way she punched back was just Marnie trying to get us to lay off by reminding us that we don't have perfect love lives either—to put it mildly." I paused to use a plastic baggie to pick up one of Chica-the-Brave's tootsie rolls. "It was tough to listen to though."

"The truth always is."

Once we'd cleaned up after both dogs, Danni and I were ready to head back to talk to Marnie. We marched straight to her door, Grizzly and Chica-the-Brave in tow.

I knocked and Marnie swung the door open a moment later. She stood in her doorway, arms crossed over her chest, and said nothing. When Grizzly leaned forward, buried his head in his paws, and whimpered, Marnie burst out laughing.

"I accept your apology, Danni." She then turned to me.

"I'm sorry Chica-the-Brave can't do this for me. I handled that badly. I apologize. Danni and I think it was the shock of seeing someone we love battered and bruised. We still hope you'll choose not to risk it again, but it's not for us to tell you how to live your life."

She stepped back to allow us to enter her apartment and waved us into the living room. Three mimosas in champagne glasses sat on the glass coffee table. Danni and I took seats on the black leather loveseat, Marnie across from us on the couch. Marnie handed out wet wipes for our hands, then passed out the drinks. "I knew you guys would see the light. Also, Danni, I have to admit I almost peed my pants trying not to laugh when you said to me, 'Focus, woman!' It was so funny coming from you since you usually treat me so gingerly." We leaned in and clinked our glasses to Marnie's toast, "To friends." Grizzly had curled up in a wide patch of sunlight on the white throw-rug, wrapped around Chica-the-Brave like she was the center of a cinnamon roll.

Marnie took a long sip of her drink, then said, "I was watching you guys out my window. Heather, I saw you confront the little boy's mother, with the look of an avenging angel. What could she possibly have done to deserve that?"

When I told her, Marnie fell off her couch laughing—one of *her* signature moves. She'd temporarily forgotten about her bruises, and needed both me and Danni to help her back up. Once she got resettled, I said, "Marnie, Danni and I agree never again to tell you how to live your life. You're a big girl."

Marnie raised her eyebrows. "I'm the one who is supposed to say that." She grabbed a pencil from the end table, and flicked a pretend cigar ash at me.

"Oops. You know what I mean."

"I do. And because you two saw so quickly that I deserved an apology, I've decided to tell you the truth about me."

Danni and I exchanged a glance.

"I'm actually a skinny woman in a fat suit."

Danni said, "What?"

Typical Marnie humor. I said, "Seriously. What is it?"

She smiled. "Seriously, I am the only child of a mathematics professor and a former professional ballerina. My issues with food began when I was five, the year my mother turned cold toward me. To this day, I don't know what caused the change in temperature, but I have a couple of theories. One is that my parents, who were very formal and proper, weren't fans of my silliness, and efforts to make them laugh. The way they responded embarrassed and frightened me. I felt like I was losing their love. My other theory is kind of Freudian. I've looked at the family photo albums, and before I put on the weight, I was an exquisitely beautiful child. So, I've wondered whether my crazy mother might actually have been threatened by me. All I know for sure is that once she went sub-zero, I started sneaking food because it made me feel more secure—it was how I comforted myself. As I started to put on pounds, my father grew more remote, as well, so I put on more."

I was shocked to hear Marnie open up about her weight. I started to perspire as though I were the one revealing my secrets.

"As a little girl, I loved to dance, and I begged my mother to let me take lessons. Her response was that it wouldn't be fair to the corps de ballet to have a person of my girth disrupt the visual harmony of their performances. Of course, she knew the dance school would include me in any productions I qualified for, based on the merit of my dancing alone. It was Mother who didn't want me up on a stage. I asked about jazz and tap, and received the same response. She wondered what was wrong with me that I was too selfish to see the problem. She suggested piano, which I studied until I was old enough to refuse—at thirteen. To this day, I won't touch one. In fact, I can't abide being in the same room with a piano."

"I'm so sorry," I said. I felt pressure around my eyes and knew I wouldn't be able to hold back my tears much longer.

"Oh, there's more. My father never said a word about my weight in my presence. He would just cock his head, ever so slightly, if I asked for seconds of anything. He would invariably glance at my plate to see how much I'd taken, before my fork was even in my hand. When I was growing up, it was the only thing I ever heard my folks argue about. The debate seemed to be about whose fault it was. Now, on the few occasions they visit, he still looks through my pantry, and in my fridge, as if to say, 'I rest my case.' "

"Oh, Marnie," was all I could think to say, as the tears started down my cheeks. But she continued, dry-eyed.

"The truth is, I have a treadmill in my bedroom—grist for a joke when I have a guy over. I throw some clothes on it and deadpan about using it as a closet. Actually, I run on the thing for forty-five minutes every morning, but not because of my weight. I carry my fat mainly in my belly, which is the most dangerous spot in terms of cardiac health. Do I wish I weren't fat? I think Danni can answer for me. Do you wish you weren't a dwarf?" Without waiting for Danni to respond, Marnie said, "The answer has to be no. Because wishing such a thing would be wishing away my identity, and all my experiences. I would be a totally different person, since the 'me' I am would be eviscerated. I've never once wished I didn't exist."

"Yeah. That's right," Danni whispered.

"I've read the literature, so I understand how my childhood trauma explains my addiction. But that's all it does. It makes sense to me that I'm trying to fill up the hole that should've been brimming over with unconditional parental love. I appreciate knowing, but that doesn't make the hole disappear." She paused for a moment. "It makes me insane when I hear people say things like, 'It comes down to calories in versus calories burned,' or 'It's all a matter of self-control.' That's like saying to a drug addict, 'It's simple. Just quit using the cocaine.' Or to a chain-smoker, 'Easy-peasy. Just quit.' Or to an alcoholic, 'You just have to choose to stop drinking.' No intelligent person would say any of those things. But everyone vilifies overeaters."

So, there it was. Marnie saw her weight problem as an addiction. I had no doubt she was right. She was a brilliant woman, and probably at least as introspective as anyone else. Her explanation made sense to me. Of course, she knew that recovery was a possibility. But it was clear she wanted to deal with it in her own way—and in her own time. I could actually feel my heart aching for her.

She continued, "So, I'm damn well going to give myself unconditional love, since that's likely the only place it will ever come from." She took a sip, then tipped her champagne flute to us. "Friends, we all have the same issue—for different reasons, our packaging just doesn't demand true love. And no decent man has bothered to look inside. The way the world works, probably none ever will." Marnie stopped to drain her glass, and set it down on the coffee table. Then she turned to me. "Now it's your turn. Your story of the evil fiancé explains you a bit. But I suspect there's more."

I used the backs of my hands to wipe the tears from my cheeks. I looked over at Grizzly and Chica-the-Brave without focusing on them as I composed myself, but I still felt nervous about getting the words out. I swallowed hard, and forced myself to speak. "You're good, Marnie. There is more. When I was ten years old, I was sexually abused by a good friend of my parents—on Christmas Day. He had stopped by our house with gifts from himself and his wife for my brothers and me. When everyone else went outside to try out the boys' skateboards, I stayed in my room to introduce my new doll to my older ones. The guy must have told the others he needed to run in to use the bathroom or something. But where he came was into my room. He didn't even try to make it seem normal. He picked me up and held me against his front, and I could feel his bulge, although I didn't understand it. He ran his hands under my shirt, then underneath my underpants. He said never to tell, or he'd hurt my little brothers. Then he hurried into the bathroom, no doubt to finish what he'd started."

I was amazed I'd been able to tell the story without falling apart. And as I looked at my friends, I knew immediately why it was, and why Marnie had been able to tell us her story. We were all in the presence of unconditional love.

Marnie slammed her fist into her other hand, and said, "I'd like to finish what he started. Fucking asshole." After a pause, she said, "Did you tell your parents?"

"Yeah. And they believed me right away, since they knew I wouldn't make up something like that. Also, they could tell how upset I was. My folks decided not to call the police because they didn't want to drag me through that whole thing. Although Mom started taking me to a therapist a few days later, I've really never gotten over it. The breach of trust was so sudden and unexpected, it made me wonder how anyone can really trust anybody, in any setting—much less in a romantic relationship. When I was with my ex-fiancé, I thought I'd conquered it. But he did rather set me back to square one."

Danni, who was trembling and biting her lower lip, said, "I'm so sorry."

Marnie said, "Give me the pervert's name and I'll have some of my hook-up friends take care of him. Maybe the guy from last night—at least we know he's good with his fists."

"Oh, Marnie, don't talk like that," said Danni while she cringed.

"Fine. Then just give me the ex-fiancé's name, and Danni and Grizzly and I can go give him a fright he won't forget."

"Thanks. I'll think about it. The thing is, I've never told anyone about the abuse before—except for my parents and my therapist. Apparently, my dad had a frank conversation with the guy and threatened him with a police complaint if he ever came near our family again. I never saw him or heard from him after the day it happened. If my brothers ever got wind of it, they'd react like you did, Marnie. They'd go after him and not worry about being subtle about it, which would probably mean little to him and ruin their lives." I took a deep breath. "I am glad I told you guys. It's not something I thought I'd ever be able to do." I gave them a little smile. At that moment, I felt exactly as though an elephant had been sitting on my chest for years and had finally decided to get up.

"What happened to you was so wrong that all I can think about is revenge," said Marnie. "So keep that in mind, Heather. It may not be important to you, but it would make me feel a hell of a lot better."

I promised again to consider it.

She added, "The truth is, we can understand each other a lot better when we know shit like this." She turned to Danni. "Your turn. But remember, you already told us about the suicide attempt, so that one doesn't count. Lay it on us, Danni. What's the real reason you're not dating?"

"I am dating." She said it in such a soft voice, I wasn't sure I'd heard correctly.

"What?" Marnie and I said at the same time.

"I'm dating. What's the big deal? People do it, you know. And I understand this much, Marnie, all sex isn't hook-ups."

"You've had sex?" asked Marnie.

"None of your business. And why shouldn't I?"

Marnie laughed. "You should. But how did you manage to keep your dating from Heather and me?"

"Actually, you've both met him."

I said, "I don't understand. I can't remember meeting your boyfriend. And that's something I'd recall, Danni."

Danni gave me a little smile. "It was you who introduced him to me and Marnie."

Marnie and I both sat back, searching our memory banks. Marnie said, "Not the cute guy who walked in with the two morons the day we moved in?"

"Yep. His name is Sam."

"But, Danni, his friends were horrible to you," I said.

"That's why he came back to my apartment later that night—to apologize again. See, those guys were just old high school friends from Central Illinois. They were staying with him to save on a hotel so they could sightsee in Chicago. As soon as they left, after Grizzly growled at them, Sam asked them to find another place to stay.

"I see," I said, unconvinced for the simple reason that I always felt protective of Danni, although I tried to hide it. "What does Sam do?"

"He's at Northwestern in a five-year social work doctoral program, with two more years to go."

"How long have you been seeing him?" asked Marnie.

"Actually, we had our very first physical contact over a year ago."

I shook my head as I did the math. "That can't be right. That would've been before we even moved in."

"Wait," said Marnie. "He's the guy who saved you

on the train platform, isn't he?"

"Same guy."

"Damn. I remember you saying there was something familiar about him when he brought us the beer and the two idiots."

"But we've just been dating since we moved in. So, almost three and a half months."

"What do you do together? Do you go out on dates?" I asked, then immediately felt stupid. *Why shouldn't they?*

"Yes. Just like a regular couple. I told him I prefer we go out on Friday nights, rather than Saturdays, because I knew Marnie would be unavailable on Fridays. I reserved my Saturday nights for the three of us."

"I'm glad of that," I said. "You know, it's pretty amazing that neither Marnie nor I have bumped into you two when you were together—considering we live in the same building."

She sat up straighter and held her hands together on her lap, the picture of composure. "That was intentional. Actually, there were a couple of reasons. First of all, I wanted to make sure it was real before I told you."

Marnie said, "Three and a half months is probably real."

Danni smiled. "I know."

"And the second reason?" I said.

"I know you guys aren't dating."

"You thought we'd be jealous?" asked Marnie.

"More like I didn't want you to feel worse."

I leaned over to give her a hug. Marnie smiled and threw her a kiss. "Oh, Danni," I said. "I'm just thrilled for you." And I really was. But I was also suspicious of the guy and couldn't help worrying she'd be hurt.

"Me too," said Marnie. "And anytime you want tips on positions—"

Danni rolled her eyes.

Chapter 22

I wasn't so oblivious that I didn't realize I might be doing the same thing to Danni that had gotten me, and her, in trouble with Marnie the previous weekend. But I couldn't help myself. I waited to make my move until I knew Danni was out on her customary long weekend afternoon walk with Grizzly. I took the stairs to the second floor, confident I wouldn't run into Marnie, who favored the elevator. Praying he'd be home, I knocked on the door of apartment 217.

Sam, wearing blue jeans and a light-green polo shirt, opened the door. "Hello, Heather. I've been expecting you."

That threw me off. As I reached out to shake his hand, I said, "Why?"

"Come on in."

I glanced around at his simply furnished rooms, neat in all respects except for the dining table, which was covered with piles of books and papers. He followed my gaze, then said, "The place is a mess. Sorry. I've been working on my dissertation. Let's sit in the living room."

The sitting area offered the choice of the plaid full-size couch, or one of the two corduroy upholstered armchairs. I took one of those, rather than disturb the large, slumbering black poodle on the sofa, and Sam sat down across from me in the other. "Would you like something to drink?"

"No, thanks. I'm good."

"Terrific. What can I do for you?"

"First of all, you can tell me why you said you'd been expecting me."

He gave me a gentle, close-mouthed smile, his brown eyes soft and thoughtful. "Danni figured you'd stop by to check me out at some point."

"Check you out in what sense?"

"In the sense of your urge to protect her."

"Shit. I didn't realize I was that transparent. I hope she doesn't think I'm acting maternal."

"It's not that. Danni doesn't view it as a negative that you care about her and her inexperienced heart. She just knows you well enough to have predicted your visit."

"Oh, my." I considered hightailing it out of there, but stubbornly decided to dig myself into a deeper hole, instead. "Well, since we've cut right through to it, I do have some questions." He started to say something, but I cut him off. "Listen, Sam, I'm fully aware of the fact that I'm intruding. So, feel free to tell me this is none of my business. Of course, you are both adults, and fully competent to make your own choices."

"Ah. You don't want a repeat of the Marnie intervention."

"Danni really does tell you everything."

"I doubt that. But we do share a lot with each other, since we've grown close." He leaned toward me and said, "What are your concerns, Heather?"

I realized I'd been tapping my right foot, but Sam's warm demeanor allowed me to stop. "To start with, I don't think I ever forgave you for the scene in Danni's apartment the day we moved in."

"I haven't forgiven myself either. Those boys were old friends from high school, who seem not to have evolved emotionally from their fifteen-year-old selves. They aren't close friends. In fact, I'm quite sure I'll never see them again—at least, if I have anything to do with it. It was when I went back to see Danni to apologize later that evening that she and I had our first long conversation. You know what an amazing woman she is."

"There's no doubt of that." I crossed my ankles and worked to look composed. "She says you've been seeing each other regularly since then, although Marnie and I knew nothing about it. Are you trying to keep your relationship below the radar?"

"I'm not. But Danni didn't want to tell you and Marnie because she knows neither of you is dating, and she didn't want to rub it in your faces that she is."

"Right."

"We do go out to dinner or a movie, almost always on Friday evenings since the three of you wouldn't be doing anything together in light of Marnie's activities on that night of the week."

"Logical. I tend to stay in and relax with a movie with Chica-the-Brave, knowing I'll see my friends on Saturday evening. That explains it."

"Danni and I talk, at least briefly, almost every night. And she and Grizzly often join Buddy and me for early morning walks on weekends." He glanced at the slumbering animal. "Heather, any day I can be with Danni, or speak with her, is a good day."

"Okay. Now I'm really going to step over some boundaries, so feel free to clam up." At that point, I could feel the start of the familiar chest constriction. "But,

Sam, you're an attractive man of average stature."

"Thanks. But I don't think five feet, five inches qualifies as average height for an American male."

"You know what I mean. You're not a dwarf."

"Now I think I will get myself a glass of water." He stood. "Anything for you?"

"Water would be great. Thanks."

As Sam walked into the kitchenette, I noticed that while not a tall man, his build was classic. He was trim with broad shoulders, and looked good in his blue jeans. He returned and we each took several long sips of our waters.

"Heather, I have one sibling, a beloved sister, two years younger than me. Joanne has Down Syndrome. Maybe she's the reason I tend to evaluate people based on character, kindness, and courage. Perhaps I would've been like this even if Joanne weren't in my life. I really have no way to know. But what I do know is that Danni is the most interesting, and understanding, and the bravest woman I've ever known."

I took the long sip of water I needed to go on. "Me too. I want her for a close friend, and I always will. But, Sam, she thinks her relationship with you is romantic. She believes your outings are dates. I just want to make sure you two are on the same page."

He pursed his lips and looked up at the ceiling for a moment before answering. "With all due respect, Heather, that sounds a little condescending." He paused. "Listen. When I look at Danni, I see a beautiful woman. I see her radiant smile, the playfulness in her blue eyes, the way her hair falls over her cheeks when she tosses back her head to laugh." Sam's face actually lit up as he described her. "Danni is the most delightful woman I've ever had the good fortune to meet. I certainly hope she thinks my interest is romantic."

"Are you saying her dwarfism didn't give you pause at all?"

He took a moment, looking down at the glass in his hands. He cleared his throat. When he looked up at me, he said, "I'd be lying if I claimed the stares didn't bother me, at first. But she doesn't let them bother her. So, I had to decide whether to protect my fragile ego at the cost of the most wonderful woman I've ever met. The truth is, every time I step into Danni's presence, I feel uplifted. She imparts joy, optimism, and fearlessness, none of which I've ever before seen in a single person in such abundance—and I don't plan to lose her over little things like the length of her limbs, or the rudeness of others. I adore her."

I was pretty sure my mouth hung open. The truth was, before I walked through his door, I hadn't been sure a man like Sam could be interested in a woman of Danni's stature. But now I was thunder-struck that someone could be so true. Sam was in love, and I felt amazement and profound envy. Of course, I didn't want Sam. But I dared to think there might be someone out there with a Sam-like heart who could feel that way about me.

I rose, and when Sam extended his arm, I gave him a hug rather than a handshake. I headed for his door, then turned to him and said, "Thanks, Sam. I'm really happy for you guys."

Out in the hallway, I let out a deep breath. But as I ran back up through the stairwell, I was still a little bit worried for Danni. Although I had no doubt Sam was sincere, I couldn't help wondering how long it would last. Of course, I appreciated that I was doing some heavy-duty projecting.

Chapter 23

Early during the last week of September, Jeanne tapped on my door, stepped in, and announced that she had a bit of information on Annie I would probably appreciate knowing. Before I could slow her down, Jeanne said, "She turns thirty on Friday. I'll bring in a cake from my favorite bakery."

"Thank you. That sounds great."

She remained standing in my doorway, and I realized she wanted me to tell her what the partners planned to do to celebrate Annie.

"Marnie and Danni and I will take her out to dinner—whichever night this weekend she's not celebrating with Bradley."

Jeanne said, "Lovely," stepped back, and closed the door behind her. I felt only a little manipulated by Jeanne since her pushing was always toward the good.

Marnie and Danni and I had planned to go out to dinner in Evanston on Saturday night, but downtown Chicago would be much more convenient for Annie. I stopped by to confirm the revised plan with my partners, then asked Annie if she could find time to be our guest for dinner on the weekend. Fortunately, her date with Bradley was planned for Friday, her actual birthday. I asked Annie if she had a favorite restaurant, and she explained that she seldom went out to eat and would be thrilled with whatever I chose.

Riding home together on the train that evening, we kicked around some ideas for good restaurants and agreed on Valentino's.

****

The three of us were alike in that we were all frugal to a fault. So, on Saturday evening, we took the train downtown, then grabbed a cab for the short ride to the restaurant. Although we arrived ten minutes early, the hostess seated us right away, and promised to bring Annie to our table.

I always enjoyed seeing my friends dressed up for an evening out and was just complimenting Marnie and Danni on their outfits when I saw Annie walking towards us. She actually looked like a different person in a pale blue sleeveless silk drop-waist dress with a knife-pleated skirt that rippled when she walked. The dress hit a couple of inches above her knees, accentuating her long legs. Her wrap was an intricately embroidered off-white shawl. She was also wearing more dramatic makeup than what she wore to the office—if she wore any. I'd always thought her coloring was such that she didn't really need any improvement. It wasn't that she looked overly made-up. It was more that she was stunning.

Danni said, "You're gorgeous, Annie. I don't remember that turning thirty made me beautiful."

Annie laughed. "That's because you were already beautiful."

As a waiter pulled out a chair for her, we all said, "Happy birthday!"

"Shall we sing it?" asked Marnie.

As she placed her napkin on her lap, she looked at Marnie and said, "Thanks. But please don't. I get embarrassed."

Marnie said, "We won't. But it's hard for me to believe you get embarrassed."

"Oh, not for myself. I'd be embarrassed for you guys." She smiled.

"As well you should be," I said. "What will you have to drink?"

"Just white wine. I don't drink hard liquor."

"On principle?" asked Danni.

"I don't get drunk on principle. I don't drink the hard stuff because I don't like the taste."

A waiter came by to take our drink orders, and I noticed he looked at Annie the same way men often looked at me. It wasn't so much a leer as an intense focus—more like interest or appreciation. Our white wines arrived a few minutes later, and we all toasted Annie.

"I know you're from the south side of Chicago," said Danni. "Have you lived there your whole life?"

"When my parents had my brothers, they were just starting out and didn't have much money. They were happy to get a spot in a newer housing project."

"You didn't tell us you have siblings," said Marnie.

"You didn't ask me," Annie said while adjusting her shawl.

"That's true. So, they're older than you?"

"They're twins, actually. Malcolm and Martin are three years older than me."

"I like the names," I said. "Did they hang out with you when you were kids?"

"Not really. They were both into anything athletic, so they tended to run around with the neighborhood boys, finding pick-up basketball and baseball games."

"How did you all get along?" asked Danni.

"We lived in a rough neighborhood, so they played the role of my protectors. They'd always say, 'Nobody messes with Angelina,' and the phrase stuck. By seventh grade, they were both football players, so everybody took them at their word. I didn't really need to learn how to fight, but I kept my eyes open and had a pretty good idea how to defend myself."

"Defend yourself?" asked Danni.

Annie smiled and shook her head. "You guys have no idea what I'm talking about. Do you?"

Marnie said, "My home life was also rough, but it was psychological beatings."

"That's bad, for sure. But not the same," said Annie.

Danni said, "Obviously, my short arms and legs weren't exactly lethal weapons."

"I'm clueless, too," I said.

"I think I'd prefer not to spend this evening educating you guys about life on the mean streets. But I will say I'm closer with my brothers now that we've all grown up."

"Did they become football players?" asked Danni.

"No. When they turned eighteen, they both joined the Army. They did the math, and decided they'd be safer in Afghanistan than on the streets of our neighborhood. It worked out well for them. They're both career Army, and happy to be where they are."

Our waiter stopped by and Marnie ordered a couple of appetizers, calamari, and polenta bites with wild mushrooms and fontina. Then she said, "You told us you went to SIU, but how did you decide to go to college?"

Annie took a sip of her wine, then eased herself back in her chair. "No one else in my family had gone. Mama worked in retail. Once my dad passed, she took as many hours as she could get, and lived for a chance at overtime. She didn't have a formal second job. She did babysit whenever she wasn't at work—but only if the child could be dropped at our house. She always made sure she was at home in the evenings and on weekends."

"So, it just came naturally to you to love reading and studying?" asked Danni.

Annie nodded at her, then said, "Not at all. I was just a regular girl. I liked dolls when I was little, TV and music as I got older, then boys when I reached my teens. Of course, most of the boys didn't want to spend much time with me, fearing a whupping from my brothers."

"Then how did you come to be serious about your studies?" I asked.

"I can answer that for you, but only if you three will tell me sometime how you did."

I smiled. "Danni's story on that is probably the most interesting. But sure. We can do that."

"In that case, I'm happy to share. But let's order our dinners first, since I don't think octopus legs are going to be my thing."

"I'm sorry, Annie," said Marnie. "I should've asked you."

Just as Marnie finished speaking, the waiter placed on the table the appetizers Marnie had ordered and a basket of a variety of hot breads, a plate of olive oil, and a crystal bowl filled with tiny ice cubes and butter pats. Annie said, "Now, bread is my thing."

"Demonstrably unfair," said Marnie. "How can you love bread and be so slender?"

"Metabolism."

"Then I definitely hate you."

After we'd ordered our entrees, Annie said, "Are

you sure you want to hear more about me?"

"You're the most interesting person at this table," said Marnie.

Danni cleared her throat, and Marnie added, "Except for the dwarf."

Danni and Marnie laughed, and my old habit of shaking my head at the two of them made a reappearance.

"When I was in fourth grade, the whole class of ten-year-olds was called into the auditorium one afternoon. Our principal introduced two church ladies from southern Illinois, and one of them told us about a summer camp in her area. She ran through a power-point presentation of pictures of the place as she talked. It was in the mountains of the Shawnee National Forest, and had several lakes for swimming and boating, and one small pond called Serenity Pool, which campers would ride their horses to, go swimming, cook their dinners over a fire, and then spend the night before riding back to the cabins the next day. There were ten separate units with six cabins, each designed for either four girls or four boys, depending on the session. The campers would also get to do archery, crafts, and lots of hiking. All of the children on the pictures had big smiles on their suntanned faces, and the sky was the color of that blue dishwashing liquid."

I frequently couldn't tell when Annie was kidding. She paused to take a bite of one of the warm rolls.

"Then the lady said the magic words, 'Anyone in your class who would like to attend the camp may do so at no charge. Our church will drive you to the camp in our van and pay for all of your meals and crafts. It's up to each of you whether you choose to earn the free week at camp.'

"Well, at that point, I would've sold my brothers to go, but earning camp had nothing to do with money. There were just two requirements. In the second semester of school that year, you had to earn a 3.5 GPA, and you had to read seven books from a list the ladies handed out and do a two-page report on each storybook and what it meant to you. Bear in mind that, up until that day, I was a C student, which was purely a matter of lack of effort. I had no particular reason to do better than that, so I didn't. But starting that night, I attacked my homework like my life depended on it."

"Did you earn camp that year?" asked Danni.

"That year, and every one after it through twelfth."

The waiter returned, and we took our time deciding on our dinner orders.

"Were there other Black campers there?" I asked.

"Just the ones who took the bus down with me. But we were dispersed among the units, so I was the only one in our group that first year."

"How did that go?" asked Marnie.

"Fine. After I established myself." She raised her eyebrows.

"Tell us," said Danni.

Annie nodded. "Well, the first year, I was in a cabin with three girls from Kentucky who were classmates and close friends. They spoke with heavy twangy accents, and I suspected they were like the crackers I'd heard about from Ala-freaking-bama. Naturally, I was a little bit afraid of them. The first night, they put a frog in each of my sneakers while I was asleep. Luckily, I saw the critters before I smushed them with my feet, but I was livid. Since my brothers always protected me, it must've been through osmosis that I'd learned about bullies. I knew I had no choice but to fight back, or they'd pick on me for my whole week at camp, ruining everything I'd dreamed of.

"I waited until we had all stepped out of the cabin to head to the lodge for breakfast. We walked together down the dirt road, the three of them chatting with each other, while they ignored me. I hurried a few feet ahead of them and turned to look at them. 'You guys put frogs in my shoes. Don't ever do anything like that again.' The tallest of the three said, 'Who's gonna stop us?' I walked up to her, stuck one foot behind hers, and pushed. Then I threw myself on top of her and put my hands on her shoulders. It wasn't hard to keep her down."

Danni finished the appetizer on her plate, and pushed her dish away. "But you were outnumbered."

"Apparently they were too surprised to think of it. I was holding down the one I figured was the ringleader. She kept yelling, 'Let me up!' I said, 'Repeat after me, nobody messes with Angelina.' She finally said it, and I let her up. Then I turned to the next girl. I started towards her, and she yelled, 'Nobody messes with Angelina.' Same reaction from the third." Annie paused to take another bite of her buttered roll, then looked away for a moment, before returning to us.

"How did they treat you after that?" I asked.

"Never had a problem with them again. In fact, it turned out that they liked adventure as much as I did. People started calling us 'the fearless four.'"

Marnie said, "I believe at least one of the four was fearless," and tipped her wine glass to Annie. "What did the four of you do?"

"Crazy stuff. We talked a counselor into letting us

go on an all-night hike with her. I climbed the tall flagpole at the front entrance to the camp when the flag got caught up there and no one knew how to get it down. We got one of the wilder counselors to let us gallop our horses through a field after a trail ride. And we all climbed through the scariest horizontal split rocks, 'Certain Death' and 'Say Your Prayers,' which no one else was willing to try."

I said, "I'm a little claustrophobic. There's no way I'd put myself in the center of a rock sandwich." Marnie and Danni nodded. "Did you see those three again after your first year?"

"Oh, yeah. We were always able to get a cabin together. I only understood about seventy-five percent of what they said since their accents were so heavy. But we had a ball."

Danni let out a long sigh. "Okay. Annie wins the most interesting person at the table competition."

"Doubtful," said Annie. "You guys just haven't told me about your childhoods. I don't think it's possible to have an uninteresting childhood."

"You might be surprised," I said.

Marnie looked at me and said, "I am curious about how you dealt with your cover-girl looks as a kid, Heather."

"Seriously?"

"Yeah. How did you?" asked Danni.

I studied my placemat for a minute while I thought about how to explain. "Honestly, it was a non-issue until I got to college. As a child, I was a nerd and a tom-boy. I only wore a dress for church, or my school uniform. I kept my hair in a long braid down my back, all through high school. Since I went to an all-girl academy, I saw no reason to waste my money on makeup, for a bunch of girls. And I was pretty shy. Actually, I'd say I was an introvert on the playground, and an extrovert in the classroom."

"I was like that," said Danni.

"And then?" asked Annie.

I smiled at her, and again took a moment to organize my thoughts. "I got more socially confident once I moved away from my hometown. College through law school, through today have all been pretty much the same. I try to dress appropriately—like everybody else. I wear just enough make-up to look like I bothered. I've never in my life gone for super-short skirts or low-cut tops."

"Yeah. That would be overkill," said Marnie.

"So that's my boring answer." I looked among my friends, who seemed to be expecting more.

Marnie said, "Thanks for the bare-bones information. We'll worm the rest out of you eventually."

I laughed, relieved to be moving on.

Once our meals arrived, we got to talking about politics and discovered Annie thought pretty much like we did when it came to the hot-button issues. Afterwards, I asked Annie if she'd like a dessert or an after-dinner drink. She said, "Remember, I only drink wine. But I'll have dessert if they offer anything with bread in it."

Marnie rolled her eyes, "Now you're just rubbing it in."

As luck would have it, the dessert selection included bread pudding with Bourbon sauce. In response to Annie's question, the waiter explained that the pastry chef couldn't leave out the sauce because it's infused into the pudding.

Annie smiled, then said, "Fine. I'll try it. But only if you three will help me eat it. Honestly, one more bite for me, and it'll be gluttony."

"I feel the same way," said Danni. "But I'm willing to risk it to help you out, Annie."

"I'm in," said Marnie.

We finished off the dessert, and my partners and I took care of the bill.

We'd agreed ahead of time to take a cab to Millennium Park after dinner for a little walk before heading to a bar. As we made our way toward the restaurant's front door, Danni went first, which made it impossible for the rest of us not to notice the stares. Annie, who was directly behind Danni, must've gotten the brunt of it. Apparently, by the time she and Danni reached the revolving door, she'd had her fill. Annie turned on her heel and looked from one to the other of the people seated near the door who were still gawking. Without raising her voice, she said, "Have your mothers taught you no manners?" as she dramatically shook her head at them.

Once we got out on the sidewalk, she knelt on one knee to address Danni. "How long has this been going on?"

Danni answered quietly, "My whole life."

"Well, if it happens in my presence, I'm calling it out."

"Annie, I respect what you did," I said. "But Marnie and I have decided to leave that up to Danni. So far, she's preferred to ignore the rudeness."

"We come from different places, Heather. Ignoring bullies isn't on my play-list."

Danni said, "Thanks. You do whatever feels right to you, Annie. I won't be any more or less embarrassed either way. I like to think I carry my invulnerability with me—like a turtle's shell."

I'd waved as soon as we came through the door, and the cabbie finally made it to our side of the intersection. I jumped in the front seat with the driver so we could all fit in the one car. After a five-minute ride, the cab got stuck in traffic a block west of Michigan Avenue, so I paid the fare, and we slipped out the doors on both sides.

There was an alley half-way between where we alighted and our destination, which was an entrance to the park on the east side of Michigan Avenue. Just as we reached the alley to our left, I sensed a quick movement, and two scruffy-looking, thirty-something White guys who smelled of urine were in our faces. I heard a loud click, and one of them flashed a knife. The other said, "Your purses! Now!"

Mine was wrapped over my shoulder and I immediately began to pull the strap over my head, but I got it stuck in my hair barrette because I was shaking so badly. Danni also fumbled with hers, which was also wrapped over her shoulder. Marnie said, "I don't carry a purse."

"Then give me your money, bitch," said the first man, the one with a light growth of beard and the knife.

Annie stepped forward, her dressy evening bag in her hand. "You are welcome to my purse full of money." She looked right at them, and added, "But I'll just keep my baby's picture," as she snapped open the purse, and reached inside.

Marnie said, quite loudly, "Avert your eyes, scoundrels. I need to dig down into my bra to get my cash." She pulled her wrap-style dress down in the front to reveal most of one of her photogenic mammaries, and the men couldn't help but look.

Just at that second, Annie took a spread-eagle stance, arms straight out, gripping a handgun with both hands. We heard the unmistakable sound of the hammer being cocked. She said, "Get the hell out of here, assholes. Now!" As they ran back through the alley, she yelled after them, "And for Christ's sake, remember, nobody messes with Angelina!"

A small crowd gathered on the sidewalk, and I saw someone making a quick call on a cell-phone. The last thing we needed was for the police to arrest Annie for possession of a firearm without a permit. I managed to flag down the cab we'd jumped out of only moments before which had advanced no more than a car-length in the crowded intersection. As I jumped back into the front seat, I heard some of the passersby saying, "Who's Angelina?"

Once we slammed the doors, the traffic light changed and I asked the driver to take us to a bar on the near north side. If we'd remained in the vicinity, there was no way the police wouldn't find a group of four women made up of a dwarf, a tall Black woman, an obese woman and a tall blonde. Apparently, the cabbie hadn't seen what happened. In any event, he didn't say a word as we sailed north on Michigan Avenue. We all held our silence until he dropped us off at the bar. By then, we were ready to explode with our opinions on what had happened.

Marnie said, "Very cool, Annie Oakley. I hope my breast display helped." She winked at Annie.

"Who is Annie Oakley?" asked Danni. When no one

answered, she said, "Wait. Marnie, you knew Annie had a gun in her purse?"

"I kinda figured."

"How?"

"'You're welcome to my purse full of money, but I'll just remove a picture first.' Who says something like that?"

I mumbled, "And who says, 'avert your eyes, scoundrels, so I can dig into my bra'?"

Marnie ignored me and continued. "Unless, of course, she really wants to get into the purse. We all just heard about Annie's over-protective Army brothers. So, I just assumed it was a pistol—or a hand grenade."

I said, "Very funny, Marnie. But guys, they just wanted our purses. If I'm remembering correctly, you need a permit to carry a concealed handgun in Chicago. Do you have a permit?"

"No."

"Seriously, Annie, our purses aren't worth your law license."

Danni said, "I'm still in shock. Literally. My hands are trembling, and my tongue is dry. Heather, I don't have the same confidence that they wouldn't have taken our purses *and* stabbed us. From my perspective, that knife blade was awfully close to my face."

Annie waited until we'd all spoken. "Anything else?"

No one said a word. "Okay then. They were bullies, Heather. And Danni's right. There was no guarantee for our safety even if we threw all our money at them. Their eyes looked funny to me. Probably drugs."

Danni said, "Why did it look like you'd done that before?"

Annie smiled. "Actually, in the year after undergrad, I trained at the Police Academy. That was before I decided to go to law school."

Marnie screwed up her face. "Seriously?"

"Of course not. I would've told you."

Annie's idea of humor was just like Marnie's. "Then what explains your cop-like stance?" I asked.

"I have a television."

"I see. But an illegal handgun?"

"I don't have a handgun, legal or illegal."

"Now you're definitely messing with us," said Marnie. "We saw it. We heard it."

"It's a toy."

"It didn't sound like a toy," I said.

"It's a very good toy. My brothers got it for me."

"Wonderful," I said. "Do you know how many Black people have been shot by White cops for less than that?"

Annie held my gaze. "In fact, I'm familiar with each and every case. The thing is, I know how to handle myself with White people."

I'd embarrassed myself. As if I could possibly know more about police brutality. I didn't say another word about it.

Marnie said, "I'm glad you're on our side. Now that we know Annie isn't a felon, and that she may well have saved our lives, can we continue our little party inside of this bar, rather than this lovely, but chilly, sidewalk?"

Danni said, "Yes," and headed for the front door. Before she reached for the handle, she turned to us and said, "But someday, I want us all to go to Millennium Park together. I'd love to stand in front of the Bean with you guys, so you could each see in your reflection how you'd look as a dwarf."

"I wouldn't miss it," I said, as I held the door open for Danni. I couldn't begin to fathom what an experience like that might mean to her—or to us. But I suspected it would be too damn poignant to bear.

"I'd love to do it," said Annie.

"Me too," said Marnie. "For now, let's celebrate being alive. And guys, for Heaven's sake, please try to remember that nobody messes with the birthday girl."

By that point, I was worn out from all the excitement, and just wanted to sit down with a glass of wine. As we entered the bar, Marnie spotted a table opening up and grabbed it for us.

Chapter 24

Because we'd promised Danni to get together again to visit the Bean—this time we hoped uninterrupted by knife-wielding robbers—we headed for Millennium Park one delightfully Indian-summerish Saturday in mid-October. Marnie, Danni and I took the train downtown, and the balmy temperature enticed us to hike, rather than Uber, from the station to our point of rendezvous with Annie, the stairs between the lion statues at the Art Institute. We all wore jeans and hiking boots or running shoes, so the walk was a breeze—a rather slow breeze.

The sun felt so fine on our faces that the three of us simply lounged on the steps until we spotted Annie. She took the stairs two at a time to join us, looking like a teenager in her casual clothes and hi-tops.

"Hey," said Danni. "Thanks for making the trip downtown."

"Sure. Incredible weather, isn't it? My mother and Eloise are cleaning out the garden for the winter."

"I see you're not carrying your evening bag," said Marnie.

"I seldom pair it with jeans and a t-shirt."

"On to the Bean," I said.

As we all rose, Annie said, "Its official name is Cloud Gate."

Marnie said, "Well, that's just pretentious."

"Apparently the designer is getting used to the nickname. I think the general population has a way of sucking out the pretension and inserting fun," said Annie.

We made our way down a sidewalk bustling with tourists and young families out to enjoy the phenomenal weather. We rounded a corner, and it came into view. "It has a fluidity, but it doesn't remotely resemble a cloud," I said.

"That's because it's a Bean," said Danni.

As we continued down the sidewalk that led us to the east side of the sculpture, Danni said, "Have any of you seen yourselves in a fun-house mirror before?"

"I have a vague recollection of something like that," said Marnie. "I must've been just a little girl." She paused. "Yes, I once was little."

"Maybe," I said. "I'm really fuzzy about it, but I do recall it scaring me."

Danni said, "In the immortal words of Heather, just before we walked through the hostile courtroom on our second day in business, 'Brace yourselves!' "

The little plaza that surrounds the Bean was filled with people taking selfies, laughing, and generally enjoying the gorgeous view in a spot that showcased the Chicago skyline. Knowing what we were about to witness, I swallowed hard. It was one thing to try to imagine going through my life with a condition like Danni's, but it was an entirely different matter to lay eyes on myself as I would've lived and breathed as a dwarf. Still, I couldn't expect to be Danni's friend if I didn't even have the guts to glimpse my body in a truncated form. I'd showered her with my share of platitudes and encouragements, but the truth was, I didn't have a damn clue what it would be like to inhabit a body like hers. This exercise wouldn't bestow that knowledge either, but I hoped it would be of value to at least try to take a peek.

We approached the sculpture, four abreast, like some kind of military assault. I was so nervous that my eyes raced to the very top, which reflected only the sky. I slowly walked my gaze down, to take in the tops of the reflected skyscrapers. No one else said a word, and I was afraid to look at my friends, but I finally forced myself to focus on our reflections.

We were all truncated—short bodies, weirdly elongated heads. Although we didn't look remotely like ourselves, the clothing gave us away as to who was who. I zeroed in on myself, and tried to imagine that image being me. The harder I tried, the less possible it seemed. But what I could appreciate was that my height and my build—but especially my height—was a gift I didn't deserve, but absolutely relished. An image flashed before me of a scene in a courtroom. I always wore two-inch heels because I thought they were dressier than flats for court. As a result, I was generally as tall as my male opponents, or at least close. One day, my adversary, who was probably six foot six inches, absolutely towered over me, and it annoyed the hell out of me. It was obvious it wasn't a helpful thing to be required to look up at your courtroom rival. But the truth was, most women did. Not just Danni. Most women.

Maybe it was because I felt so frustrated that I couldn't really experience what I was staring at, that I placed my left hand on Danni's shoulder. Could there be solidarity in trying to comprehend something I was too limited to get? At that moment, I loved my friends with a ferocity I'd never felt before. I would've killed for them. But I couldn't *be* them.

I finally worked up the nerve to glance their way. Annie, to my right, had tears shining on her cheeks, and I leaped to the conclusion that her level of empathy was far beyond mine. Of course, it was.

On my other side, Danni looked serene.

I had to take a half-step forward to see Marnie, and she wore the solemn, aggressive face of a warrior. Of course she did.

I, however, just felt hollow and useless—contemptible, really. How dare I believe I could be their friend? My level of privilege was so off-the-chart, I couldn't even be on the same graph with them. I recalled Marnie's comment about me from the first day we met. It went something like, "I have a ton of assumptions and prejudices about you—which are probably true." Of course they were true.

I got myself so worked up about it that my stomach started aching pretty badly. Seeing nowhere to sit, I simply sank down onto the concrete and assumed a Lotus position. Danni immediately leaned into me. "Heather, are you okay?"

I had no answer. Should I have admitted to her that I was crap, and always would be? How could I have shared with them my angst over my lack of understanding when the three of them surely possessed an easy knowledge of that which I wasn't able to comprehend? I burst into tears.

Marnie said, "What the hell, Heather? What happened?"

I couldn't formulate words through my sobs.

Danni eased herself down beside me, and the others

followed suit, so we became a nest of sitters, surrounded by standers and millers. Annie handed me a tissue. "What's wrong?"

I blew, then sniffled until I was able to speak. "I'm so sorry. Something about seeing my truncated reflection made me feel shame."

"What?" asked Danni.

I hesitated, not knowing what to say without making the disparity of our body-privilege status feel even worse. "It just hit me how I'll never be able to understand how I would feel if the distorted version of me I just saw were my real body." There was no way I'd bring up the obesity thing, or the race thing, since our visit to the Bean was intended to be all about the dwarfism thing.

Danni took both of my hands and looked into my eyes. "Listen. I didn't ask you to make this little pilgrimage with me to make you feel bad."

"I know."

"I just thought it would be fun to have the chance to see the way you guys would all look as dwarves."

Annie said, "Heather, you aren't personally responsible for our beauty standards. And the fact that they place you at the top of the heap really isn't your fault."

Marnie shook her head at me, then rolled her eyes for emphasis. "It's not entirely logical for you to feel guilty that you don't look like Danni—or me, for that matter. I joke about it a lot, but I'm quite happy in my skin. Danni is happy in hers."

"If we didn't look like we do, we wouldn't be who we are. You once told us you try to use your superpower for good, rather than evil," said Danni.

"I said that?"

"It was appropriate in that conversation," said Danni. "I'm sure you're familiar with the expression, 'For of those to whom much is given, much is required'?"

"John F. Kennedy," said Marnie. "Also, Luke 12:48, 'For unto whomsoever much is given, of him shall much be required.' But I'm not sure it was the best way to state the sentiment. It kind of suggests that those who aren't blessed with a lot of advantages are free to be selfish."

Danni said, "That's because the phrase limits its focus to the moral responsibility of advantaged folks."

"I know," said Marnie. "I just like to criticize anything that's articulated better than I could've said it."

Annie leaned in toward me and said, "From what I've heard about the beginning of your law firm, it was you who dragged Marnie and Danni out of their caves."

That shocked me. "How could you know that?"

Annie nodded to me and said softly, "Jeanne." As though that were a thorough explanation.

"But, how—"

"It doesn't matter, Heather," said Danni, who was still holding my hands. "The point is, and without getting too biblical—" She glanced at Marnie. "You've been blessed with a form that guarantees you a certain amount of privilege in our society. But you used your power for the good. And Marnie and I decided to risk major changes in our lives, too. And it worked."

"That's right," said Marnie. "We've each done our part, including you. Now, let it go."

Danni released my hands and folded hers demurely on her lap. "Although you can never *be* us, you've worked to understand some issues we face, that you don't. You didn't create our materialistic, beauty-crazed culture, but with us, you did what you could—in a brave and deliberate way—to thwart it. We succeeded. And we'll keep challenging injustice together. But we're also just your friends."

Annie pursed her lips, then said, "Honestly, I don't think it's healthy to refuse to be happy."

It felt a bit odd discussing my deepest feelings with our employee. But I decided to get over myself and respect that she'd also become my friend. "Well, I've never claimed to be emotionally healthy. The truth is, I'm always in turmoil about whether I'm doing enough good in the world."

"I'll bet you were raised Catholic," said Marnie.

"How did you know that?" I looked at her as I pushed my long bangs to the side, behind my ear.

She rolled her eyes.

Danni said, "What do you mean by 'enough good'?"

"It's been bothering me since we planned today's event. Two things. First, being so close with you and Marnie—and now, Annie—I think I have survivor's guilt."

"Can you see that might be a little insulting to us?" asked Annie.

I was embarrassed to be talking so much about my psyche, and Annie's comment got my stomach going again. Nevertheless, I wanted to go through with the conversation. So, I thought about what she'd asked before responding. "I can. It's implicit in my feeling guilt that there's something lesser about being a dwarf, or plus-size, or Black. Annie, please believe me that I have no such thought." I paused. "No such conscious thought. My focus is how society treats each of us because of what category we're in. You guys all take some shit from ignorant people—a lot of ignorant people—that I don't get. I think that's why I have the guilt."

Danni said, "I guess it's okay to carry that *if* it propels you to make some positive contribution because of it. And, Heather, you're doing that." She looked at me intently and spoke as though she were pleading with me to accept what she was saying.

"I don't know," said Marnie. "I think you've taken too large a dose. It may move you to be a good-deed-doer, but it seems to be eating you up."

"Kind of."

Marnie said, "Obviously, that's because you wear your privilege-guilt like a crown of thorns. It's as though you believe life is so good for you that you have to atone for it. That's actually crazy, Heather. Nobody needs to apologize for her very existence."

Danni said, "That's right. You have to figure out how to let that go." She waved like she was sending someone off on a trip. "Adios guilt." Like so many things Danni did, it was charming.

I laughed. "Okay. I'll try."

Annie said, "You said there are two things that plague you. So, what's the other?"

I shook my head, embarrassed to be the center of the conversation for so long. "Enough about me."

"Come on, Heather," said Danni, as she patted my hand. "We really want to know."

I looked from one of them to the other and saw what I took as genuine interest. "Okay, guys. This will probably sound just as crazy, but I worry a lot about whether I'm doing enough with my life."

"Catholic high school, too," said Marnie. "Right?"

"You're good. But I can't imagine it's only

Catholics who have this issue."

"Not 'only.' But I've run across it primarily in that realm. Well, that and the Jews," said Marnie.

Annie said, "What exactly are you two talking about?"

I said, "Am I being sufficiently of service in the world?"

Marnie said, "That thought has never crossed my mind. I just live my life, do interesting work, and have marginally interesting friends." She winked at me. "I send dollars to Amnesty International and Docs Without Borders. Oh, and I recycle, big time. Who am I supposed to measure myself against, anyway? Also, are we graded on the curve?"

"I'm with Marnie," said Danni. "I've always thought that living a good life meant being kind to everyone and doing my best. I suppose I could do more for the community of Little People, but I don't feel called to it—at least, right now. But I do recycle."

Annie jumped on the bandwagon. "I'm just trying to get through it by being a decent person and keeping my loved ones first and foremost. Honestly, saving the world isn't even on my to-do list."

Danni said, "When I hear you say that, Annie, I think it may be. If everyone just got through it by taking a path of love and decency, wouldn't everything be good?"

I said, "Danni, you're a wise woman."

Marnie looked offended. "Hey! What about me?"

"Oh, you're a wise-ass woman."

"Thank you, Heather. I appreciate your appreciation."

Annie said, "Now that we've all shared our thoughts

on the tiny little issue of the meaning of life, I think Heather's asking us to help her figure out how to stop agonizing over this."

Marnie said, "I'd start by suing the Catholic Church—but they probably don't have any money left because of their other teensy, weensy little problem."

"I think you need a mantra," said Danni, emphatically.

"Such as?" I asked.

"Let it go."

Of course she was right. They all were. "Do I sing it or chant it?"

"You just do it," said Annie.

As she'd done before, Danni held out her closed hands, then slowly opened them as though she were releasing a little bird or a butterfly. Then as she parted her lips slightly, one little sound came out with her breath. "Poof."

I felt a huge surge of relief when it dawned on me that Annie's comment could have segued into an observation about privileged people asking non-privileged folks to "take care of" our feelings of guilt. Of course, I'd read about this phenomenon, but now I was watching myself do it. My friends were all smart women. They knew. I took a deep breath, and decided to believe they forgave me.

As we all rose, Annie said, "Does anybody want to know my reaction to seeing myself truncated?"

"Of course, we do," said Danni.

Marnie said, "I see a bench opening up. Much less pathetic than sitting on the concrete."

Annie ran ahead of us to grab the bench for our group. As we reached it, all I could think of was how I'd commandeered the experience and hadn't even asked the others what they were feeling. I worked hard to get a grip. I let my guilt go and appreciated that I could still ask them. We were lined up on the bench, each of us looking at the Bean in the distance as we chatted. I said, "How *did* it make you feel, Annie?"

"Grateful."

"Why?" asked Marnie.

"Oh, I don't know. I suppose I just appreciated some of the challenges for little people a bit more. Imagining myself with dwarfism is one thing. Seeing myself with short limbs was much more real. I don't think most folks spend much time appreciating having average height, or limbs of typical length. So, one more thing for me to be grateful for."

"What about you, Marnie?" I asked.

"Honestly, I couldn't do it. I could no more mentally inhabit that short, truncated body than I could a body like Heather's. So, I'm sorry to say, I didn't really have a reaction—except, of course, that this outing gave the rest of us a chance to play Heather's therapists." She laughed, but no one else did.

I sighed. "Well, you're all good at it."

Marnie laughed again.

I was sitting between Danni and Annie, and I placed a hand on each of their knees. "No. Seriously. You guys all helped me a lot. Believe it or not, I'm already working on letting things go." I held my closed fists out in front of me, opened them and said, "Poof." I turned to Danni. "What did you feel?"

Danni stood, looked toward the Bean for a moment, then turned to face us. She gave us a big smile. "Are you kidding? I felt joy, naturally. It's a gorgeous day in an exciting city, and my three best friends took the time to travel just to be in this place with me. Of course, it makes perfect sense that you would each have a different reaction to seeing yourself in the Bean. You are different people, after all." She paused. "But what I felt—what I feel—is bliss."

Chapter 25

One bitterly cold afternoon in mid-November when I was grateful that I worked indoors, Jeanne stuck her head in my doorway and asked if she could speak with the partners about taking some vacation time.

We gathered in the conference room, where we all took our usual seats around the table. Jeanne was wearing a royal blue skirt suit, which looked lovely with her coloring. Her small earrings were stones of an identical color. I said, "Jeanne, it's really no problem if you'd like some time off for the holidays. I'm sure we can manage without you for a while."

"Thank you, Heather, but I require six weeks of leave, from November 26th to January 3rd. I've arranged for a temporary secretary, Mary Maloney, an old friend of mine. I'll train her for a day or two—or whatever it takes—before I leave. I'm sorry to have so little flexibility on this, but I'm committed to spending time in Florida and Texas with some very old friends."

"We'll miss you," said Danni.

"I hope you have a blast with your friends," said Marnie.

"The truth is, we have some sad things to work through together, but I'm confident I can be of help."

I frowned. "I'm sorry it won't be a pleasure trip, Jeanne. Of course you may have the time off. As you know, you are entitled to four weeks paid vacation. Will you be okay about the other two weeks?"

"Yes." She nodded for emphasis.

"Because we'd be happy to include an advance if that would help you out."

"Thank you, Heather. I believe I'll be fine."

"Let us know if you change your mind on that," said Marnie.

Danni said, "As far as I'm concerned, the worst thing about this is that you won't be around for Sam's New Year's Eve party. We're planning to invite all of our office. We're hoping Annie can bring Bradley so we can finally meet him. And Sam's been so excited he'd get to meet you."

"That's lovely, Danni, and I'm really very sorry to miss it." She looked at Danni in a way that confirmed her regret was not only genuine, but deep. "I hope I can meet Sam and Bradley sometime in the new year." Turning to Marnie and me, she added, "But you two must make a special effort to attend. Surely, you know how much it would mean to Danni."

"I'm available," I said, then smiled at her.

"I wouldn't miss it," said Marnie.

"Wonderful. Now I need you to swear to me that you'll be there."

Marnie and I exchanged a look. Danni said, "Well, it's not *that* important, Jeanne."

She ignored Danni and said again, "Swear?" She stared at Marnie, and then at me.

"Pinkie-swear or regular?" asked Marnie.

"The real kind," said Jeanne, apparently in all seriousness.

Marnie raised her right hand and said, "I swear."

I echoed her, having not a clue why Jeanne was

being so insistent.

Jeanne said, "Lovely." As she rose from her chair, she added, "Thank you all for being so understanding. Good and kindness will flow through you all the days of your lives."

"Isn't that biblical?" asked Marnie.

Jeanne smiled. "Not exactly." She slapped her hands together. "Now, back to work."

Chapter 26

None of us had seen the others since we'd all left for our parents' homes on the morning of December 24th, the first of the days we'd given ourselves off. Marnie and I had planned to share an Uber to Sam and Danni's New Year's Eve party, since Danni would've left hours earlier to help with the set-up. But I'd awakened that morning with chills, and by mid-afternoon, I didn't have a muscle that wasn't aching. I was still in bed when I rang Marnie. "Hi."

"Hi, Heather. I'm trying to decide whether to put my hair up for tonight. What do you think?"

"I think you'll be beautiful either way."

"I know that. But I'm going for festive. So, what?"

"I like it down."

"Thanks. So, what's up?"

"Not me. I'm coming down with something."

"What are your symptoms?"

"Achy all over. I had chills this morning."

"Any nausea or vomiting?"

"No. It's not a stomach bug, at least so far."

"Good."

I tried to get more comfortable by rolling over onto my side. "I think I'll call Danni and ask her to give my regrets to Sam. I really shouldn't be going out tonight."

"Except that you don't have a choice."

"How's that?"

"You promised Jeanne you'd go. You swore."

"I know I did, Marnie. But Jeanne isn't going to be angry with me that I got sick."

"Hang on, Heather. I'm on my way."

I couldn't believe Marnie was going to fight me on this. Moreover, I wasn't in any condition for a confrontation. I padded through my living room in my slippers, unlocked my front door, then settled on my couch under a wool blanket I'd dragged with me. Within a minute, Marnie was standing over me.

"You look fine. Let's plan to meet downstairs around seven."

I pulled the blanket up to my chin. "Do my words just bounce off you? I told you I'm not well enough to go out."

"And I told you that you have to." She kept her arms folded over her chest the whole time.

"That doesn't make any sense, Marnie. Why do you care so much?"

"I don't. But Jeanne does."

"I wasn't sick when I agreed to go."

She leaned over and put her hand on my forehead. "No temperature. And you said you have no nausea or vomiting."

"So?"

"So, you can put on a happy face and do your duty. You won't throw up in the punch bowl. And you'll probably live through it."

"Why do you see this as my duty?"

"It's simple, really. For some reason, it's very important to Jeanne that we both go. Jeanne wasn't kidding around when she asked us to swear that we would. Surely you remember the look on her face."

"I do. She probably just didn't want Danni to be disappointed."

"Honestly, Heather, I don't care what her reason was. She sees it as imperative. Jeanne would never insist on something with such gravity if she didn't think it was important—somehow."

"It still defies logic to me. But I suspect you won't stop badgering me about this until I relent."

She shook her head. "Certainly not."

"Fine. I'll go. But I'm leaving one minute after the ball drops."

"Because that's when you turn into a pumpkin and six white mice."

"Of course, I do."

Later, I was able to get dressed, but I didn't have the energy to do anything with my hair, so I just combed it and used a little gel to push it back from my face. I popped a couple of aspirins.

The address was in Winnetka, a famously well-to-do-in-an-old-money-sense suburb north of Evanston. Because his apartment, like Danni's, was too small for such a large gathering, Sam was hosting at the home of a friend's parents who were in Europe for the holidays. The car pulled into a circular drive in front of a large, elegant old red brick two-story house. The light pouring out of the front windows was a warm yellow, and I spied a fire dancing in a brick fireplace in the living room. Danni must've seen us get out of the car, because she rushed to welcome us with hugs as we walked in the front door. She looked like a little fire herself, with her auburn hair, and wearing a sophisticated red and orange patterned velvet, knee-length dress and black patent-leather, high-heeled dress boots, which I assumed she'd had specially made.

"Danni, you're gorgeous," I said.

"Thanks, Heather. Let me take your coats." A tall young man appeared, retrieved the coats from her, and removed them to who-knows-where. I was then able to get a good look at Marnie's dress, a dark green silk brocade, which was a great color for her.

"You look stunning," I said.

She brushed off the compliment with, "You too," without really looking at me. I had chosen a simple, red velour sheath with spaghetti straps. As a result of our neglecting to coordinate our color choices, when Marnie stood next to me, we were a couple of Christmas ornaments. That turned out not to be a problem because, as she went looking for the bar, a couple of men introduced themselves to her, and she disappeared with them. I noticed soft jazz playing, and saw that there were probably twenty people or so present, with more pouring through the front door.

Danni grabbed my hand and told me Sam wanted to see me. As we approached, I watched him, looking very handsome in his tweed sports coat and gray wool slacks, talking with another man. His friend wandered off just as Danni and I reached him.

"Danni, thanks so much for bringing Heather over." He leaned down and gave her a kiss on the cheek. He turned to me and gave me a quick hug. "Welcome to the home of someone I've never met."

"It's lovely," I said.

"And very kind of them to share it with us. I'm so pleased you could be here, Heather. Annie and Bradley haven't arrived yet, but they have quite a drive. I was thrilled when they said yes to our invitation." He whispered to Danni, "Is your surprise ready?"

I looked at her and raised my eyebrows. "What?"

She gave me a quick smile. "Follow me."

I had no idea what was up, but dutifully followed her past the long dining room table laden with all manner of fish, meats, cheeses and intriguing side dishes. We continued through an archway lit with clear twinkle-lights and into the impressively modern chef's kitchen. I was taken with the wood beams overhead, the intricate flow of swirls on the pale gray granite top of the center island, and the gleam of the terra cotta ceramic tiles adorning the walls and the floor. The ovens were on, making the room toasty warm. It took me a moment or two to notice the small breakfast booth at the far end of the room, where Danni's twin sat, reading something on her Kindle.

Danni said to her sister, "She's here!"

Delaney looked up, her smile every bit as bright as Danni's. She slid out of the booth, walked toward me, and gave me a long hug. "Heather, I'm so happy to see you again."

"Really?" I said, stupidly. Even though Danni had assured me that her sister actually liked me, my heart's muscle-memory was warning me to be wary of the woman.

She laughed. "I'm so sorry for the way I treated you when we last met, Heather. You've proven to be everything I'd hoped for. And I can't tell you how thrilled I am for all of you about your firm's success."

Danni said, "Listen. I need to get back to our other guests. I have a chilled bottle of champagne and glasses for you two stashed in this cupboard." She pointed, and I leaned down to retrieve the items. "Why don't you two spend a little time together before joining the party?"

"I would love that," I said, then popped open the champagne bottle and filled our glasses. Delaney, wearing an elegant, deep purple, off-one-shoulder dress, and with her hair up, slid back into her side of the booth, and I scooched in directly across from her.

We clinked our glasses, and Delaney said, "To the new year."

"I had no idea you were flying in for this. Danni must've been thrilled."

"Actually, I drove up with her after our Christmas with Mom and Dad."

"How long can you stay?"

"I have to leave tomorrow afternoon."

"Right. I suppose investment banking is pretty demanding of your time."

"It was."

"Was?"

"I asked Danni not to tell you, since I knew I'd see you tonight. I've left my old job. I'm finishing up on a special teaching degree to get my credentials to instruct at the nine through twelve level. I should be ready to apply for positions by May, and I hope to get into a classroom by summer session. If not, then definitely in September."

"Oh, my God, Delaney! That's fabulous. What made you decide to make the quantum leap?"

"You did, Heather." As she smiled, her blue eyes lit up her face, just like Danni's did.

"I don't understand."

"As Danni probably told you, our parents have always been incredibly supportive, but they don't have any extra money to help Danni if something comes up—

medically or otherwise—which she may require assistance with. So when I completed my education, I decided to pursue a career that would allow me to save up to be able to finance whatever she might need."

"Oh my. I don't think she knows that."

"She doesn't. And, of course, I don't want her to." Delaney gave me a look which made it clear I was sworn to secrecy.

"Of course."

"But now that the three of you have been such a smash with your law firm, complete with health insurance and 401(k)s, I'm confident Danni's needs will be met."

"They will. But, frankly, didn't she have the same security at your uncle's firm?"

Delaney took a long sip of her champagne. "Hardly. First of all, she wasn't allowed to be in a position to ever make partner, so her income was pretty much capped. But more worrying was the fact that our uncle is near retirement. Once he leaves, there's no guarantee the firm would even keep her on."

"I hadn't thought of that."

"I had. It's not just that she's financially secure, Heather. As you know, Danni is in court or taking a deposition almost every day now. Honestly, I've never seen her so happy."

"She does love the practice. She's been ecstatic to be in a courtroom ever since the day she presented her first motion. But I think Sam has a lot to do with the current level of *joie de vivre*." I smiled, then took a swallow of my drink.

"He does. But I believe you're acquainted with the fact that apparently ideal romantic relationships can go sideways." She raised her eyebrows. "Don't get me wrong. I think Sam's a gem. But work she loves will sustain her—no matter what."

"Which is why you can now do the work you're passionate about."

"Precisely." She lifted her glass to me. After we each took another sip, she said, "What about you, Heather? Is the firm all you hoped it would be?"

I thought for a moment. "It's so much more than that. I knew I'd love practicing with Marnie and Danni. Then charming, unpredictable Jeanne and Annie came along, and iced the cake. It's like living in a Dali painting. Each of the women is so interesting that, just when I think I have one of them figured out, she surprises me again."

"So, you're confident Annie will work out?"

"No question. I expect we'll be able to invite her into the partnership within a couple of years."

"That's great, Heather. You know, Danni says the same thing—that your offices are an enchanted space." She gave me a soft, closed-mouth smile. "You know, I've been wondering about you."

"In what respect?"

"About your love-life."

"Seriously?"

Delaney laughed. "Yeah. I guess that sounded weird. It's just that Danni's told me about the faithless fiancé."

"Oh, I see."

"I've been wondering if you're looking to have a relationship. I mean, if you don't mind my asking."

I bit my lower lip as I tried to decide whether I really wanted to discuss my private life with a virtual stranger.

But I decided she probably already knew quite a bit about me anyway, so I dove in. "I'm ambivalent. I know for certain I'd like to raise a child. I may start to look into adopting over the next year. My problem with men is that I don't know if I'll ever get over my break-up. Danni filled you in on that. Right?"

"Mm-hmm."

"I'm afraid I prefer never dating again to being seduced by another phony. I obviously can't tell the difference between true and false love. I suppose the best way to put it is that I don't trust my judgment anymore." I took another swallow of my drink. Then Delaney picked up the bottle and topped off our flutes.

"I'm sorry." She paused. "I'm certainly no expert, but I think if you have any interest in having a partner, you'll always be leaving yourself exposed."

"You're saying I should take a chance?"

"I'm saying, if you want to have a romantic relationship with someone, you have no choice but to take a chance. It's a good idea to be cautious, but you can't move forward if you're paralyzed by skepticism. The real question is whether a romantic relationship is something you want."

"I am thinking about it." I took a moment to study my full champagne flute. "What about you? Do you have a partner?"

"I do. We've been together almost four years."

"That's great! What's his name?"

"My wife's name is Marilyn. Right now, we're in the middle of deciding whether one of us gets pregnant or we adopt. Either way, we're ready to start our family."

Embarrassed that I hadn't left room for this possibility, I nodded, probably blushed, and quickly raised my glass to my lips. Then I said, "Is she here?"

"I wish she were. I'd love to introduce the two of you, but she had to fly to Minnesota to spend New Year's Eve with her family."

"Congratulations!"

"On what?"

"On being where you are in your relationship, and on your marriage. Falling in love is one thing. After that, it's like a slippery bar of soap in wet hands—hard to hold onto. Keeping a grip on it for four years is an achievement." I was feeling unusually relaxed, and remembered I was drinking on a completely empty stomach. I pushed my glass away.

"Yes." She nodded, then looked away for a moment before returning her gaze to me. "To continue with your unusual analogy, I can hold onto the soap if I stay focused. But inadvertent inattention is every bit as risky as consciously dropping it. And, of course, all the focus comes at a cost. I've come to believe that keeping a relationship healthy is no different than maintaining the fitness and wellness of any other organism. And I think we tend to get out of most things in proportion to what we put into them. Frankly, healthy relationships are a hell of a lot of work."

"I can't disagree with that." I sighed. "Thanks for sharing. Danni is lucky to have you for her sister."

"I am, and always have been, the lucky one to have her." Delaney patted my hand and stood. "Time to get back to the party?"

"Right. Let's." I left Danni's champagne bottle on the table and set the flutes in the sink, not knowing where they'd originally come from. When we reached the dining room, Delaney headed for her sister, who was sitting near the fire in the living room, and I looked around for Marnie or Annie. I caught a glimpse of Marnie, who was sitting on a couch in an alcove just off the formal living area, animated in her conversation with two young men sitting across from her, and one beside her. She used her hands expressively, and the men were laughing hysterically. There was no way I'd interrupt her.

When I glanced toward the front door, I saw Annie and a handsome Black man, a couple of inches taller than she, handing their coats to the same gentleman who had taken ours from Danni. The guy hurried off with the wraps. Annie had gone with the African princess look again, decked out in a gorgeous deep blue and gold wrap-type gown and head covering, with large gold hoop earrings. He wore a sports coat and slacks, and had a low ponytail that reached his mid-back. I hurried up to them to greet Annie and introduce myself to Bradley.

"Annie, hi! You look gorgeous." Turning to her friend, I said, "You must be Bradley. I'm Heather. I'm so happy to finally meet you."

As he shook my hand, he said, "The pleasure is all mine."

"How was your long drive?"

"Delightful. I was with Annie."

"I can understand that. She is rather a bright light at the office, as well."

"Guys, I'm right here. You don't need to speak about me in the third person. Heather, I love the red on you. You should wear it more often." She surveyed the rooms. "I see Marnie found a group of admirers. I won't interrupt her, or she'll murder me on Thursday. But there's no way she'll get out of here without meeting

Bradley."

"She can't wait," I said.

Annie and Bradley and I visited for a while and I learned about his work teaching and coaching. In the short time I had with him, I found him to be an easy-going guy, who was probably comfortable in most surroundings. Anyone who could stand up before a classroom full of fifteen to eighteen-year-olds, and enjoy doing it, had my admiration. Danni approached us and asked if she could borrow Annie and Bradley to introduce them to Sam and Delaney.

I wandered over to the dining table, wondering how food would go down. A young man standing there studying the selection quietly said, "I feel guilty—in the home of a one-percenter. Looking at a sumptuous spread of plenty."

"I beg your pardon," I said.

"Sorry. I was just mumbling to myself."

"You mumbled quite clearly." I smiled.

He stretched out his arm to reach over the table to shake my hand. "Hello. I'm Charlie Merton."

"Heather Hightower."

"Of course. Danni's partner. She's told us so much about you that I feel I know you already."

"Who's the 'us'?"

"Sam's university friends."

"Ah. So, you're also studying at Northwestern?"

"Was. And will be. I've been working toward my doctorate in social work. It's a combined masters/PhD program. But I took a year off to do some volunteer work in Appalachia—West Virginia. I just returned so I can resume my studies next semester."

"So that's why the extravagance of the table leaves

you feeling guilty?"

"I suppose it is. Food insecurity is more common in the United States than most people imagine."

Charlie was a pleasant-looking man with an open kind of face, around my age, but taller than me, and quite thin. He wore glasses with narrow frames in a brownish-gold color that matched his thick hair, the front of which fell over his forehead making him look a bit rakish. He was the only man at the party wearing a sweater and khakis, rather than sports coat and slacks. I realized he was the same person who had been taking coats at the door.

"Will you be able to overcome your guilt to taste a bite of something?"

"I'll have to. Actually, I have hypoglycemia, so I'll need to get a bit of protein in me or risk disrupting Sam and Annie's party by planting my face in the food."

I pointed. "There are cheeses down there."

He looked up at me with such a gentle and appreciative smile, it was as though I had offered him one of my kidneys.

"Thank you, Heather."

He took some creamy gouda and a slice of blueberry stilton, with a few crackers, and I grabbed a few morsels of fruit on toothpicks. "Will you sit with me?" he asked, indicating a corner spot off the dining room where two armchairs faced each other, separated by a small mahogany table.

"Of course."

After I sat, he returned to a corner of the dining table to retrieve two pre-poured glasses of water for us. I was relieved, having had so much champagne. He said, "Heather, I'm honored to meet you. The way you managed to get Danni and Marnie out of their positions, and then made everything come together for your law firm is remarkable. I haven't met many people as brave and generous as you are." Again, he gave me his deeply appreciative soft smile.

I wondered exactly what Danni had said to Sam's friends. "Thanks, Charlie, but it was their talents that made it a success. I'm proud to know them." I changed the subject. "What were you doing in Appalachia?"

"I worked for a non-profit that assisted families with basic needs."

"Such as—" Still too warm from sitting in the kitchen, I downed half my water while he answered.

"We secured and delivered food for families and the elderly, and schoolbooks for the children. We assisted with paperwork so folks could apply for medical benefits and social services, and we did a lot of after-school tutoring. Also, I started a low-level soccer league. Really low level."

Either Charlie's glasses were too loose, or he just had a habit of pushing them up on his nose with his index finger. He'd already done it three times, and it was pretty cute. "Do you think you made a difference?"

"I'm not sure that I did. But I'd hoped to. I'd been studying social inequality issues on a macro-level— basically policy. But I felt I needed some on-the-ground experience with people living in poverty to help me understand in practical ways. When I was an undergrad, I wrote a paper on unintended consequences of do-good policies. My case study was about the little children in a country in the Middle East who were being forced to weave intricate oriental rugs. The children were losing their eyesight from all of the fine work. Well-intentioned people convinced the government to disallow the practice. But since the families relied on the income from those little children to allow the siblings and elders to eat, the little ones turned to a different occupation. They became sex workers."

"Oh, no. That's terrible."

"What was disturbing was that the experts hadn't looked far enough down the line. They hadn't thought through what all of it would lead to. So, I decided to study policy."

"How much longer do you have?" I took a chance and ate half a strawberry.

"I'll probably finish my dissertation in the next year to eighteen months. But enough about me. What interests you, Heather?"

I found it a challenging question. Unlike everyone else, he wasn't asking about my work or my background, so I had to take a moment to think. "I'm curious about how science interacts with social justice. What interests me is how policy decisions affect people on the ground. So much is going so badly, and it feels like we're always one step behind the next disaster. My leisure reading tends to be about issues like that—early childhood education, healthcare access and outcomes, global warming—"

He smiled. "Important issues."

"I also enjoy creative writing, so I've been trying to educate myself about it by studying short stories for ideas on how to execute on my themes and character development arcs—things like that."

We talked—subjects along these lines—for another half hour. I would've been content to spend the remainder of the evening sharing ideas with Charlie, but

I knew it would be particularly rude to neglect my friends since Sam and Danni planned the party specifically to bring us all together and to introduce us to Sam's friends.

"Charlie, please excuse me while I say hi to some people. I'd love to visit with you longer, but duty calls."

"You should. Have fun, Heather." He smiled. "I'm going to make sure I'm completing all of my assignments from Sam and Danni. Somebody has quite a number of champagne corks to pop before midnight."

I nodded and walked off in search of Marnie. She'd moved into the living room and was seated on a couch in front of the fireplace with one of the three young men I'd seen her with earlier. He had shed his sports coat, and wore a light-weight blue sweater. His build—like someone who puts in time at the gym—and slightly receding hairline belied his youthful face. I guessed him to be in his early thirties. His medium brown complexion and black, curly hair suggested either Italian or Hispanic heritage. As I made my way to them, Annie and Bradley appeared to have the same destination, but kept getting stopped by people who seemed to really want to meet them.

"Hi, Marnie."

She looked up, beaming and a little flushed. "Oh, Heather, I'm glad you're here. I want you to meet Ivani."

The man rose and the two of us shook hands. "It's a pleasure to meet you. Marnie's been telling me all about you, Heather."

"Yikes."

"Not at all. Congratulations on the law firm."

I took a seat on the edge of the hearth. "Thanks. But Marnie and Danni are the reason it's working out. Are you one of Sam's Northwestern friends?"

"Guilty. Actually, I'm in the same program as Sam."

"Are you from around here?"

Marnie said, "Do you mean, is he an immigrant?"

"I meant the Chicago area." I gave her a look.

"I am. My parents moved here from the Dominican Republic before I was born. They've lived in the north suburbs since then."

Annie and Bradley stepped up, introduced themselves to Ivani, and took the two chairs across from the couch. Marnie said, "Ivani, Bradley teaches high school, and I've told you about Annie."

"Yikes," said Annie.

"That's what I said."

Marnie laughed. "I just told him about the day you threw your dreadlocks at me."

Ivani studied Annie for a moment. "I think you'd look good in dreads."

"Thanks. I think. Anyway, I haven't thrown anything at her since that day."

I said, "This is such a great party. I wish Jeanne could've been here."

"I hope I'm not speaking out of school," said Ivani.

"Bradley will know if you are," said Annie.

Ivani smiled. "The way Marnie talks about your office manager, I think she is something special."

Annie said, "Who? Marnie or Jeanne?"

"It's my supposition that Jeanne is. I know Marnie is."

Marnie said, "Aw. Shucks." But the way she looked at him said, "Thanks so much. You, too."

"Is anyone into New Year's resolutions?" I asked.

Marnie said, "Just another way to disappoint yourself."

"I don't think it's a bad idea to take a few minutes to reflect on putting some conscious effort into self-improvement," said Bradley.

"Coming from a man who's already fully there," said Annie.

"Would that were true," said Bradley.

"Hmm," said Marnie. "Annie doesn't exactly throw around compliments. I'm going to keep my eye on you, Bradley."

He shook his head. "Isn't Jeanne the one who has the reputation for speaking in hyperbole?"

"No one can argue with that," I said.

"I've never made a New Year's resolution before in my life," said Annie. "But I'm committed to one for this year."

"Self-improvement?" asked Ivani.

"More like law firm improvement."

That caught my attention. I couldn't wrap my head around us actually discussing firm business in front of Bradley and Ivani. All I could think to say was, "Really?"

Annie smiled. "I'll make a proper proposal to you guys and Danni. I have no idea whether it will be possible this year, but I'd really like to do some pro bono work at some point in my career. Maybe I could volunteer for an immigration case. I understand they're always looking for people to help."

"That feels right to me," said Marnie. "Then again, I've had a few glasses of wine, and I never mix business with alcohol."

Annie said, "Let me just add that I won't be asking the partners to finance this. If you guys approve it, I would do it in addition to my billable hours." She let out a long sigh. "I just feel so disproportionately blessed." She turned her gaze to the fire, then added, "Maybe it's the time of year."

I didn't respond because I thought it was important to say just the right thing, and I hadn't figured out what that was.

"My only resolution is to present the plan to you. I'm really not presuming anything."

I knew I had to say something since everyone was looking at me. "Alcohol intake notwithstanding, I can say that I look forward to seeing your proposal. In our own small way, I think Marnie and Danni and I have tried to build our law firm on a foundation of social justice—or at least feminism. But that doesn't mean we can't do more."

Thankfully, Ivani steered the conversation to a new topic. "I have to say how incredibly impressed I am with Sam's girlfriend. She's been hanging out with us— Sam's friends—for months. We all think Danni's incredible. And there's no way we could've missed how Sam is with her. It's an every-minute-of-every-hour they're together kind of adoration."

Marnie said, "It's like the flu then."

"Excuse me?" asked Ivani.

"The falling in love disease is spreading through our office." She looked directly at Annie.

"Well," said Annie, raising her chin. "Just for saying that right out loud in front of all these people, I hope Jeanne catches it in Florida, or Texas, or wherever the hell she is, and then sneezes on you, Marnie."

"That's my cue," I said as I stood. "I always leave when group conversations turn to private things."

"Are you sure you're not planning to seek out the

tall guy in the sweater?" asked Marnie, as she raised her eyebrows.

I looked at her, smiled, and shook my head. "I'll see you all a little later. Maybe by then you'll return to proper, non-embarrassing topics of conversation."

Annie said, "I'm not embarrassed. I do love Bradley and I don't care who knows it. Why do you think I dragged him on an hour and a half drive? I intended to show him off to my friends and Sam and Danni's friends, and I'll keep on doing that until the clock strikes twelve."

"Why stop then?" asked Ivani.

"That's when the kissing starts."

"Fair enough," I said, as I walked toward the dining table, only a little chagrined that Marnie had called my next move.

Chapter 27

Fifteen or twenty people milled around in the dining room, the luscious spread now obscured by bodies. I glanced into the kitchen and saw that it too had filled with partiers. I wormed my way through, smiling and saying, "Excuse me," until I found Charlie, alone in the booth, apparently counting empty champagne flutes. It struck me that my earlier nausea had totally disappeared. I slid into the bench across from him. "May I help?"

"Heather. I'm so glad you found me in my cave."

"Interesting choice of noun. That's what Marnie and Danni and I took to calling the back offices they were relegated to before we started the firm."

"Knowing Danni, and having met Marnie, I can't imagine anyone thinking it was a good idea to hide them."

"I know. Did I interrupt your work?"

"No. Just finished counting. My job is to get fifty of these filled and on trays by 11:45. Then others have been recruited to pass them around in time for the magic hour."

"Are you getting to enjoy the party?"

"I am now." He pushed his glasses up on his nose.

I smiled. "I looked for you because I was hoping for more conversation."

"I'm glad you did."

I folded my hands on my lap, but my right knee was

bouncing up and down, one of my nervous habits. Fortunately, it was hidden by the table-top. I said, "I've been thinking about your work in Appalachia. Have you travelled anywhere else?"

"My father was with the foreign service, so it would probably be easier for me to tell you where I haven't been."

"That has to be an exaggeration—I hope."

Charlie laughed. "I haven't been anywhere in Asia or Africa. Never set eyes on Australia or New Zealand. But my family traveled all over Europe, Canada, and Central and South America. It wasn't that the government posted my dad in dozens of countries. My folks just made sure we did a lot of touring from each of his assignments."

"Do you have siblings?"

"I wish I had."

"Why's that?"

"We moved so often it was hard to keep a friend. If I'd had a brother or sister, we could've palled around. Do you have siblings, Heather?"

"Two younger brothers. I adore them, but we've never been particularly close. They were born within eighteen months of one another, and five and six years after me. They did become best friends. Frankly, I think of Marnie and Danni as my sisters now. I can see us growing old together—tottering around the office, gray-haired and wrinkled, strategizing and laughing about our cases."

"Do you imagine Annie will still be with the firm?"

"Oh, yeah. I think she's a lifer."

"And Jeanne?"

"I'm not sure how old she is, but yes, I believe she'll

be in the saddle as long as she possibly can. But no gray hair for her. She dyes it black, and she looks fabulous."

"Will that satisfy you?"

"What do you mean?"

"Is that the contribution you want to make to the world?" He looked completely earnest.

For a moment, I was taken aback by the question. I pushed my hair back behind my ear as I took a moment to consider what I wanted to say. "If I hadn't thought about that a lot, I might take offense, Charlie. That because your work is service-oriented, you may not value mine."

"That's not what I meant, Heather. I would never presume—"

"I know. It's funny because my undergrad major was sociology, but it just didn't intrigue me. So, when I thought about the next level of school, I was drawn to law because I knew I'd have the opportunity to do a lot of analysis and writing—which did excite me. But I've certainly questioned my choice."

"Where have you landed?"

"I'm at the stage where I think there's real value in our special combination of lawyers. I believe that creating a business, paying our employees above the prevailing rate, and thinking of all of us as friends, is worthwhile. But I fully realize I may just be rationalizing."

"I don't think so, Heather. You may be underestimating the impact you've already had on people—the ones directly involved, and the ones who are watching what your firm is doing. I have nothing but respect for your work." He pushed his glasses up again, then smiled.

The compliment did it. My knee finally stopped bouncing. "Thanks. Actually, we may be able to put a plan together to take on some pro-bono cases this year. Annie says she's making it her New Year's resolution to submit a proposal to the partners. I handled one or two asylum cases a year at my old firm, but Annie doesn't know that. Because I have that background, I could easily supervise the cases if Marnie and Danni agree the firm should volunteer for some. I admire the way Annie doesn't hesitate to make suggestions. I can't even imagine a finer first associate for us."

"I'd say she's lucky, as well."

"You're very kind, Charlie."

A young red-haired man in a gray-green sports coat whom I hadn't yet met showed up beside the booth, struggling with the weight of a cardboard box full of champagne bottles. He said, "Time to get pouring."

"Heather, Jim. Jim, Heather." Charlie slid the trays of flutes out of the way so Jim could place the box on the table.

I nodded to Jim, who nodded back. I said to Charlie, "How can I help?"

"I'll tell you what. I'll pop the corks and hand the bottles to you and Jim to fill the glasses and set them back on the trays." We got to work, and moved hurriedly. Once we'd filled each flute, Charlie said we should step out of the way of the servers, who would be arriving momentarily. We both slipped out of the booth and had finally reached the living room when Sam's sudden, loud announcement jolted me. His voice came through on a speaker.

"The countdown to the New Year starts now. Ten...nine..." I looked for the source of the announcement and glimpsed him with one arm around Danni and a microphone in the other hand. Annie was just beside them, facing Bradley, holding both of his hands. "Eight...seven...six..." I had no time to think. Should I shake Charlie's hand? Hug him? "Three...two..."

He leaned toward me and surprised me by saying, "May I kiss you?"

"One!"

I had no idea why I nodded yes. I'd known the man for only a couple of hours. He touched my bare shoulders as lightly as if his hands were butterflies. His lips reached mine for a chaste kiss that sent tingles down my spine the way a rough hug and a long French kiss is supposed to. His lips were uncommonly soft and warm upon mine. I swallowed hard as I took a step back and smiled. "Happy New Year, Charlie."

"And to you."

The others launched into *Auld Lang Sine*, and I joined in, tears filling my eyes. My dearest friends were in that room. Someone passed around one of the large trays filled with sparkling champagne flutes we'd filled, and finally reached Charlie and me. We toasted and sipped, eyes on each other. After a couple of minutes, several of Charlie's friends came out of nowhere to hug him, just as Marnie and Danni rushed up to me. Marnie made a double toast, "To friends. And to Jeanne. We wish she were here." I drank again.

Loud dance music came on and several couples started the flow into a large family room I'd barely noticed before. Charlie returned to me and asked if I'd like to dance. I nodded as I shed my heels and flung them toward the pile of footwear expanding beside the wall.

Charlie took my hand and led me in.

The room was tucked behind the kitchen, with three of its large walls made wholly of windows. Because the back yard was illuminated, the bare, mature deciduous trees and the full growth evergreens seemed to lie just beyond my reach. Someone had pushed back all of the furniture, displaying a highly polished hardwood floor in the rectangular room. It struck me as reminiscent of an old-fashioned ballroom. It was perfect.

Whoever dimmed the lights had my undying gratitude because I'd never been an exhibitionist kind of dancer. It was more something I did alone in my living room in rare moments of unbridled joy, with Chica-the-Brave cocking her head in wonderment. It had been so long since I'd had a man's arms around me that I couldn't even remember it—and had no desire to try. Living in the present—feeling as though I were part of a gorgeously cascading night—was more than satisfactory. I had the strange sensation of something inside me loosening.

Most of the couples around us looked to be unconnected dancers, each enthralled in their own ecstasy, the beat and the melody flowing through them. Who exactly was dancing with whom wasn't readily apparent. But Charlie's eyes never left me, even when, as embarrassed as I was delighted by his attention, I glanced around the dance floor to witness the flashes of colorful garments and bodies, some with heads lolling, eyes closed, others gyrating to the pulsing rhythm.

Light from strobes washed over the crowd, white dots with some songs, splashes of deep color with others. Charlie proved to be as tender a dance partner as a kisser. He was helpful, smooth, and confident as he guided me through steps I barely remembered, but all of which seemed to involve twirls and dips. As he and I moved to the music, I glimpsed Sam holding Danni up to him with his arms around her waist. She threw her head back like a figure-skater, hair flying out behind her. We left the dance floor a couple of times, desperate for glasses of water, but it was too loud for conversation.

After what seemed like an hour of cardio and eardrum-challenging songs, the DJ started in on the slow dances. The room remained dim, and only the tiny white dots of light splashed over us. Surprisingly, being in the arms of a man I liked but barely knew felt not the least bit strange. We danced until the music finally faded and people found their shoes and began to say goodbyes.

I felt flushed from the alcohol, the dancing, and Charlie's attention. I guided him to a spot near the front door so I wouldn't miss saying good night to any of my old friends or new acquaintances. Annie and Bradley were among the first to leave in light of their long drive. They both looked so happy as they gave out hugs and handshakes, I imagined them still swaying to the music all the way back to Eloise. By the time the number of guests had thinned to a handful of couples, it was almost 3:00 a.m. Marnie approached and whispered that she wouldn't be Ubering back with me because Ivani had offered to drive her home. Charlie asked if he could give me a ride to Evanston, but I declined, not wanting to spoil my unexpectedly lovely evening with any decisions or disappointments. I did give him my number and knew even then it would be hard to wait for him to call. We hugged our goodbye at the front door.

As I rode home, alone in an Uber, I realized that what was so engaging about Charlie reminded me of

Jeanne in that every word he spoke and every movement he made seemed purposeful. He struck me as unusually relaxed, possessing a serenity reminiscent of a few spiritual people I'd come across. Being with him had made me completely forget my muscle aches. Or maybe it was all the champagne.

Chapter 28

I slept in on New Year's Day and awoke with neither chills nor aches. After luxuriating in a long, hot bath, I pulled on my sweats, ready for a relaxing at-home-alone day. As part of my plan to not think about Charlie, I grabbed a novel I'd been looking forward to, cozied up on a couch in front of my space heater with Chica-the-Brave, and spent the entire day reading. Around 9:00 p.m., there was a knock on my door. I opened it to Marnie and Danni, neither of whom was in sweats or pjs.

"Hi. What's up?"

"Not you, apparently," said Marnie.

"I was just enjoying a novel and a quiet day. What about you two?" We all moved into the living room and arranged ourselves on the couches, Danni beside me, and Marnie across from us. Chica-the-Brave made herself comfortable with her little head resting on my lap.

"How did you like the party?" asked Danni.

"It was fabulous. Thanks again."

"Did you run off with the tall guy?" asked Marnie.

"Obviously not. Since I'm sitting right here."

"Let me rephrase that. I saw you with him most of the evening. When you danced, his eyes were pasted to yours, and vice versa—after your miraculous recovery from your body aches."

"You could've asked me to introduce you to him."

"I would've. But my time was occupied."

"Mm-hmm."

"So, who is he?"

"I can answer that," said Danni. "Charlie is Sam's best friend. He's studying social work at Northwestern. Sam says Charlie's the real deal."

"Meaning?"

"To Sam, that means he's a straight-arrow. Unpretentious. With a genuine social conscience that propels him to do more than feel bad about the state of the world."

"Well, Danni, that's all lovely for his humanitarian award nomination, but will he pass muster as a boyfriend for Heather?"

I laughed. "He's hardly my boyfriend. We talked a lot about real issues, and I enjoyed hearing his ideas. He's a very thoughtful person, gentle and sensitive, I think. He asked for my number, but I don't know if he'll call."

Marnie mocked me. "You don't know if he'll call? Heather, I saw him kiss you, and it was quite a tender scene."

"Wait. Why weren't you kissing your new friend at that moment instead of spying on me?"

Marnie dramatically raised her chin and looked down her nose at me. "It just so happens that Ivani has a girlfriend. He told me about her as soon as we started talking. She would've been with him last night, but for the fact that she's still home visiting her family. He said they're breaking up, but he intends to be faithful as long as they're remotely still together. So, he just gave me a quick hug at midnight."

"What happened when he drove you home?" asked

Danni.

"The sweetest thing ever. He walked me to the front door, took my hand, and asked if I'd be willing to see him again, once his breakup is over. No hug. He shook my hand. It was the most romantic moment of my life."

"I love that," said Danni, as she clapped her hands together.

"Were you out with him again today?" I asked, as Chica-the-Brave popped down, pranced over to Marnie, and jumped up to sit beside her on the other couch, where she was rewarded with a belly-rub.

"He called at ten o'clock, so of course, I was sound asleep."

"Of course."

"He said, 'Do you think we could go out today—just as friends?' I thought, do hummingbirds hum?"

"Still don't know," said Danni, shrugging.

"What did you guys do?" I asked.

"We went downtown to ice skate in the park. Ivani said he loved the idea of it, but hadn't actually done it before. Fortunately, that was one class my evil mother had allowed me to take—well, just for one winter. I was able to keep us upright, which did require me to hold his hand—not nearly as exciting as it would've been if we hadn't both been wearing thick gloves."

"I wish I could've seen it." We all glanced at my window, having heard a few gunshots in the distance. If it hadn't been New Year's Day, we would've been concerned.

"Actually, Heather, I think we were pretty smooth, although you know how much I hate to brag."

"Of course."

She smiled. "We took a long walk down Michigan

Avenue, around the curve at Lake Shore Drive, and through some high-end neighborhoods full of graystones still wearing their holiday finery. Finally, we found a place for an early dinner."

"I'm surprised anything was open on New Year's Day," said Danni.

"I know. It must've been the only place. The owners had planted their business in the basement of a large stone building on the end of a residential street. We held onto the rail for dear life, since the steps were fairly steep, and not what you would call totally ice-free. But once we walked through the door, we were in heaven."

"I always thought heaven was up," I said, as I rearranged myself to tuck my legs under me. I grabbed a pile of three small throws and placed one over my lap. I offered the other two, but Marnie and Danni both shook their heads.

"Definitely down. Since we were both frozen solid by then, we were thrilled by the toasty air we stepped into. The hostess seated us beside the stone fireplace where the blaze was literally roaring. I had a hot buttered rum for the first time in my life, and Ivani went for a hot cocoa, which came in an enormous, thick mug, and topped with a halo of whipped cream so shiny it looked like a plastic replica."

"But it was good. Right?" asked Danni.

"Everything was incredible. We had bowls of steaming clam chowder, French bread, and salads. There's something about sustenance when our bodies are stressed that makes it delectable."

"I know," said Danni. "It's like the taste of the beans and hot dogs we made over a fire after a long day of hiking when I was little. You can't bottle that ingredient, but it's the world's best seasoning."

"Exactly." She picked up Chica-the-Brave and kissed her on the head. "Ivani didn't drop me off until almost seven o'clock."

"Did you get another handshake?" I asked.

"It was unbelievable. When Ivani touched my hand, it was almost as good as sex. In some ways, far superior." She smiled, and let it linger.

I said, "So, Marnie, will you continue with your Friday night activities?"

"Of course not. Once you've tasted champagne, you can't go back to crap drinks."

Marnie said, "What did you and Sam do today?"

"We played games."

"Sexy games?" asked Marnie.

"Of course not. Real, old-fashioned games."

"But those aren't really two-person games, Danni," I said.

She sighed. "We improvised. Plus, we took Grizzly and Buddy for a long walk in the bitter cold. The dogs looked ridiculous in their matching red plaid snow booties, but we had to protect their paws from the ice and salt on the sidewalks. Then Sam made us a fabulous meal. Now that Marnie's mentioned it, the food may have tasted extraordinary because we'd just come in from Antarctica. But Sam really is a terrific cook. It was heaven just hanging out."

"I'm glad, Danni. Would you two like some snacks or something to drink? I could whip up omelets." I started to get up, but each of them shook her head.

Marnie said, "Actually, I just wanted to hear about your boyfriend."

"He's not my—"

Danni interrupted. "I hope you do get to know Charlie better. Whether he's just a friend or something more, he's definitely worth spending time with."

I gave her a smile. "Yeah. I think so. Guys, I can't tell you how happy I am that you both got to visit heaven today. I had a lovely day, too. But more like purgatory, trying not to think about Charlie—which, of course, made it impossible."

"Only a Catholic would make that analogy," said Marnie. "Anyway, anticipation is a big part of the fun. Really, Heather, I hope you can just relax and see where it goes without getting hung up on your special worry."

"I hope so, too."

Marnie started to get up from the couch, then plopped back down. "Before I go, I want to let you guys know something I discovered a few days ago. You two were still out of town, and I was bored to death one night, so I poked around on the Internet." She paused for several seconds to lose her shoes and tuck her legs up under. "Have you guys ever Googled Jeanne?"

"Of course not," I said.

"It never occurred to me," said Danni. "Have you?"

"Would I have brought it up if I hadn't?" asked Marnie.

Danni laughed. "So, what? Is she on the FBI's most wanted list?"

"Not on it, per se."

"What are you talking about, Marnie?" I asked, pulling the throw higher.

"Jeanne isn't who we think she is."

I raised my voice a bit. "The only thing I think she is is a hell of an office manager, a supportive friend, and someone who often speaks poetically."

"Oh, she's all of that," said Marnie.

"Don't tease us. What does your opposition research show?" I asked.

"Number one, I only tease hot guys. And number two, I am not now, and never will be, in opposition to Jeanne. But I will admit I've been curious about her background because she's always so vague and secretive about it. It turns out she's not on Facebook or any other social media."

"But that's not unusual for older people," said Danni.

Marnie leaned in a little. "That's true. So, anyway, there was nothing on Google except her date of birth and the years of her marriage. But while I was scrolling around, I caught a glimpse of a woman who looked to be her twin. The woman's name is Jeanne Cooper."

"That is interesting," I said.

"It could be a coincidence," said Danni.

"It's no coincidence. They have the same birth date, and the dates of their marriages are identical."

"So, you're saying our Jeanne once went by the name of Jeanne Cooper?" I was trying to make sense out of it but couldn't fathom why she'd need two identities.

"Yeah."

"But for what purpose?" asked Danni.

"She never wanted any publicity, but I was able to find a couple of articles about her."

"What?" I asked, a little too loudly.

"She's a psychic. Not one of those phony ones with the crystal ball and the palm reading schtick. The real thing."

"How do you know she's really psychic?" I asked.

Marnie leaned in a little farther. "Jeanne

311

Coopersmith has worked as a legal secretary, then an office manager, since she was in her early twenties. But, as Jeanne Cooper, until two years ago, she spent a month or so every winter flying all over the South and Southwest to help the FBI and state and local law enforcement agencies solve crimes. Apparently, she's been especially useful at finding dead bodies and coming up with clues about how they got that way."

"I can see why she'd want to keep that a secret," said Danni. "A lot of people would think she's a little bit nuts to believe in the voodoo stuff."

"It's not voodoo for Jeanne. Her talents have proven very useful. The two articles I found from local newspapers, one from Georgia and one from Texas, mentioned her and a couple of other psychics, and how their intuitions had solved crimes. None of the clairvoyants would agree to be interviewed, and the law enforcement agencies never reveal much about how the work of these people helps solve cases."

"That makes sense to me," I said. "After all, once they've found the body, it doesn't really matter that it was a psychic who led them to it."

Marnie leaned still farther toward us, and I feared she might fall off the couch. She lowered her voice. "There's more. I found a follow-up article that appeared in the Georgia paper. It said she married the son of an elderly woman whom Jeanne had pinpointed in the woods outside an assisted living facility. The lady had been missing for a couple of days, and the son, desperate, pressed the police, whose searches weren't producing anything, about what else could be done. Jeanne was flown down from Chicago on a private jet and taken to the nursing home, an elegant, upscale place, surrounded by acres and acres of land. Apparently, she sat in the woman's room for ten minutes and then led the rescue team directly to the lady, who had lain down in a ditch and covered herself with leaves for warmth. She was dehydrated and disoriented but otherwise uninjured."

"That's pretty impressive," said Danni.

"The police paid Jeanne her customary, modest fee and she rejected the man's efforts to give her more of a reward. All of this information came from the man, who was so relieved that he spoke to a reporter at the scene. Jeanne was back at her secretarial desk the next morning, none of her co-workers the wiser. The man had been quite taken with her, flew up to Chicago regularly to court her, and married her in 1976, according to another follow-up article."

Danni asked, "Did they stay married until two years ago, when she told us her husband died?"

"Yeah. Same guy," said Marnie. "But here's the kicker."

She paused, and I held my breath.

"He was the owner of Dalmatron Industries."

"*The* Dalmatron?" I asked.

"The same. After he died, Jeanne sold the business for millions of dollars."

"And the 'very old home that requires constant repairs to keep it habitable'?" asked Danni.

"A 1920's era mansion overlooking Lake Michigan."

"Why didn't she tell us?" asked Danni.

I was having trouble visualizing Jeanne as a millionaire.

"I've been thinking about it," said Marnie. "Maybe she imagined we wouldn't hire her. And maybe she's keeping busy with work because her grief would overwhelm her if she sat at home doing nothing."

"I don't think it has to change anything about our relationship with her," said Danni.

"Certainly not," said Marnie. "We're all entitled to our secrets. Although mine are probably the most X-rated."

"But you don't know that, do you?" asked Danni. "I mean, if they are secrets, none of us knows."

"I dislike all this talk of secrets." I said.

Marnie said, "The lady doth protest too much, me thinks."

I just shook my head, as any additional words could've been construed as more protest.

Danni said, "It will take me a little while to digest what you said about Jeanne. And if she's psychic, won't she know that we know?"

"Maybe," said Marnie. "But I don't see how we can un-know it." She shrugged.

"Are you sure you guys don't want to stay for a while and talk this out? The omelet offer is still good."

"I wish I had the energy, Heather," said Danni. "But I'm wiped out. Anyway, it'll take me awhile to absorb all this information about Jeanne."

"Work tomorrow, guys," said Marnie. "Oh, by the way, Annie told me she'll need to bring Eloise with her to the office."

"Terrific," I said. "I really enjoy having that little girl around." I paused. "Shall we meet in the morning to catch the seven twenty-five?"

"Definitely," said Marnie. Danni nodded.

The two of them walked out of my apartment, Danni whistling and Marnie humming along—things they'd picked up from Annie, I assumed, since they never did either before she joined us.

Ten minutes later, my phone rang while I was brushing my teeth. When I located my cell under my book, I saw it was Danni. I quickly rinsed my mouth before I picked up.

"Hi, Danni. Did you leave something here?"

"No, Heather. I was just thinking more about what I said about Charlie."

"You want to retract your compliments?" My chest tightened.

"Not at all. I just feel like I should tell you the rest of the story."

"Okay." I sat on the corner of my bed and Chica-the-Brave moved over to lean against my hip.

"Everything you saw in Charlie last night at the party, and what I told you a few minutes ago, is true."

"Good. So, what's the skeleton in his closet?"

"From my perspective, the skeleton is in his ex-fiancée's closet."

This confirmed it would be bad news. "Oh." I bit my lip as she went on.

"Up until about a year ago—just before Charlie left for Appalachia—he was engaged to Pamela."

"Pamela?"

"Yeah. A girl he met on campus."

"So, what happened?"

"They agreed to call it off because they came to realize their life goals just weren't compatible."

"What are you talking about, Danni?" I was absent-mindedly stroking Chica-the-Brave's head and back.

"Charlie was very open about it when he told me. Pamela was just finishing her MBA and wanted them to make a lot of money so they could afford a nice condo in the city and lots of travel. But Charlie is perfectly content with a low-paying, service-oriented job. He's a frugal guy, and just wants a simple life. As an example, he's one of the few people I know who believes the damage to the environment by unnecessary air travel directly translates to his avoidance of long flights. Plus, he's hoping to have a family."

"Pamela didn't want children?"

"Apparently, she hadn't given it much thought because she'd been so busy with school and her part-time job at a bank. She wasn't ready to commit to having kids. She also feared she'd grow bitter about Charlie's relatively small contribution to their income."

"She ended the engagement?"

"It was mutual. I think they were both embarrassed they hadn't realized sooner they actually aspire to different things. I've heard that Pamela is a really good person. It was just that she'd grown up poor, and wants to enjoy a more luxurious life than her parents had. The break-up was tough on both of them."

"I see. But why are you telling me this?"

"I adore Charlie. And you know I love you, Heather. I just don't want to see either of you hurt."

"So, you're giving me a heads-up on his dream lifestyle before I fall for him, discover mine is different, and break his heart—again."

"And yours—again. Yeah. That's pretty much it."

"Okay. Thanks, Danni. I do like Charlie. And I'm attracted to him. But he hasn't even asked me out for a first date. So, I'll just tuck away what you said and take it a step at a time."

"Good plan. I'll see you in the morning, Heather."

"Good night. And thanks." Even though I hadn't done a thing to burn calories all day, I felt exhausted. I slipped under the sheets and my Aunt Agatha's quilt. Chica-the-Brave arranged herself so her little head rested on my leg.

Chapter 29

Jeanne wasn't due back until the next day, so Mary greeted us as we walked into our suite. She said, "Annie's here, and her darlin' daughter is sitting in the conference room with books and drawing materials."

We all three stopped by to welcome the little girl on our way to her mother's office to tell her how much we liked Bradley. Although none of us had a court hearing or a deposition that day, we were all swamped with work. We had sandwiches delivered for our lunch, and Annie took Eloise out to a nearby diner to break up her long day.

Late that afternoon, I needed to stretch my legs, and I also wanted to visit with Eloise for a few minutes since we so seldom got to see her. I walked into the conference room and sat down at the table across from her. As I said, "Hi," she looked up from the book she was reading, and said, "Hi, Ms. Hightower."

"Are you enjoying the book?"

She carefully inserted a cardboard bookmark, closed the book, and turned it so I could read the cover. "I loved that book when I was your age."

"Really?"

"Mm-hmm. But it was kind of shocking that a child could be so different from her parents that she didn't really fit in with her own family."

"That's true. They don't match. She loves books like

I do, and my whole family does. Thank goodness. It would be terrible if my mom ripped up one of *my* library books."

"Does the book make you feel sad?"

"I don't know if you remember this about the story, but the main character outsmarts her family when they're mean to her. So, it's more about girl-empowerment."

I was surprised at how clearly Eloise saw what kept the story from being miserable. "Yes. Thanks for reminding me."

"It's one of the most delicious things about the book."

I nodded. "Definitely. So, did you have a good Christmas, Eloise?"

"Yes. Did you?"

"It was lovely. But I especially enjoyed New Year's Eve."

"Because of the party my mother went to with Bradley?"

"Exactly. What was your favorite part of the holidays?"

"Having Bradley and Mama home with Grandma Ann and me." Eloise grew more and more animated as she spoke. "We all got up on Christmas Eve morning and had pancakes and hot chocolate for breakfast. Then Bradley went up in the attic and brought down three boxes of Christmas decorations! Well, Mama had put the tree up the week before, but we didn't have time to decorate it until Christmas Eve. Bradley and Mama strung all the lights, because they're electrical and she didn't want me to get shocked." She rolled her eyes. "Actually, I think I'm old enough to deal with Christmas tree lights. Anyway, my grandma and Mama told me about each ornament as I unwrapped it out of the newspaper, although there were a few they couldn't remember. Of course, I knew about the ones I made, and I put those right in front where everybody could see them."

"Did you use garland or tinsel?"

"We made our own garland out of popcorn. Grandma Ann used her needle and thread to make enough to go around the tree like three times, and I got to eat tons of popcorn. But if you're asking about icicles, we don't use them because they're bad for the environment."

"I've heard that, too." I assumed Eloise to be an extrovert, like her mother, because she grew livelier and more engaging the longer we talked.

"Then I went to my room to wrap the crafts I made for everybody so I could put them under the tree. And when I went back downstairs with the gifts, Mama was just putting on a Christmas movie."

"Which one?"

"The one with the pathetic little stick tree."

"I love that movie. That night, did you put out cookies for Santa?"

She rolled her eyes, again. "Actually, I did. But it was just to make the adults happy. The funny thing was, it kind of made me happy too, to remember my childhood days. Of course, the chocolate chip cookies and the carrots for the reindeer were gone in the morning." She winked at me and reminded me so much of her mother.

"Do you have a favorite among the presents you got?"

"This will sound stupid. I got a lot of nice things.

But the truth is, my best gift is seeing how happy Mama is this year. Ms. Hightower, you have no idea how much better everything is in a family when the mother is super-happy."

"I believe you're right. I'm really glad for you, Eloise. You are a very wise young lady." As I rose to leave, I said, "I want to thank you again for the drawing you made for me on your last visit. It's still up on my wall where I can see it every day. It was really sweet that you drew yourself next to me."

"That isn't me, Ms. Hightower."

"Oh. I just assumed."

"If I was drawing myself, I would've filled me in with shiny black."

"Of course you would. Do you mind telling me who it is?"

"I don't know." She shrugged. "Jeanne just told me to draw you with one little girl, and what to draw on the pictures for Ms. Ames and Ms. Dooley."

"Did she say why?"

"Nope." Eloise glanced downward, and I realized she wanted to get back to her reading.

"Well, thank you again. And happy New Year, Eloise."

"Happy New Year to you, too!"

I walked back into my office, closed my door, and fell into my chair. I swiveled it to stare out my window. The sky was a deep blue with light-striated clouds floating by. I was too confounded to enjoy the view, so I tried to read the shapes like a Rorschach Test, and got nowhere. I turned and glanced at my wall, now realizing that the answer had been taped up there on a sheet of paper since Eloise's last visit. Tears streamed down my cheeks and I knew my mascara must be running, so I dashed to the restroom to freshen up, then impatiently waited to approach Marnie and Danni until Annie and Eloise had left for the train. I knocked on Marnie's door, my picture in hand, and asked her to join me in Danni's office for a minute. Once we were all seated, Marnie said, "What's up?"

"I just wanted to share with you guys a conversation I had with Eloise today."

"Great!" said Danni, who was sitting at her desk with a pile of documents in front of her. "I always love to hear her insights."

"Okay. Here goes." I recounted the entire conversation, but without my conclusion.

Danni said, "When Eloise gave me my picture, I asked her who the other figures were."

"What did she say?" asked Marnie.

"That she didn't know. So, I just assumed they were random people, just there to contrast with my short stature."

"You should've asked the follow-up question," said Marnie. She then reached over and took my picture out of my hand and stared at it.

I asked Marnie, "So, did you ask about yours?"

"Nope. I'm stupid, too. I thought it was obvious it was a drawing of me, with Eloise…Oh, shit."

Danni suddenly turned pale. "Are you okay?" I asked. It seemed they'd both gleaned the meaning in the same instant.

Emotions flashed across Danni's face in sequence, from fear to astonishment, to joy, back to fear. I asked again, "Are you okay?"

Still not answering, she opened her top desk drawer

and pulled out a sheet of paper, a page from a yellow legal pad. She handed it to Marnie, who shared it with me. The drawing was a decent rendering of Danni wearing a big smile, standing next to three girls in pigtails, all taller than her, all holding hands. "They're all average size. How could I possibly—"

Marnie said, "Babies are really tiny when the mom gives birth, Danni. You'll be fine."

I turned to Marnie. "Did you keep your drawing? I don't remember seeing it in your office."

"That's because it's in my bedroom, a place you've never been."

"Why is that, anyway?" I asked.

"Doesn't matter. I've decided to redecorate. New bed, new furniture, new linens. Then I'll give you a tour."

"And the drawing?" asked Danni.

"Oh, I'll have that framed and hang it right back where it's been, on the wall over my dresser." She paused to study the two pictures. When she looked up, she said, "You know, it's a funny thing. Whoever would've dreamed when we first met that evening at the bar in Chicago that a little over two and a half years later, we'd all be relishing pieces of paper from a yellow legal pad?"

At that point, we were all grinning like idiots. We couldn't help ourselves.

Marnie glanced down at the pictures again, then looked up quickly. "Wait a minute. Did you guys notice there are no men in these pictures?"

Danni's smile faded. "What does it mean?"

"I don't think it means anything," I said. "Jeanne was probably just focusing on the issue of children. In fact, I think I told her about the Women Lawyers' Club's plan to set up a day care center."

"So?" said Marnie.

"So she knows there is some interest among us in possibly having children."

"I'm not convinced," said Marnie.

I raised my voice. "How could you be convinced? None of us knows what the hell's going on."

"Heather's right," said Danni. "I'm exhausted from my first day back. Let's hit the road. We can agonize over the meaning of the drawings on the train."

We all grabbed our briefcases and purses, then retrieved our coats from the closet in the reception area. I happened to glance at the secretarial space. "Someone left an envelope on Jeanne's desk chair."

"That's interesting," said Danni. "It wasn't there an hour ago."

Marnie stepped into Jeanne's work space and lifted the manila envelope. "It says, 'to Jeanne, from Eloise.'"

Danni and I glanced at each other.

Marnie started to lift the metal tab.

"You can't do that," said Danni. "It's private."

Marnie dramatically turned the envelope around a couple of times. "It doesn't say 'private.'"

I said, "Nevertheless, it would be unethical to open Jeanne's mail."

"It's not mail," said Marnie. "If it were, it would be a felony to intercept it. But look." She held it up again. "No stamp. No street address. No U.S. Postal Service involvement."

"Marnie!" said Danni.

But she already had it out, another page from a yellow legal pad. She read it to herself, then slid the paper back into the envelope, clasped it shut, and returned it to Jeanne's desk chair. "That explains everything."

"What?" I said.

Marnie lifted her chin as she said, "I will not be a party to your doing something unethical."

"Come on, Marnie," said Danni. "We're already accessories for not stopping you. We may as well know what the note says."

Marnie shook her head emphatically. "No. I would never involve you guys in something as nefarious as what I just did."

"Stop fooling around," I said. "I won't be able to rest until I know whatever you know."

"Heather, there's no way you'll ever know whatever I know."

"Why do you say things like that? How can you be so confident you know more than I do?"

"I'm not boasting. But with my photographic memory, everything I ever knew, I still know. Normal people forget things."

"Oh. Well, I'm referring only to the contents of Eloise's note."

Marnie had come out from behind Jeanne's desk, and leaned against a wall. "Fine. Do you want it verbatim?"

"Yes," said Danni.

She dramatically cleared her throat. "Um-hm. *'Dear Jeanne, I'm sorry you weren't here today. I hope you had a good holiday. I did. The last time I was here you told me what to put on the second set of pictures for my mom's bosses—the couples' pictures. I didn't have time to finish those, so I took them home to do. Now they're done. But I would like you to look at them to be sure they are right, before I give them to Ms. Hightower, Ms. Dooley and Ms. Ames. So, I'll make sure I bring them with me the next time I come to the office. Happy New Year! I miss you! Love, Eloise'"*

"Oh, my," Danni and I said at the same time.

Chapter 30

The next morning, I was looking forward to opening the office door and finding Jeanne, already typing away, looking up and giving us her cheery, "Good morning, girls!" But when we entered, the rooms were dark. No sign of Jeanne.

As she hung her coat in the closet, Marnie said, "I wonder if her return flight was delayed."

"Check the messages," said Danni. "She would've called."

As the fluorescent lights flickered on through our space, I slipped into Jeanne's spot to check the phone. Nothing.

"This is so odd," said Danni. "We should call her cell."

Marnie said, "Let's give her a half hour. She may just be running late, and I don't want her to think we're annoyed that she's late for work for the first time in her life."

"Good point," I said, as I slipped out of my coat and took Danni's from her. "I'll give her a call around eight thirty, when Annie gets in." I made the coffee, then got to work wading through a pile of briefs. It was around eight-fifteen when the phone rang on our general number. I picked up, and imitated Jeanne's salubrious "Hightower, Dooley and Ames. How may I help you?"

"I'm trying to reach Heather Hightower." It sounded

like an older man.

"You've reached her." I grabbed a pen to make a note of whatever he wanted.

"Oh, good. I'm Sergeant Michaels with the Tampa Police Department. I'm afraid I have some very bad news for you, ma'am."

I didn't know anyone in Tampa, so he wasn't making any sense. "Excuse me?"

"Jeanne Coopersmith passed away yesterday afternoon—at the airport, actually."

I felt my heart sink. "What? How?"

"She had a heart attack. Died within minutes."

"Oh, no."

"We got your name and the name of a lawyer in Lake Forest, Illinois, from business cards she had in her purse. On yours, she'd printed the words 'my girls,' so I assumed she'd want me to call you. Are you her daughter?"

"No. I'm—" I could feel the blood draining from my head. I saw myself free falling into an abyss. I needed to get a grip. "Right. What should we do?"

"Nothing. Her lawyer from Lake Forest has all the information on her wishes. He said he'll give you a call. His name is James Phillips."

"May I have his number?"

"I don't see why not. I gave him yours—although he said he already had it."

"What?"

Sergeant Michaels gave me the number, then said, "I'm really sorry, ma'am," and hung up.

Annie passed my office on her way to hers. "Good morning, Heather!" She was greeting me as she walked, but apparently the look on my face was enough to stop her mid-stride. She stood in my doorway. "What's happened?"

I couldn't speak. Literally. My tongue had turned to cotton, my lips to balloons. But the effort to utter a word did unleash my tears. Annie shouted over her shoulder, "Marnie! Danni!" as she approached my desk.

"Jeez! Why in the world are you hollering at—" said Marnie as she reached my door.

Danni was right behind her. When the two of them set eyes on me, the explanation for Annie's scream was obvious. Jeanne wasn't sitting out front, and I looked like I'd just watched a truck run over Chica-the-Brave.

"What happened to Jeanne? Is she okay?" asked Danni. The three of them were standing at my desk, staring at me.

I still couldn't get my mouth to unfreeze. They looked so desperate, I was finally able to spit out, "Dead."

"No!" screamed Marnie, just before she sat and began pounding on my desk.

Danni fell into the other chair, and put her head in her hands.

Annie simply crumpled, and ended up sitting on the floor, her mouth hanging open.

Watching my friends falling apart seemed to give me the strength to force out more words. "Heart attack." I sucked in a deep breath. "Yesterday." Then, "The airport."

"Damn it. Damn it all," said Marnie, through tears.

We were sisters who had just lost our mother. We really were Jeanne's girls. And the news that we would never see her again was unbearable, as such news always was. We did nothing but cry and curse for a half hour or more, our only interaction being hugs and the passing of my tissue box.

"She was a mother to me," said Marnie.

"More than a friend, for sure," said Annie.

"She was like an angel who watched over us," said Danni. "Even though we didn't even have her for quite two years, I got the feeling she loved us from the first day we met."

"She said as much," I said.

"No one has ever been more encouraging to me," said Marnie. "No one. Ever."

Annie said, "Eloise only visited with her that one day, but that evening she told me she loved Jeanne. She's included Jeanne in her prayers every night since. I think children see with the clarity of pure hearts." She paused. "Oh my God! Eloise will be devastated."

"There are never sufficient words," said Danni. "Our hearts are broken, and none of us will ever get through another day without feeling the ache of her absence."

I made a limp smile. "That was very Jeannesque, Danni."

She tried to return my slack attempt, but dissolved into tears again.

I said, "I think we should all pack up our things and head home. We can't work today."

"You guys go ahead," said Annie. "I think I'll do my cursing and crying here rather than in front of my mother."

"Of course," I said. "I'll just make a quick call to Jeanne's lawyer, and let you guys know what he has to say. Then I'm ready to go."

The three of them clung to each other as they left my

office. I could feel a tightness, and then an ache in my chest, and wondered how painful it had been for Jeanne. I dialed Mr. Phillips, and was put through after a brief wait. "Hello. This is Heather Hightower."

"Oh, Ms. Hightower. I'm glad you reached me. I was just about to call you." There was genuine warmth in his voice.

"You're Jeanne's personal lawyer?"

"For quite a few years. And a very old friend of hers and her late husband."

"Ah."

"She was a very special woman. To tell you the truth, Ms. Hightower, I'm just crushed. And I know you must be, too."

"Yes. Marnie, Danni, Annie and I all are. I'm sorry for your loss."

"Thank you. And I for yours." He paused. "So, what I wanted you all to know is that Jeanne entrusted me with all of her personal affairs. This morning, I've been reviewing the document expressing her wishes upon her death, and also her will."

"What are her wishes?"

"Cremation. Ashes to be strewn by me over Lake Michigan, just behind her home." He paused. "I suppose I'll need to rent a boat to do it properly. But I digress. I'm sorry to tell you that she insists on no obituary and no memorial service."

"That's a shame. It'll be hard not to have a remembrance ceremony of some kind."

"She told me you'd say that. Jeanne said she hoped you would remember her often, but that the idea of a wake of any kind rather creeped her out."

I couldn't imagine Jeanne using that phrase. I

believed she was more likely to say something like, "I don't appreciate the overindulgence in sentimentality." But all I said was, "I understand. We all loved her very much."

"Well, she told me on many occasions that she loved you, 'her girls.' She's asked that her will be read here in my office's conference room within two weeks of her death."

"That's very quick, isn't it?"

"Yes. But there's nothing to prevent it. I'm perfectly willing to do it a week from tomorrow, Saturday the eleventh, since you all work during the week."

"That's very considerate."

"Shall we say ten o'clock next Saturday morning?"

"If you can hold on for a moment, I'll check with the others." It took me a couple of minutes to explain, and get everyone's agreement. "Mr. Phillips?"

"Yes. I'm still here."

"I apologize for the delay. Ten o'clock works for us. Can all of the other people do it then?"

"That won't be a problem. I'll send my address by email. Of course, I have yours in my file since it's where Jeanne worked."

"Right. Thank you."

"I'm sorry we'll be meeting under such sad circumstances. Nevertheless, I look forward to introducing myself to Jeanne's dear friends."

"Thank you."

Marnie and Danni were ready to head to the train, so we all got together in the reception area. I reported what Mr. Phillips had said.

"Wow. That seems fast," said Marnie.

"And so like Jeanne," said Annie. "Everything

organized and ready to go."

"She was a treasure," I said.

"There will never be another Jeanne," said Danni. She paused, then added, "I don't want to sound cold, but don't we need to find an office manager pretty darn soon?"

"It's not cold," I said. "It occurred to me, too. How do you all feel about Mary?"

"She's like Jeanne without the hyperbole. I like her," said Marnie. "Plus, her Irish accent will give us an international flair."

"Yeah. She's been great," said Annie.

"Danni?" I asked.

"She does a solid job. The fact she was also Jeanne's long-time friend cinches it for me."

"Right. Another connection," I reached down to grab my briefcase, and said, "Let's get going. I'll call Mary from home to let her know about Jeanne and ask her to think about taking the position."

We all hugged, and Marnie, Danni and I left for the train, wiping tears from our faces as we walked. We would devote the day to grieving privately in our apartments. I imagined we'd spend the rest of our years grieving together.

Chapter 31

On Saturday, Annie was already sitting in Mr. Phillips' waiting room when we arrived at ten o'clock. I would never have guessed his age from his telephone voice, but he must've been in his eighties. He was thin, stooped, and wore a gray three-piece suit just a shade darker than his thinning hair. "Hello. I'm James Phillips. Please do me the honor of calling me James. I've had the pleasure of meeting Annie. Ms. Hightower, it's wonderful to finally meet you."

He shook my hand, and I said, "Heather, please."

He turned to Danni, and leaned over to take her hand. "Delighted, Ms. Dooley."

Danni said, "It's nice to meet you. Please call me Danni."

Finally, he stepped up to Marnie. Before he could address her as Ms. Ames, she said, "I'm Marnie." They shook hands and he held onto hers with both of his, which may've been an endearment, or may have been to steady himself.

We followed him into a small, windowless conference room and sat at a round mahogany table. Danni's seat had been readied for her with a pillow.

"Where are the others?" I asked.

Mr. Phillips looked around, apparently confused by my question. "What others?"

Marnie asked, "Aren't there any distant, greedy

relatives?"

Mr. Phillips laughed. "No relatives, greedy or not."

"So, we're it?" asked Danni.

"Everything Jeanne wanted to say is for your ears only."

It struck me for the first time that Jeanne might have bequeathed part of her fortune to us, and I didn't like the way that made me feel. If Mr. Phillips would just get on with it, I wouldn't have time to think about what a large bequest would mean.

His folded hands rested on the table, and he turned from one of us to the other as he spoke in a soft voice. "This past October, Jeanne came to see me about revising her will. As I mentioned, she has no relatives, so originally, one hundred percent of her estate was to be distributed to a number of charities. She was very clear about the changes she wanted, and I got them made for her right away. A week later, she stopped by on her lunch break to execute the document with witnesses from my staff. Then she made what I found to be a fairly unusual request. She said she had a letter explaining things, and she wanted to read it aloud and have a recording made so that the beneficiaries—you all—could hear the details in her own voice. I have a copy of the letter for each of you, and I'll hand them out after you've heard directly from Jeanne."

"Are we expected to be able to listen to this dry-eyed?" asked Annie.

I was thinking the same thing. Although I'd shed an ocean of tears over the past days, it certainly wasn't an exhaustible supply. There was no way any of us could hear Jeanne's distinctive voice without losing it.

"No, indeed. And thank you for reminding me,

Annie." Mr. Phillips rose, walked over to a credenza, and returned to the table with a tray holding a tape player and five square boxes of tissues. Evidently, he didn't think he could manage it, either.

We all stared at the little machine as though Jeanne were inside with a tiny megaphone. Her voice came through so clearly it was like she was sitting across the table from us. My eyes stayed glued to the tape player.

"Dearest Heather, Marnie, Danni and Annie,

If you are hearing this, I've already taken my last breath, and live only in your memories. I accept this reality with hope that I will linger in this glorious world a bit longer because of you four girls. Perhaps it was presumptuous, but I thought of you as my girls since our first meetings. I was never fortunate enough to have children of my own, but I could not have loved you more if you were my own offspring.

It is quite possible that my passing has resulted in some local news coverage about me. If not, you will learn a bit about my little secrets at the reading of this will. I never meant to deceive you about my wherewithal or my special gift. My reason for the secrecy was simple. I treasured my career as an office manager, and did not want to give you pause about hiring me or keeping me on.

Through no effort of my own, I've been blessed with a small fortune. As my lawyer and good friend will advise you, I've decided not to leave it to you, my beloved girls. It has long been my deeply held belief that all work is noble, and that even the 'job' of philanthropy is not an adequate substitute. We grow through our struggles. I hope you understand that I decline to deprive you of the joy of making your own successes in your own ways.

There is one exception. I am bequeathing $500,000 to your law firm to be used solely for the creation and maintenance of a day care center for your women lawyers' club. It is also something you may all find, in the fullness of time, you will want to use.

Each of you will receive one or more pieces of jewelry which I have selected from those my beloved husband presented to me over the years. My hope is that you may see fit to wear them, and that they will occasionally remind you of me and the too-brief time we shared. Please hand these down to your own dear daughters.

In addition, I would like Eloise to have my writing desk.

Finally, I want to let you in on something I've discovered due to my gift of connectivity. You may not believe what I am about to tell you, but I love you all too much not to share it. I don't subscribe to any organized religion, and I have no expectation of an after-life in the traditional sense. But I know with certainty that some kind of continuation of life is real. Even after all these years, I still have no insight or understanding of how it works. I tend to think of it as an energy which somehow remains after death and connects the still-living with people who were once alive. Since the age of ten, I've had the ability to walk into the room of a deceased person and receive a fairly clear sense of how the person perished.

Over the years, my impressions proved to be accurate enough that I was considered to be a reliable partner by numerous police departments and other law enforcement agencies. I wish I could've helped them full time, but I've never had the stamina to permit such extended work. As you might imagine, being a vessel of the energy has been exhausting. Plus, I loved my day job.

It is my guess that the energy of the deceased is always present in the world in some manner, but only a small number of us were given the gift (or curse) of the ability to tap into it. There are others like me, but we tend to keep quiet about it. I suspect that it is also somehow through the energy of deceased persons that I have sometimes been able to see the future with a reasonable degree of clarity. When it looked bright, and I thought it would be encouraging for someone to know about it, I would make my little 'predictions.' I hope you did not think me insane!

My point in telling you this is that I promise to remain connected to you—if it's possible.

Annie, be aware that your dear Eloise told me some things which led me to wonder if she may also be a vessel. If she is, you'll want to support her on her journey. She adores you and Bradley, and will welcome your help.

I'm so sorry I've left you. Please know that I deeply loved each of you. I'll continue to be with you if I can. In any event, please keep me alive in your memories, and tell your daughters about your elderly office manager who spoke in flowery superlatives, and the enchanted space we shared in the early days of your law firm.

With deepest love, and very best wishes for your futures,

Jeanne

When the tape ended, I grabbed a second handful of tissues and smeared them over my face trying to clear off the tears, mascara, and snot which were still flowing.

Once I'd blown my nose a half-dozen times, and was able to restore my vision, I saw that all of the others—including Mr. Phillips—were doing the same thing.

He stood and took the tape player in his hands so gingerly that it was as though it was an actual part of Jeanne. As he left the room, he said, "I'll be back in a moment with the pieces of jewelry that are in my safe."

None of us said a word. He returned a few moments later with another tray. This one held an assortment of velvet jewelry boxes in a variety of colors and sizes. He mumbled to himself as he read through a list and slowly and deliberately handed them out. One for me; one for Marnie; three for Danni; and two for Annie. We opened them to see stunning rings and bracelets and necklaces in diamonds and a host of other more colorful precious stones.

"Ladies, beneath the velvet insert in each box is an appraisal. I recommend that you insure your gifts as soon as possible. In fact, I can give you the name of the insurance agent Jeanne always used. Very reasonable. From Jeanne's comments, I gather that she wants you to wear them often, rather than secreting them away in a safe—which just makes the insurance more important."

Annie asked, "Why do I have two, and Danni, three?"

"We can explain," said Marnie.

Mr. Phillips smiled. "Very good. Then you've deciphered the hidden meaning."

"Well," said Marnie, "Heather figured it out after a conversation with Eloise."

"What in the world are you talking about?" asked Annie.

Mr. Phillips said, "I think your friends will enjoy

explaining it to you, Annie." He stood. "Now, unless there are other questions, I promised to join my wife for brunch at her favorite restaurant."

I raised my hand a few inches above the table, then said, "There is one more thing. I think we would all really appreciate having a picture of Jeanne. I can get copies made. I really don't know if this is an appropriate request."

"Of course," said Mr. Phillips. "I know just the one. I'll send it to you, Heather, and you can have the copies made."

"Thanks so much."

"You are most welcome. I'll forward the check for the childcare center once I get everything in order with the distribution of the estate. And, Annie, I'll call you to arrange to have Eloise's desk delivered. The appraisal is in the desk drawer. I suggest that you also purchase insurance for that. It's quite a fine antique."

"Thank you. Eloise will treasure it."

"Marnie and Danni, I'm so happy to have finally met you, as well."

"Thanks," said Danni.

"Have a nice brunch," said Marnie.

As we walked through the reception area, Marnie said, "Everyone stop and put your uninsured jewels in your purses. Annie, do you have your toy with you today?"

"Of course not."

"Then everyone stay close as we walk outside."

I said, "Marnie, Lake Forest is one of the safest rich-people havens in the state."

"You never know, Heather."

Once we were out on the sidewalk, Annie said, "You

guys have to tell me. I have two pieces of jewelry. What does it mean?"

I remembered the charming restaurant Jeanne had taken us to for a celebration the day Marnie's former client called to tell her he would be sending all of his files to her. It was where we first decided to hire an associate attorney. "Why don't we also have brunch? We can go to Magellan's. It's just a couple of blocks—straight ahead." I turned to Annie. "It's kind of a long story—not something we just want to blurt out. Okay?"

"I suppose. But will it answer my question?"

"Oh, yes," said Marnie. "Hopefully, you won't go into shock like Danni did when Heather first cracked the code."

"Why did you go and say something like that, Marnie? How am I supposed to wait now?"

"Believe me," said Danni. "It'll be worth it."

"Fine," said Annie, as she sped her walking to a sprint. "Can't you guys walk any faster?"

From ten feet behind her, Danni said, "No. Come here, Annie. Walk with me."

Annie made a deep groan, then joined Danni. "Wait," she said. "Does the mystery have anything to do with the fact that Jeanne was apparently a psychic?"

"Little bit," said Marnie.

"How long have you guys known that?"

Danni said, "Marnie discovered it a few days before Jeanne died. She told Heather and me the night before."

"I still don't understand."

"It's been an extraordinary morning, Annie," said Danni. "I promise that what we are about to tell you will only make it more extraordinary."

"All right. I'm trusting that this will be worth all the

build-up."

Marnie and Danni and I looked at each other. Then Marnie said, "I think we can pretty much guarantee it."

Chapter 32

It's been eight months and we are still feeling Jeanne's absence as a strong presence, but we've grown better able to talk about her without sobbing. We've taken to crediting her with all manner of small interventions. When a falling object from a window-washer's scaffold narrowly missed Marnie, it was Jeanne's doing. When Danni got the last stand-by seat for a flight to visit her sister, she admitted that she silently thanked Jeanne. When Bradley proposed to Annie, we kidded her that Jeanne had nudged him over the hump. When Sam proposed to Danni, we made the same lame joke.

Marnie is seeing Ivani regularly and exclusively. I've had a good number of dates with Charlie. While I always enjoy spending time with him and find him to be especially genuine—and attractive—I'm not sure he's "the one." I'm still inordinately cautious, and, like his ex-fiancée before me, I worry a little that his life goals may be more altruistic than I'd be comfortable with. Naturally, that embarrasses the hell out of me. Time will tell.

We never did ask Eloise what Jeanne had instructed her to draw for the second set of pictures—the "couples" set—nor did we request the drawings. Danni pointed out that asking would require us to admit to Annie that we'd read Jeanne's letter from Eloise. Marnie insisted we could explain that adequately so Annie wouldn't lose all respect for us, and I agreed. The truth is, we would rather be surprised.

We all enjoy including Jeanne in our banter and our adventures. It's odd, but whenever anyone mentions her, in silliness or in fond remembrance, my right hand flies to my heart as though her name has become my anthem. I've grown to treasure the reflex, and I hope it lasts as long as I do.

When I look out my office window, I can see down the block to the courthouse lawn where the American flag flutters against a variable sky. In the foreground, I often glimpse Annie, or Marnie, or Danni crossing the street, being greeted by lawyers who stop to shake hands or nod and smile in brief greeting. Frequently, whatever it is Marnie says makes the other person throw back their head and appear to roar.

The Women Lawyers' Club has started the renovations on an old flower shop which will become the first iteration of Ms. Jeanne's Nursery and Child Care Center.

I'm sitting at my desk when the top page of my legal pad flutters for no apparent reason. I feel a cool breeze touch my face and neck.

"Jeanne?"

A word about the author...

Judith Fournie Helms grew up in southern Illinois, and attended college and law school in Chicago. She became a founding partner of a law firm based in Chicago with offices on both coasts, and was recognized by her peers as a "Super Lawyer" and a "Leading Lawyer." Retired from the practice of law, Judith writes novels and short stories at her home in Virginia where she lives with her husband. She is also the author of the 2018 novel 'The Toronto Embryo' and the 2021 novel 'Grudge Tiger.' www.judithhelms.com

Thank you for purchasing
this publication of The Wild Rose Press, Inc.

For questions or more information
contact us at
info@thewildrosepress.com.

The Wild Rose Press, Inc.
www.thewildrosepress.com